WINTER MAGIC

THE THORNE WITCHES BOOK 3

T.M. CROMER

Cover art: Deranged Doctor Designs
Line+ Editor: Formidable Red Pen
Proof Editor: Trusted Accomplice

FINDING YOU

THIS TIME YOU

INCLUDING YOU

AFTER YOU

THE GHOST OF YOU

To Lauren
Thank you for your friendship and invaluable assistance!

To my faithful followers
Thanks for your never-ending support!

*A*s Zane Carlyle rolled off of her and patted her leg, Winnie Thorne experienced a keen sense of disappointment. The sex between them had been godawful. The guy possessed nine inches of what should be a pure-pleasure stick, yet he didn't know how to wield it.

"Was it good for you, Win?" he asked with the cockiness of a well-endowed twenty-one-year-old. Apparently, one who thought he was a sex god because of what he'd been blessed with.

"Not so much," she muttered.

His sandy-blond head whipped up from the grassy bed it had been resting on. "What?"

"Not so much." Winnie was nothing if not honest. "I'm damned disappointed if you want the truth. All that bragging and that glorious glimpse I had when—well, never mind about that—but still, total disappointment, dude."

"Are you kidding me right now?" he demanded, rolling away and yanking on his jeans.

"Zane, don't take this the wrong way, but you couldn't find a g-spot if you had a map." Laughter bubbled up, and she swallowed a giggle at his outrage. "And for future reference, you might want to make sure your partner gets off. First would be nice, but women are happy to get off in general."

His pale-faced shock gave her a twinge of remorse for her brutal honesty. Perhaps she should have tempered it. Guys had delicate egos. She laid a comforting hand on his arm only to have him jerk out of her reach.

"I'm not trying to hurt your feelings. I'm only trying to give you a heads up for the next time you have sex," she said.

"I can't believe this!" Zane pulled his shirt over his hard, muscular chest in quick, spastic movements.

Covering up all that beauty was a shame. From the time Winnie was old enough to have such thoughts, she'd always admired his physique.

He'd topped six feet back in high school and seemed to still be gaining ground. Currently standing at about six-three, Zane was imposing in height and build. Hours of farm work and physical exertion—lifting hay and bags of feed, exercising horses in addition to his spot as captain of his college swim team—had built muscle upon muscle.

"You're the only woman who's ever complained. Perhaps *you're* the terrible lay," he sneered.

She winced then sighed in resignation. Yep, it was always the woman's fault when a guy didn't know the intricacies of good sex, never mind great sex, which was rare with any guy in general to her understanding. Other women talked. And based on her limited knowledge, it was an extraordinary man who took time to learn erogenous zones and put that knowledge to good use in fantastic foreplay.

"Yeah, that's it. I'm the terrible lay. It's all on me." She snorted and rolled her eyes. "Sorry you drew the short straw."

"I should've remembered your only goal in life is to be a ball-buster to every guy you meet."

She frowned. Where the hell had that come from? Since when was she a ball-buster? "Now that's just a blatant lie. Almost as blatant as the lie where you claimed this was going to be the best night of my life."

His scowl darkened considerably.

She could almost feel the black rage radiating off him. Winnie took a step back, worried he might strike her. After all, she didn't really know him other than by reputation and a sprinkling of dates.

"Christ, this was the biggest mistake of *my* life. I wish I'd never asked you out. If I could go back to the second before I bumped into you in the grocery store, I'd go down a different aisle."

She hadn't expected his words to cut so deeply. Perhaps because she'd been dreaming about doing the deed with Zane since high school when she'd cloaked herself in magic and snuck into the locker room to watch him shower. Never had there been a more erotic sight. The water had glided over every sinewy plane of his body that she'd longed to follow with her hands. Since that day, he'd been her secret fantasy. But wasn't that the problem with fantasies and daydreams? The reality was always worse.

"And tell me, how much experience do you have anyway? Must be quite a lot to compare to if you thought what we did was so terrible." His tone was as ugly as his words.

And the insults kept coming. Not immune to hurt, Winnie struggled to remember that he lashed out because she'd disparaged his prowess.

"To think, I've always thought you might be the *normal* sister," he said with a scornful look.

Her back went up.

People could say what they wanted about *her*, but her family was off limits.

Her rage fueled the magical power contained within her body. The nucleus of her cells fired up, making her insides feel like a volcano ready to blow. How she contained her desire to turn him into a slug was beyond her own comprehension.

"You wish we'd never gotten together?" she asked with cold fury.

"Yes," he spat.

3

She stepped up to where he stood. "Done," she snarled.

Hands shaking, Winnie fastened the buttons of her blouse as she left the clearing and headed through the woods, toward her home. Today had been a massive mistake, but she intended to rectify that as soon as she got to the attic of their house. There had to be a spell in the family grimoire to wipe this day from existence.

"And, Win?" Zane called.

She spun back to glare at him across the distance. "What?"

"When you realize what you could've had, don't bother calling me. I won't pick up."

Without bothering to answer, she fled. As she ran through the woods, a sob caught in her throat. Goddess, if there was a way to make him forget, she'd make it happen.

Once she'd reached home, she jogged up the steps and headed straight for the Thorne spell book. As she thumbed through the pages, she happened upon what she'd been looking for and tapped the page. "This should work nicely."

"What should?" A statuesque blonde woman appeared in the doorway and caused Winnie to scream. "Why are you so jumpy, child? Are you up to no good?"

"No, Aunt GiGi. I... well, you..." Winnie detected amusement in the other woman's bright violet-blue eyes. "Okay, I was up to no good."

"Wonderful!" GiGi clapped her hands. "How can I help?"

"I thought we weren't supposed to do things for personal gain? Why would you want to help me?"

"Are you gaining anything from the spell you're intending to cast?"

"Not me personally. I was going to wipe Zane's memory."

Perfectly arched brows shot up, and her aunt silently studied her.

Sweat pooled under Winnie's breasts and in the small of her back. No way she could bluff her way out of this one. She went with the truth. "Zane said he wished he'd never asked me out."

"You've only been out four times. It's a little early for a lover's spat."

4

"We, um, we… today, we decided to… um…"

"Are you trying to find a way to say you had sex with the boy?"

"Yes," she expelled on an exhaled breath.

GiGi smoothed a hand over Winnie's hair. "While young, you are both consenting adults."

Winnie screwed up her face.

Tone hard, GiGi asked, "It was consensual, correct?"

"I didn't put a spell on him to do me if that's what you're asking!" Winnie retorted.

GiGi lost the cool composure she'd always worn like a cloak about her. Tears streamed from eyes crinkled with laughter. The sound of her merriment echoed off the wooden rafters. When she could finally draw a breath, she said, "I was talking about him forcing *you*, child. *Not the other way around.*"

Heat flooded Winnie's face, and she ducked her head. Uh, yeah, maybe her mind had gone there because plenty of times over the last four years she'd thought of conjuring a spell to attract Zane's notice.

"You liked this boy, didn't you?" GiGi asked. The humor was replaced by a gentle understanding.

Tears stung Winnie's eyes. "I thought I loved him. But he wasn't who I thought he was."

Her aunt heaved a heavy sigh full of understanding. "They never are, dear. Show me the spell you intend to use to wipe his memory."

ZANE CONTINUED TO PACE THE CLEARING LONG AFTER WINNIE RAN away. Man, he'd screwed up. Because he cared what she thought, because he'd wanted the sex between them to be off the charts, he'd had an adverse reaction to her honesty.

The act itself had been sadly lacking on his part. He couldn't hold on once inside her warm, tight passage. As a result, he'd come without getting her off. The person Zane most wanted to satisfy was the one person he hadn't. Normally, he was a considerate lover.

He also regretted saying Winnie was easy. She'd told him he was only the second guy she'd been with, and he believed her. But after his poor performance, he'd hoped that, in her innocence, she wouldn't know any better. That she'd be happy with his pathetic sex.

Her words had stung his pride. Mainly because he'd intended to make it up to her when he caught his breath. She hadn't given him a chance.

Zane scrubbed his face with his palms. He needed to apologize. Winnie didn't deserve his ugliness. Maybe if he confessed he hadn't lasted because the feel of her combined with the sight of her beautiful, taut body had him ejaculating faster than he could blink, she'd understand.

A scrap of material caught his eye. He bent to pick up the lacy thong, the exact color of her ice-blue eyes. He intended to keep the little triangle of material. It would be his private trophy to take out when no one was around. It would help him remember and savor the delicious feel of her in his arms. With a quick check of the area, he stuffed her panties into the inside pocket of his jacket.

As he took a step in the direction of the Thorne estate, a wave of dizziness struck. He balanced himself with a hand against the closest tree.

What the hell was that?

He shook his head and straightened.

Another step brought another wave of dizziness.

After five more steps, he forgot why he was heading toward the property bordering his family's.

He spun about. Why the hell had he entered the woods?

The world started to whirl, and he collapsed on his ass. Bile rose up into the back of his throat, and he expelled the contents of his lunch next to the old oak where he'd carved his and Winnie's initials after their first date.

Winnie. He needed to remember something about Winnie.

Zane raised a shaky hand to his brow.

Like a kaleidoscope of reverse images, the day's events replayed backward in his mind, each memory blurred and faded into obscurity.

6

Fear clawed at his insides and ripped him up as, one by one, the last two weeks disappeared from his mind.

A half hour had passed before he could gather the strength to stand. He glanced around the woods, worried as to why he might be out here to begin with.

A marking in the bark of a nearby tree snagged his attention. Zane staggered over to the mighty oak and traced the letters there. Who had carved his and Winnie's initials? Was this his cousins' idea of a joke? Had they drugged him and done this, knowing he had the major hots for Winnie Thorne?

"If you fuckers are out there, I swear I'm going to kick your asses!" he hollered.

Not even a rustle of leaves answered him.

"Coop? Keat?"

Nothing.

His eyes returned to the initials surrounded by a heart. The tickling in the front of his brain worried him. It was as if his mind struggled to recall something. *But what?*

2

*T*he sign read, Zane Carlyle, Attorney at Law.

Well, if that wasn't a clear indication Zane had returned to town and planned to stay, Winnie didn't know what was.

Working up her nerve, she pulled open the door and stepped into the small reception area. A perky redhead sat behind a chrome and glass desk. It appeared to be the only piece of furniture Zane had updated so far, probably the only modern thing this musty, old office had seen in close to fifty years.

Before either woman could speak, Zane came from his office with his headful of pale, sun-bleached hair buried in a file. He maintained a longer style that made Winnie heave an internal sigh. Something about the way his hair fell just so over his brow made her want to run her fingers through those glorious locks.

"Penny, get me McMasters on the line. He..." Whatever else he'd intended to say was lost when he saw her. "Winnie."

His gaze swept her jean-clad form and lingered on her breasts before he frowned and busied himself with his file. "Uh, what are you... can I... is there something I can help you with?"

If she didn't know better, she'd say she'd flustered him. A quick glance at his assistant told Winnie that Penny found his behavior odd as well.

"It's my understanding that you are taking over Mr. Peterson's clientele." She shrugged and threw up her hands. "I was one of his clients."

Zane pinched his nose as if the idea of working with her was bothersome to him. "I see."

A frisson of hurt ran through her, but she shoved it aside. He wouldn't be the only person in Leiper's Fork to find the idea of doing business with her abhorrent.

"Look, if it's a problem, I can see about hiring an attorney out of Nashville. It's no big deal."

"It's no problem," he said sharply as he rushed forward and tossed the file folder down on the desk. "Or it shouldn't be. Peterson's filing system left a lot to be desired. Penny and I are still trying to find a client list."

In the two times Winnie had visited the law firm of Peterson & Peterson, she'd noted the stacks of boxes lining the walls. She'd assumed Robert Peterson had been in the middle of organizing, but perhaps she'd been too generous in her thoughts.

"I have a few minutes now, if there was something specific you wished to address."

"I don't want to take you away from…" Winnie gestured to the file folder and noted Penny observing the two of them with avid interest.

"He's got nothing on his schedule for another thirty minutes," Perky Penny provided.

Zane took hold of Winnie's arm.

The resulting zing of electricity startled them both.

As he stared down where his hand clasped her elbow, he frowned. "Have we ever…?" With a shake of his head and a bemused smile, he said, "Forget it."

Winnie was shaken down to her pinky toes. The only time he'd ever grasped her arm was to help her from the car on their first date —*eight years ago*. He shouldn't have even a shadow of a memory from that time. First chance she had, she would consult with Aunt GiGi. Maybe spells had a shelf life, and if that was the case, she was in deep doo-doo.

"I was just about to grab lunch. Care to join me?" he asked.

His sunny smile chilled her and made her uncomfortable. They'd been here before. But at that time, she'd been foolish enough to believe he was after something more than a quick, unsatisfying lay. For his sake, she hoped, after all this time, he'd improved in the sex department.

Winnie offered a tight, polite smile in return. "I don't want to keep you from your lunch. I can return another time."

"I'm only running right next door to Monica's Cafe for soup and a sandwich, but I'd love the company."

How could she refuse without sounding churlish? She must've hesitated too long because all his open friendliness disappeared.

"You know what, it's okay. Penny can schedule an appointment for when it's convenient for you." He picked up the McMaster's file and tapped it on his opposite hand. "Let her know what you require."

Until he rescinded the invitation, Winnie hadn't realized how much she wanted to spend time with him. She'd gone for eight years effectively suppressing all thoughts of Zane and how he'd made her feel leading up to that horrible day in the clearing; treasured and wanted. Something she hadn't felt since then and hadn't realized she missed until now.

"Okay," she blurted.

"Fine. Just give her your number and—"

"No. I mean, okay, I'd like to have lunch with you."

The intensity in his dark, chocolatey eyes sharpened—became deeper—as they studied her. It seemed as if he concentrated on memorizing her features. A bright, engaging grin burst across his face and stunned her into silence. "Awesome."

She wanted to bask in the warmth of his wide smile. If there was one thing she remembered about him, it was that Zane hadn't met a stranger. One and all took to his open, cheerful personality, herself included.

"Have you had Monica's tomato basil soup? No? You're in for a treat." He directed the wattage of his smile at Penny. "Should we bring something back for you?"

"Cheesecake."

"You have to eat something more substantial than dessert, Pen."

Penny shrugged and laughed. "You know my motto."

"Life's uncertain; eat dessert first," Zane and Penny quoted in unison.

Zane sighed his disgust. "I tried."

"And I love you for it. Best Boss Award goes to..." She tapped out a drum roll, smiled, and turned back to the monitor in front of her. "Well, look at that. Your next appointment canceled. Take your time, kids."

Penny couldn't have been more than twenty-three or four in Winnie's assessment. Her use of the term "kids" caused both Winnie and Zane to roll their eyes and chuckle, as she'd no doubt intended.

After Zane and Winnie were ensconced in a booth at Monica's Cafe, he spoke. "It's been a long time."

"It has," she agreed as she fiddled with the edge of the worn menu.

He ducked and captured her eyes with his inquiring gaze. "You seem nervous. Do I make you nervous, Winnie?"

Goddess, yes!

But she didn't dare tell him. She'd learned her lesson about telling men the truth the day in the meadow.

"Do you intend to split your time between here and Nashville, or are you back in Leiper's Fork permanently?" she politely asked in an effort to avoid his question altogether.

His lips twitched. "I'm here permanently. Are you seeing anyone?"

The speed and bluntness of his question stole her breath away. He couldn't be serious, and yet, the determined glint in his eye said his interest was genuine.

If she lied, he'd find out the truth. The size of their town didn't allow for secrets, minus the one major secret the Thornes had managed to keep hidden for a few centuries.

"No."

"Excellent."

Her eyes darted around the crowded room as she looked for an escape. No way did she intend to have a repeat of their aborted romance. She needed an excuse—STAT!

"I definitely make you nervous," he teased. "The next logical question would be why?"

"Not at all. I have a lot on my mind."

"Odd. The Winnie I used to know as a kid never lied."

Irritation spiked her temper. Who was he to determine if she was lying or not? "You want the truth? Fine. I get the impression you are deciding whether to ask me out or not. Don't bother. I'm not interested."

A twinkle lit his eyes. "Is that so?"

She jerked her chin up. "Yes."

"Like I said, the Winnie I used to know never lied." He surveyed the menu. "What looks good?"

ZANE COULD FEEL WINNIE'S ANGER AS SHE SAT AND SIMMERED.

Once, the thought of angering Winnie would've had him bending over backwards to soothe her ruffled feathers. Now, her temper amused him. Picking a fight went against his nature. Other than the courtroom, where he relished a battle of wits, he preferred peace and an easy existence.

Yet the way Winnie's icy-blue gaze darkened to smoke made him wonder what other emotion might cause the unusual change in eye color. Passion?

As he fantasized about kissing her delicate mouth and running his hands over her creamy skin, Zane's focus on the menu morphed into an image of him and Winnie naked in the grass. He could almost hear the crinkle of autumn leaves beneath the purple blanket they lay upon. Her long black hair a halo around her as he pumped into her tight, hot body.

Sweat beaded on his brow, and he shifted in his seat. A surge of desire hit him below the belt. Where the hell had that vision come from? He could almost smell the musky scent of sex in the air.

"Are you all right, Zane?" Her husky voice only fueled his need.

Heat started on his neck and worked its way up, adding color to his face and highlighting his cheekbones. "Uh, yeah. I think I'll have the tomato soup and grilled cheese combo. How about you?"

He nearly smacked himself on the forehead. Damned if he didn't sound inane. But whenever she turned those probing eyes in his direction, he would lose his train of thought and get lost in her gaze.

"Sounds good. I'll have the same," she agreed without a glance at the menu.

While he didn't want to cut their lunch short, he hated that she seemed to find dining with him distasteful. "You know, if you didn't want to have lunch with me, you could've just said so. I'm an adult. I can take it."

Her mouth opened and closed around the words she couldn't seem to form. She cleared her throat once before reaching for his hand. When their fingers connected, he once again felt the current pass between them.

"I wouldn't be here if I didn't want to be," she finally said.

Her honesty shone bright and clear.

"Good." As she moved to pull away, he captured her hand more fully. "Because I like you, Winnie Thorne."

A flash of an unnamed emotion clouded her features before she shoved it away and smiled. "I like you too, Zane Carlyle."

An attractive waitress showed to fill their drinks. After an unsuccessful attempt to flirt with Zane, the woman took their order and disappeared in the sea of lunchtime diners before either of them spoke again.

"We established I'm not dating anyone," she said. "How about you?"

He lost the battle to suppress his happy grin. "Nope."

"You seem ecstatic to be single. Should I be concerned?"

"I'm ecstatic you asked. It means you're open for something more," he returned.

Winnie rolled her eyes. "You are such a player."

"No. Never that, Win."

Her eyes lost the amused light, and she frowned.

"What did I say?" he asked as he interwove his fingers through hers. "Obviously, I've upset you."

She shook her head. "Someone I knew once upon a time used to call me Win. That's all."

The day lost a bit of its shine. Winnie appeared to be pining for a lost love. It bothered him because it meant he didn't stand a chance with her. He'd heard the rumor that Thornes only loved once. It had never been proven truer than when Winnie's sister Summer hooked up with Zane's cousin Coop after what seemed like a lifetime. It was proven again when her other sister Autumn had mended fences with the love of her life, Keaton.

Zane dropped Winnie's hand and fiddled with the napkin-wrapped silverware in front of him. "Did you love him?"

"I don't know. I liked him a lot." She shrugged in what Zane recognized as the trademark move for her family. "I think we were both immature at the time."

Zane studied her as she sipped her water. She'd avoided his eyes when she talked about her mystery man, a clear indication she lied. Winnie either cared about the loser more than she let on, or she found this discussion embarrassing for some reason. Although he was grateful she didn't totally dodge the question, he didn't like that she couldn't meet his gaze. If he intended to pursue her, he wanted complete honesty between them.

"I think you more than liked him," he blurted.

Winnie shot him a sharp glance, but any retort was lost as their server returned with the meal. In an attempt at stealth, the woman slid a slip of paper facedown next to his plate, then she brushed a hand along his wrist.

"Seriously?" Winnie asked, reaching over to snag the offending piece of paper. She read what was written there and flipped it to face Zane before she crumpled it up and tossed it onto the serving tray. "He's on a date," she snapped.

He compressed his lips to stop his bark of laughter. Winnie's jealousy delighted him for reasons he would explore later.

"Don't you dare laugh," she warned under her breath as the server hurried away.

"I can't help it. You're so fierce."

"I've got your fierce," she muttered as she picked up her spoon.

"I bet you do. I look forward to seeing more of it."

"You wish."

"Yes. Yes, I do," he said with a deep chuckle.

He watched her from beneath his lashes as they ate. More than once their eyes connected and caused a fiery blush to color her cheeks.

"Um, Zane?"

He shot her an encouraging smile.

"Do you, um… do you ever… feel certain things?"

Because laughter threatened to choke him and he shouldn't add food to the mix, he carefully laid down his spoon and crossed his arms. It took him another moment or two to ask, "What things?"

Her dark frown indicated she wasn't as amused as he was.

"Never mind." Winnie picked up her sandwich and commenced eating.

Zane had the distinct impression she did it to prevent herself from cussing him out.

"I'll be serious, Win. Go ahead and ask."

For a moment, she continued to chew, eyeing him over her grilled cheese. With great care, she set the half sandwich down and wiped her fingers off. "Magic."

"Excuse me?"

She cast a wary glance around them and leaned in closer. "Magic."

"What about it?"

"Do you ever feel it?"

15

"Are we talking in the bedroom?" he teased, finally under-standing where she was heading with their conversation, but feeling the need to toy with her at the same time.

"Zane," she growled. "You said you'd be serious!"

He lifted his glass of water to hide his grin. Her heightened color was a thing of beauty and made him want to continue teasing her.

"You're being an asshat!"

"I feel you are being unjust, Win. I simply asked for clarification."

"Forget I asked."

"Oh, no! Now you have me curious. You can't back out now."

"I'm not getting into this with you. Obviously, you think it's a joke."

Abruptly, he stood. "Come on."

Winnie stared at his outstretched hand like it was a snake ready to strike.

Without a word, he reached for her and tugged her upright. When she fell into him, he wrapped his arms around her. A wild sense of déjà vu struck without warning, and his grip on her tightened.

A flash of her laughing up into his face flitted through his mind, but when he struggled to recall the incident, his mind went blank. Dizziness assailed him, black spots danced about his vision, and he swayed.

Winnie's concerned voice seemed to come from far away. "Zane? Are you okay?"

The noise of the diner came back in a snap.

"I don't feel well, Win. I need to go." He ran a shaking hand through his hair.

"Stay here. I'll pay the tab." She patted his chest. "Seriously, don't move."

He nodded and sank back into the booth as she rushed to the counter.

Off and on through the years, he'd had dreams of him and Winnie. Other than his wishful thinking, he'd never lent any credence to the scenes that played out in his mind. Now, he had to wonder if perhaps there was something more to it.

An instinct told him that she had a secret. Her face had been exceptionally pale, and guilt weighed heavily upon her features. And as Winnie stared at him in the mirror over the counter, Zane decided it was time to find out exactly what she was hiding.

$\mathcal{B}$y the time they returned to Zane's office, he seemed to have shaken off whatever he'd experienced at Monica's Cafe. For that, Winnie was grateful. However, she continued to be concerned by his suspicious attitude since his episode. From the moment he had recovered from his dizziness, his eyes held a speculative gleam. It was as if Zane knew Winnie was responsible for stealing his memories, though how he could remember anything about that time was a complete mystery. She and GiGi had been thorough in their spell. Unless, as she was beginning to suspect, the original spell had been faulty or was wearing thin. In that case, she was in for a world of trouble.

Winnie left him in Penny's care and beat a hasty retreat. Any magical discussion could wait until another day. She glanced back through the glass door to find him watching her retreat. The purposeful expression on his face caused her nerve endings to go haywire. If Zane ever discovered her duplicity, there would be hell to pay.

In an attempt to appear casual, she smiled and gave a finger wave.

She needed to gain his trust and had hoped a business discussion would put him at ease. Instead, they'd bypassed business altogether and now, his trust would be hard earned. But somehow, she needed to rope him into the plan to go after the Uterine amulet her uncle needed to revive her mother. A family meeting was in order. Perhaps her sisters had an idea as to how to persuade him to help.

"WHAT WAS THAT ALL ABOUT?" PENNY SAID WITH A NOD TOWARD the door Winnie had escaped through.

"I'm not sure, Pen, but I intend to find out."

"You think she's up to something? Some spy mission for Mr. Peterson's son?"

They could speculate all day, but an odd feeling whispered that the answers to her strange behavior rested with Winnie herself. "Doubtful."

"You like her," Penny crowed. "I can tell, boss."

"Who I do or don't like is none of your business," he said reproachfully as he picked up the McMasters file he'd left on her desk earlier.

She shook her overly bright red head and laughed. "Yeah, tell me that again when you're having me send her flowers or make dinner reservations at some swanky restaurant in Nashville."

Heat crept up his neck and into the tips of Zane's ears.

As young as she was, Penny was remarkably astute.

"I don't need any crap from you, Pen. We have a ton of work to do."

"Yes, sir." Her upper body snapped to attention, and she saluted him.

"Not funny."

"It's a little bit funny," she argued with a cheeky grin.

The phone rang and cut off his retort.

"Mr. Carlyle's office... yes... yes... one moment, sir." Penny put the phone on hold and frowned in his direction. "It's Mr. Alastair Thorne. He said it's important he speak with you right away."

Curious as to why Alastair Thorne would be calling, Zane had Penny send the call to his private office line.

"Mr. Thorne?"

"Mr. Carlyle, I'll cut right to the chase. I need you to come to Thorne Manor immediately. There's a situation."

"What situation? What's happened? Is Winnie okay?"

Zane could swear he heard an amused cough from the other side of the connection.

"That's what I wanted to talk to you about, son. How soon can you be here?"

"I can leave now."

"Brilliant. Bill me for your time. I'll see you in twenty minutes."

"Mr. Thorne—" Zane didn't have a second chance to ask what the "situation" happened to be before the line went dead. He stared at the receiver for a good five or more seconds, wondering what the hell the call had really been about before he placed the receiver in the cradle.

"Penny, cancel any remaining appointments for today. I'm heading out to Thorne Manor."

"Oh, did you find out what was happening with Winnie?"

He frowned his irritation. "No. Can you do as I ask for once and not be a pain in my ass?"

Penny popped the gum she'd started chewing since taking the call from Alastair. "It's a good thing I like you, boss. I wouldn't put up with this attitude from just any employer."

He stared at the floor until he quelled the desire to strangle her. "I apologize for any attitude you perceived on my account."

She grinned and popped her gum twice more in rapid succession. "I accept your apology. You'd better go. You don't want to be late."

Zane showed teeth in a purposeful attempt at a smile. "Right."

"Oh! Wait! This came while you were at lunch." Penny rushed around her desk to retrieve a brown, nondescript box from a nearby credenza.

"What is it?"

She shrugged and handed him the unopened box.

"Uh, Pen, since when *haven't* you opened mail addressed to me?"

Her confused gaze focused on the box. She looked as stumped as he was. "I don't know."

With great care, he opened the edges. When nothing untoward fell out, he reached in and pulled out the item of clothing inside.

"It's my old leather jacket!"

"Oh-kay." Penny rolled her eyes and went back to her desk—her curiosity for the box's contents having fizzled out.

"I haven't seen this thing in years, Pen." Zane turned the box over and inspected the outside for a return address. Odd how happy holding the jacket made him. "Who could've sent it to me?"

"It's a mystery." Penny's dry voice lacked the zest of a genuine response.

"Whatever. I have to go." But before he could leave, the urge to try on his old coat overwhelmed him. Zane shrugged out of his suit jacket and replaced it with his leather bomber jacket. "What do you know; it still fits."

His assistant never removed her gaze from her computer screen. "Woohoo!" The complete lack of enthusiasm on Penny's part was unmistakable.

Zane glanced at the mirror along the back wall behind her bright head. "Social media, Pen? Really?"

"I'm checking the office Facebook page," she lied with a straight face.

"Uh, huh. Try to at least remember to answer the phones while I'm gone, okay? We need the business."

"Your family is richer than God, boss. You could only come in one hour a month and still afford to keep the doors open. You can also afford to give me a raise."

"You've been employed here all of two weeks. How about we save any raises until the ninety-day trial period is over?"

"If you want to be that way about it…"

Zane shook his head, collected his keys from his suit jacket, and headed toward the door. "Be sure to lock up when you go. And before you ask, you need to stay until at least three-thirty if you want to get paid for the full day."

Her laughter echoed around the tiny office space.

Within five minutes, he was headed down the two-lane road toward his family's home. On the West side of their property line was a heavily wooded area that divided the Thorne and Carlyle estates.

A smile came unbidden.

There had been many times when he'd snuck into those woods to watch the neighbor girls play. He'd never told his cousins. Those times had been for him alone. If no one knew where he was or who he was spying on, he didn't have to take flack for his crush on the black-haired girl with the beautiful smile.

Winnie.

The girl whose laughter was like the warmest sun, and whose eyes were brighter than the mid-summer day sky. The girl who had grown into a stunning woman. A woman with a wealth of secrets. Secrets he intended to find out.

The scent of wild orchids rose up along with the musky scent of sex. It teased a corner of his brain. As if his hand had a mind of its own, it reached into the inside pocket of his jacket and felt around.

When his fingers closed around a scrap of material, Zane started to sweat. And as his hand pulled the sky-blue triangle from its hiding place, another image flashed through his mind. One of Winnie teasing him and shimmying out of her thong. Image after image slammed into his brain, jarring loose memories long forgotten. His mind whirled at the implication of his possession of her panties.

The steering wheel jerked in his hand as he recalled their argument.

Where the yellow lab in the road came from, he'd never know, but Zane yanked the wheel sharply to the left to avoid running over the pup. The crunch of metal as his BMW impacted the trunk of an enormous oak tree was the last sound he heard before his forehead broke through the windshield.

*a*fter lunch with Zane, Winnie had headed back to her workshop. Working with her lotions, balms, and healing oils went a long way to clear her head and soothe her nerves. And since Aunt GiGi wasn't answering her texts, Winnie definitely needed a way to calm the worry that had invaded her peace of mind.

She had pulled out the stopper to measure exactly three drops of peppermint oil to add to the batch of lotion she was whipping up when the door to her workshop flew back on its hinges. In her surprise, she dumped a quarter of the amber bottle into the mixture, ruining the entire lot.

Frustrated, she counted to ten before facing her unwelcome guest. Serene once more, she said, "Uncle Alastair. Your enthusiastic entry surprised me. I mean, when have you been anything but reserved?"

"My apologies, niece." His tone was anything but apologetic. "Shall I extract the peppermint oil?"

"No. What's done is done. *But* you can tell me why you decided to pay me a visit in the middle of my workday."

"There's been an incident with your young man. I thought you should know."

Winnie frowned her confusion. "I don't have a young man."

"Zane Carlyle."

Her heartbeat ratcheted up a notch. "What about him?"

"It seems he's been in a terrible accident."

She grabbed a towel to wipe off the excess oils from her hands as she rushed for the door. "Is he okay? What happened?" If the volume and pitch of her voice hurt the ears of canines in a hundred mile radius, it couldn't be helped. Her concern for Zane took precedence over making the dog population of Leiper's Fork deaf.

"No time for all of that. Grab your medical kit and come with me," Alastair ordered.

"*He hasn't been seen by a doctor yet?*"

"I just came upon him. Now, do you want to discuss this, or do you want to help the poor lad?" Alastair ground out.

Freaked out, Winnie rotated her head back and forth in a search for the bag that held her healing supplies. Where the hell had she put it?

"Here, child." Her uncle held up her black leather case, and his tone was considerably warmer. "No need to panic. He'll recover."

"How do you know?" she managed in a hoarse whisper, her voice deserting her in her fear. If something happened to Zane, her world would become a whole lot duller. Granted, she hadn't seen him in years, but she'd known he was safe and happy in Nashville. If not happy, the knowledge had kept her content.

"Because I have faith in the Goddess's plan. Come."

On leaden feet, she followed him to the yard, convinced when she got to Zane that he would be beyond her ability to heal him. When she saw him sitting on the steps to Thorne Manor, a blood-soaked rag in his hand, she cried out.

His head snapped up, and he winced. Both his eyes closed, and he rested his head back against the white column of the porch.

Winnie rushed to his side, running her hands lightly over his pained features. "Tell me what happened. Where's the pain?"

"Who are you?" he rasped out.

Frozen in shock, Winnie could only stare. She hadn't expected to find his memory impaired. "What?"

"Who are you? Are you a doctor?"

"I..." Her throat seized. Horror stole her ability to speak. She cast a helpless glance Alastair's way. The inscrutable expression on his face told her nothing of his concern, or if he even *was* concerned.

"We need Aunt GiGi. I don't know how to treat him."

A speculative look entered Alastair's sapphire eyes. If Winnie had to guess, she'd almost say a grudging respect followed close behind. Whatever was running through her uncle's mind, she doubted he would share it until he was good and ready. She focused her attention on Zane.

Zane appeared cold and closed off.

"Zane." She said his name cautiously as she reached for the wound on his forehead. "My name is Winnie Thorne. I'm your neighbor. I'm not a doctor, but I specialize in healing." She pulled back slightly as he flinched away from her touch. "I want to help you if you'll let me."

ZANE KNEW DAMNED WELL WHO WINNIE WAS. HE ALSO HAD A CLEAR idea what she'd done to him. If his head wasn't throbbing so freaking bad, he'd give her hell. But for now, a little payback was in order.

When his memories had been unlocked, his abilities had come with them. Or what he assumed were his magical abilities. A surge of raw power flowed through him and fired up his cells—right before the moment of impact.

Alastair had happened upon him at the exact second the crash had taken place. The older warlock had saved him from an accident that most probably would've taken Zane's life.

Their eyes connected across the distance. A flare of amusement lit Alastair's dark-blue gaze. One brow lifted, and a smirk danced about his mouth.

In all honesty, Zane couldn't understand why Alastair didn't reveal the truth—Zane's memory hadn't been affected by the accident. He could only surmise the other man had a secret agenda of his own.

The gash on Zane's forehead had been treated by Alastair on scene. An angry red mark and blood were all that was left of Zane's contact with the windshield. Well, that and a stiff neck. Alastair had stated Winnie needed at least *one* injury to treat.

"I don't know you," Zane rasped. "I don't want you touching me."

Hurt darkened her eyes before she pasted on a false, reassuring smile. "I understand. Maybe we should get you to a hospital?"

"I'm fine."

"No, you have a head wound—" Her dialogue ceased as she noticed the "wound" in question was now knitted together.

"My neck is stiff. That's all," he countered.

"Would you like me to take a look? I might be able to ease your pain."

Zane could see Winnie's cool confidence had taken a beating. *Good.* Before he was finished with her, she'd be the one hoping to forget *his* existence. He studied her beautiful face, noted the worried gleam in her brilliant blue eyes. Oddly, he thought they'd been brighter once upon a time. In that, his memory must be faulty.

He frowned. Maybe his memory was skewed in other areas as well? His gaze zeroed in on her lush, berry-red lips. No. He recalled her taste as if they'd kissed yesterday instead of eight years ago.

"You're the most beautiful woman I've ever seen."

Of its own volition, his hand snaked around her waist and drew her close.

Her eyes widened but didn't show alarm.

He maintained eye contact until the last second when their mouths connected.

Yes, the taste of her lips was as delicious as he remembered. Zane took his time exploring the recesses of her mouth, teasing a response with his tongue and little nips along her full bottom lip.

She moaned into his mouth, and he was lost.

The sound of a clearing throat penetrated Zane's consciousness before he could take his impromptu seduction a step further. He drew back in small increments, unable or unwilling to release her.

Wonder blazed from Winnie's wide eyes, and her mouth—*God, that delectable mouth*—rounded in an O of surprise. Her tongue darted out to wet her swollen lips, and Zane nearly groaned.

He needed the distraction of his anger—*or hers*. "What did you say your name was again? Willow?"

Her skin lost its flush of desire and turned ashen. "Winnie," she gasped. "My name is Winnie."

"Right." He gave her a lopsided grin because he knew it would irritate the crap out of her. "Well, sweetheart, whatever your name is, you've got mad skills in the kissing department. I can tell you've had a lot of practice."

Her gasp of outrage forced him to bite the inside of his cheek to keep his laughter at bay. A rough cough came from Alastair's direction.

"Since you appear to be just fine, I'll go back to work." Winnie's words would chill a normal person to the bone. But Zane's blood was still fired up from rage and desire.

"Thanks for the TLC, Wendy."

"Oh!"

She stomped off in the direction of her workshop.

Both men waited until she was out of earshot before either of them spoke.

Alastair broke the silence. "Well played, son. Well played."

"She deserves that and more for her games."

"How far do you intend to take this little revenge of yours?" With warning evident in his tone, Alastair stepped forward.

"Until she's paid for erasing my memories."

"Well now, son, you know I can't allow you to break her heart, don't you?"

"She has no heart. She's a cold-blooded bit—"

"Careful," Alastair said. The frost coating the one word left Zane in little doubt the warlock would retaliate on his niece's behalf if her

27

honor was besmirched.

"Eight years!" Zane snarled. "Eight years she cost me."

"What did she actually take from you, young man? One memory of a less-than-stellar tumble in the woods?" GiGi Thorne-Gillespie's crisp voice asked from behind.

Alastair winced and made a face. "Ouch. Did you need to be harsh, sister?"

"Is it harsh when it's the truth, brother?"

The older man coughed into his hand in a poor attempt to hide his smirk.

"So not only did she wipe my mind, she laughed about it with all of you," Zane ground out as he rose to his feet with the help of the step railing. A sense of betrayal took hold and fueled the already burning rage within him. The wood ignited under his hand. *What the—?*"

From thin air, water doused the flames.

"What was that?" Zane demanded.

"That, dear boy, is a clear indication that you are a fire element. Welcome to the world of witchcraft." Alastair laughed in the face of Zane's shock. "Until you learn to control your powers, I'd say you should practice the art of Zen." Alastair addressed GiGi. "Seems Autumn and Winnie have another pupil for their magic training sessions."

"Winnie?" Zane cast him a sharp glance. "Winnie trains witches?"

A sly, knowing smile crept over Alastair's countenance. "Is that a problem for you?"

"Not at all." No, indeed. An idea formed. Spending more time with Winnie in order to exact his revenge worked perfectly to Zane's way of thinking.

"What do you mean I need to train him?" Winnie demanded in outrage. "How do I put this? *Hell. No.*"

"Winnie, be reasonable." Her sister, Summer, stepped forward and hugged her. "I understand you have a history—although, to be honest, I can't understand why you won't share the deets when the rest of us have spilled *our* guts—but he needs to be trained, and *you* need him for the trip to Egypt."

That had been yet another command that came down through Summer's father, Alastair. Last month, Alastair made the declaration that Zane had extensive archaeology experience and he would therefore be useful when she set out to retrieve the Egyptian Uterine amulet her uncle needed in his attempt to resurrect her mother Aurora.

"I can't do it," Winnie croaked out. "I can't train him."

"Why? Other than GiGi and Autumn, you are one of the most knowledgeable witch alive." Her youngest sister, Spring, positioned herself between her other two siblings. Her curiosity shone brightly on her beautiful face. "What happened?"

Wild-eyed Winnie stared at her sisters. Their stances gave the distinct impression they were ganging up on her. Better to get her confession out of the way and deal with their anger now. Perhaps then they would understand why she couldn't take on this part of the family quest for Alastair.

Winnie groaned. "We did it."

"Oh!" Summer meeped.

"I knew it!" Autumn laughed.

"Did what?" Spring asked in confusion.

Winnie lost what was left of her frayed temper. "*It*, Spring. *It!* The horizontal mamba. The bedsheet boogie. The—"

Spring held up one elegant hand. "All right. I get it." A wicked grin lit her face. "So how was it?"

"That's the problem," Winnie said with a heavy sigh. "It was godawful."

The jaws of all three sisters hit the floor.

Winnie almost giggled. She would have if the situation hadn't been dire. They'd all heard the story of Winnie using their grandmother's cloaking spell to spy on Zane in the locker room showers years before. She'd led them all to believe—quite truthfully—that he was hung like a horse. Now, to find out Zane hadn't known the basics of satisfying a woman…well, if it had happened to anyone else, she probably would've found it humorous.

"Now do you see the problem?" she asked, desperate for them to back off.

Autumn laughed. A long, obnoxious, side-splitting guffaw. Her amusement triggered her other sisters. They resembled a pack of baying hyenas.

"It's not freaking funny, Tums! I'll have to see him every single day, knowing we boinked, and he doesn't remember a thing about it."

Their amusement choked off, and, as one, their eyes went round. If they were synchronized swimmers, they'd have their act down pat.

"Why doesn't he remember?" Summer asked with trepidation. "What did you do?"

Her annoyance at the assumption flared to life, and Winnie jerked her chin up. "Why does it mean *I* did something? Maybe the whole day was just—"

"Fess up, sister. What did you do?" Autumn demanded, her hard tone no-nonsense. Having been trained by their parents through a strict old-school regime, her sister took magic and consequences seriously.

With a helpless glance into each face, Winnie looked for support. She got none. Each sister seemed convinced she'd done something dire. *And hadn't she?* She'd effectively erased the man's memories of their time together.

"I may have cast a spell to erase the event from his mind," she hedged.

"*Ohmygod!*"

"*Goddess!*"

"*Holy shit!*"

The last was followed by a forceful sneeze. A scurry of mice appeared in Winnie's periphery. Such was the case whenever Summer swore. It took a lot to rattle her sister, but Winnie had managed it with one simple confession.

Autumn ran a hand through her mass of auburn hair. "Let me get this straight. You slept with Zane, and because it sucked, you wiped his memory clean?"

Winnie winced. "It's a little more complicated, but yeah, that's about right."

"Oh, Winnie!" Summer exclaimed. "Was all that talk of him being well-endowed a lie?"

"No!" Winnie nearly shouted. She cleared her throat and struggled to control her blush. "No. He's well equipped. He just didn't know how to use his equipment in a satisfactory manner."

A snort, a giggle, and a coughing-gasp greeted her statement.

"What happened?" Summer made a serious attempt to control her hilarity.

"We went out a few times. On our last date, we went to the clearing between our properties."

"That damned clearing!" Autumn muttered with a dark frown. "I swear it's cursed."

"You may be right," Winnie agreed with a nod. "But except for a quick grab of my boobs and a finger in my hidey-hole to see if I was ready, he had no moves. He got on and got off in a matter of minutes."

Again, her sisters' expressions reflected shocked wonder. Winnie almost took a picture in order to frame it for posterity.

"That's terrible!" Summer exclaimed.

"You ain't lyin', sister." Restless energy swamped her, and Winnie stood to pace. "He had the nerve to ask if it was good for me afterwards."

The choked laugh behind her was cut off with an "oomph." Winnie had to assume Summer or Spring elbowed Autumn who seemed to find most things funny.

"When I told him 'not so much,' he had a meltdown."

"Wait! You *told* him it sucked?" Autumn asked, incredulous.

"He asked!" Winnie shouted. "What was I supposed to do?"

"You lie, Winnie!" Summer shouted in return. "You *never* tell a guy he sucks in bed!"

"What did I miss?" Asked a deep, dry voice from the living room doorway.

All four sisters whipped around to face their visitor.

Cooper Carlyle leaned one shoulder against the jamb. He stood with his arms across his brawny t-shirt clad chest. His brows were lifted in inquiry, but his twinkling blue-gray gaze was for his girlfriend alone. "Summer? Is there something you need to tell me?"

"No!" Summer gasped. "Never!"

Coop let loose a sharp bark of laughter. "But you just said you should lie if a guy sucks in bed."

"Not you, Coop! You… me… we…"

He took pity on her and grinned. "I came to see if you were ready to head home for the night. Should I leave you to your gossiping?"

Summer bit her lip in indecision. Clearly, she wanted the scoop, but she wanted to spend time with Coop, too.

Winnie waved her off. "Go, sister. I can fill you in another time."

"But Zane—"

"Zane!" Coop crowed in delight. "Zane was the one who sucked in bed?"

A hand flew up to cover Summer's gaping mouth. "Oh, hell, I'm sorry." A sneeze and an influx of mice followed her apology.

Winnie covered her eyes and prayed for the floor to open and swallow her whole. How had her life come to this? Zane was Coop's cousin for Christ's sake! If he took it into his head to tease Zane, Coop could open a major can of worms.

"Now we know why you objected to working with him," Coop said when he had his laughter under control. "Wait until I bust his balls!"

"You may want to hold off on that, Sheriff. The Boy Wonder doesn't know," Autumn clarified.

Winnie glared. Her sisters could be a little more discreet and not tell all hell and back about her business.

Coop stilled, and a fierce gleam came into his eyes. He straightened to his full height and glared. "What do you mean by he doesn't know? What exactly doesn't he *know*?"

"It's nothing so awful, Coop," Spring soothed in her musical tones. "Winnie only erased his memory of their time together."

Coop sucked in his breath hard enough to hack up a lung. When he'd gotten his coughing fit under control, he stormed to where Winnie stood trembling in her proverbial boots. "*You did what?*"

"I took away his recall of that day's events. And maybe a few others," she confessed weakly.

"Restore them," he growled.

"I can't."

"Why can't you? If you removed them, you can replace them."

"No, I mean I don't know what the long-term consequence might be if I messed with his mind a second time." Winnie swallowed hard and closed her eyes. "I think I'm responsible for the fact he didn't regain his powers when your parents unbound the three of you," she gushed.

Silence reigned as everyone finally understood the magnitude of her actions.

"Jesus!" Coop swore. "What do we do now?"

In for a penny, in for a pound. Winnie decided to reveal the rest of her secret. "To add to the problem, he was in a car accident earlier today."

"What?" Coop gripped her arms and shook her.

Winnie winced in discomfort. "He's okay," she hurried to assure him. "Or at least he is physically."

"Stop stalling, Winnie. What happened to Zane?"

"He hit his head on the windshield and doesn't remember who I am—*at all.*"

Cooper swore long and hard before he disappeared into thin air.

"Where do you suppose he went?" Spring asked.

Autumn snorted. "Hopefully, to check on Zane and not find reinforcements to murder our sister."

ZANE OPENED HIS FOURTH BEER AS HE SAT IN THE LOUNGE CHAIR overlooking the back of the Carlyle estate. He guzzled half the bottle before he grimaced in disgust. Four damned beers and he didn't even have the beginning of a buzz. His supercharged cells must be to blame.

A crackle rent the air, and in the next instant, a glowering Coop filled the empty space. Teleporting. His cousins had told him that's what it was called, this ability to bend space and instantly be in another location.

Was that something he'd be able to do now? The idea perked him up slightly.

"Coop."

"Zane."

"Aren't you usually heading to North Carolina with the little lady about this time of day?"

"I am, but something's come to my attention."

34

Zane shot him a guarded look. "Care to elaborate, or am I supposed to guess?"

His cousin sat on the edge of the lounger next to his. "I heard you were in an accident today?"

"Yeah, no worries about that. Not even a report for you to file. It seems Alastair Thorne is one powerful motherfucker. He restored my car and healed the small scratch to my head."

"Rumor has it, you have a little glitch in your memory bank."

Zane snorted and took a pull of his beer. "No. I finally remembered everything."

"I was at Thorne Manor. Winnie said you don't remember who she is."

At the mention of Winnie's name, his rage resurfaced. "I said I remember, dammit!" A spark flared from his fingertips, and Zane shook it out like a match. He couldn't wrap his brain around the fact he could produce fire from his hand without burning the living crap out of himself.

"Why does she believe otherwise?" Coop asked cautiously.

"*Because that's what I want her to believe.* That back-stabbing, sneaky—let's just say, she's going to get what she deserves."

"Zane," Coop said, a warning in his voice. "Maybe you should think this through."

"I've already thought it through. She stole my memories for whatever messed-up reason of her own. I intend a little payback."

"I get that you're angry—"

Zane scoffed in his fury. "Angry? *Angry?* I'm not angry, Coop. I'm fucking *livid!* How would you feel?"

Coop shook his head and grimaced. "I guess I'd feel the same way. But she's the sister of my girlfriend, and I don't want to see anyone get hurt."

"Too late for that."

"What do you mean?"

"*I* got hurt. When the memories returned today, I wrecked my car and put my head through the damned windshield. That wasn't a fun day in the park, you know." Zane inhaled in an attempt to calm the fire within. "I didn't deserve her spiteful behavior, Coop. I was on my way to apologize for... well, never mind that, but before I could, everything about our time together was gone." He closed his eyes. "Our first kiss. Carving our initials into the old oak after our first date. Everything."

"You love her," Coop said in awe.

"No!" he denied hotly. After another heavy sigh and another drink, he said, "Not anymore. She took that away, too."

Coop stood and placed a hand on Zane's shoulder. "If there is anything I can do, let me know."

"We never had this discussion."

"Okay."

"Oh, and Coop?"

"Yeah?"

"If anyone asks, I don't remember who Winnie is."

It was a long moment before Coop nodded his head. "Okay. But tread carefully."

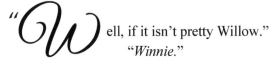 ell, if it isn't pretty Willow."

"*Winnie.*"

"Does it matter? You're only here to teach me to control my magic."

Winnie inhaled for the count of five. If she didn't get a handle on her temper soon, she was likely to zap Zane to another continent. This was the second day of training, and his stupid-ass comments were already grating on her last nerve.

Boy had she been fooled as to his character, believing him to be sweet and charming when in actuality he was the worst sort of Lothario. After their first session, she'd gone home disillusioned and full of self-loathing for ever caring about him in the first place.

With a heavy exhale, she faced him and flashed him a polite smile. "You're absolutely correct. It doesn't matter. Let's get started, shall we?"

His eyes narrowed as if he was trying to figure her out.

Winnie could've told him not to bother. She didn't have a handle on herself. She doubted anyone else would understand what made her tick.

"My uncle mentioned that you're fire element," she said brightly.

Zane didn't answer. Instead, he continued to stare.

"Yes, well." Unnerved, Winnie strode across his attic to the Carlyle grimoire and picked up the heavy tome. "I'm not sure how much you've already gleaned from your family, but we can go over the basics again and add to our lessons from there."

"Are you dating anyone?"

Winnie fumbled the heavy leather volume in her hands. "As I stated yesterday, this is called a grimoire. Every magical family has one."

"Is that a no?" he asked, amusement thick in his voice.

"Can we stick to learning here?"

"I am learning. I'm learning if you are available for a date with me tonight."

"No."

"How about tomorrow?"

"It's always going to be no, Zane."

The carnal look in his eyes made her stomach tighten in knots. While they'd only dated a few times and slept together just the once, she recognized his expression for what it was.

Zane closed the space between them.

Nerve endings on high alert, Winnie stepped back.

Once again, he closed the gap.

Her foot caught on a table leg as she backed another step. Had Zane not caught her arm, she'd have fallen over in an ungraceful heap. Winnie jerked away from his touch and opened the distance between them again.

With a knowing smirk, Zane took another step in her direction. She backed up a third time. The cat-stalking-the-mouse game continued until she found herself with her back against the wooden slats of the attic wall.

"Tell me, Wilhelmina, why is it always going to be no?"

Wilhelmina? She'd give him Wilhelmina!

Winnie slapped a hand flat on his chest. "That! That right there! You can't be bothered to remember my damned name."

"Hmm, I can see where that might be an issue while we're holding a conversation, but for what I have in mind, it won't matter."

"Well, get whatever you have in mind right on outta there! It's never happening agai—uh, it's never happening."

His lips twitched. Whether in anger or laughter, she couldn't say. Zane's neutral mask settled firmly in place. "Oh, I don't know. I think you should give it a shot. Being with me might just be the *best night of your life*."

Winnie released an unladylike snort. "Where have I heard *that* before," she muttered. In a louder voice, she said, "Back off, Don Juan. No means no."

Zane stepped backward as if she'd pulled a gun on him. Hands in the air, he kept a wary eye on her from his position in the middle of the room. "Got it."

If only everything in life were that easy. "Good. Let's get on with it."

"I thought you didn't want to have sex?"

"I meant the magical training," she ground out.

"What else could you possibly mean?"

If she didn't know better, Winnie would think Zane was toying with her. But why? If he truly couldn't recall any part of their relationship, why mess with her at all? How had his personality changed so drastically in the time since she'd known him?

Sadness swarmed her. The truth was, she hadn't really known him. He'd always presented as a warm, caring man, but on more than one occasion, she'd seen a side of him that she doubted he showed many people. She'd seen the anger and ugliness spew from his own lips.

"Are you okay?"

Winnie hadn't realized she'd zoned out for the few minutes she'd been lost in the past. Embarrassed by her space-cadet routine, she held out the grimoire. "You need to familiarize yourself with the spells in this book. They will come in handy."

"Win?"

Her head snapped up, and she locked eyes with him. "Why did you call me that?"

"What?"

"Win. It's… you…" She sighed her frustration at his blank look. "Never mind." Perhaps his use of the nickname was like muscle memory in his brain. He might not be aware he'd called her by the name he'd given her eight years before.

Somehow, she had to find a way to leave the past behind her. That way lay heartache and resentment.

With a put-on bright smile, she knelt at his feet. "Come."

Twin spots of color appeared high on his cheeks. "Uh…"

The second Zane stuttered, he gave away his thoughts.

Winnie's cheeks heated to burning. "Oh!" As she tried to gain her feet, she pitched forward. Her face came into direct contact with the front of his fly. In an effort to catch Winnie, or possibly to save his crotch from major incident, Zane's hands flew down toward his genitals. But their trajectory got waylaid, and his hands tangled in Winnie's hair.

Zane's fingers tightened, and he tugged her head back. When their gazes connected, his burned bright with an unnamed emotion. For a long moment, neither moved as the tension sizzled in the air about them. Winnie knelt, frozen in place by the predatory gleam shining from Zane's eyes.

Without warning, his expression shifted, became moody and contemplative. He bit his lip as if he were holding back words he longed to say. What did he have to be moody about? And for that matter, why *was* he moody? This was Zane. Mr. Happy-Go-Lucky who was fazed by nothing.

"Zane? Are you all right?" She rose and touched his forearm. Her voice was loud and breathy, giving away the fact that she was disturbed by his nearness.

"I'm fine. Let's get on with today's lesson. I have work to do."

The about-face and gruff attitude burned Winnie's ass. It had only been ten minutes, but she was sick of his behavior. When he wasn't stalking her like he wanted to rip her clothes off, he was behaving like a petulant child.

"Have I done something to upset you?" She didn't bother to keep her irritation hidden.

His lip curled in derision. "Upset me? Why would you think I'd ever be upset with *you*?"

"Oh, I don't know. Your *animosity* right now? Why don't you tell me what it is you think I've done? Because from where I'm standing, I've only tried to help you."

"Are you kidding me right now?" His arms were raised, and his hands were curled into white-knuckled fists. "I… Gah!"

She wasn't prepared for the fury behind his words. Apprehension crept in. The only thing she'd ever done was to erase his memories. But if Zane couldn't remember who she was, he shouldn't have the slightest recollection of what they'd done. Yet the rage radiating from him was eerily similar to the day in the glen.

The only other possibility was that Zane was mentally imbalanced. Whether he'd always been that way and Winnie had been sheltered from his behavior, or it was a recent development, she'd never know. But if his current tangent was a side effect of his accident, then someone should be made aware.

"How about I go get one of your cousins for you?" She tried for soothing tones, but Zane was having none of it.

"I'm not a mental case," he barked. "Stop staring at me as if I am."

"I didn't say you were."

"You didn't have to."

ZANE NEEDED TO GET A HANDLE ON HIS ANGER. BUT WHENEVER HE was around Winnie, he thought of sex. The thoughts of sex brought him back to the day they'd made love. Which in turn, had him recalling that she'd stolen his memories with a deceitful trick. The acid in his gut churned, and bile rose up to the back of his throat.

How could she do that to him? He'd thought they started something special back then.

While Zane never had a problem with a good-natured jest, he drew the line at being a chump. What Winnie had done was unforgivable. Although, if he were to be fair, his terrible words in the field had been unforgivable, too. But words and actions were two different things, weren't they?

Yeah, he was angry. Bitterly so.

"Look, I'm going to go. You obviously don't like me, and I—"

"No!" he exclaimed before he could stop himself.

Her wide-eyed look of concern spurred him into an explanation.

"I'm sorry. It's not that I don't like you, Winnie. It's that I like you too much," he lied smoothly.

Winnie's eyes grew larger, and her mouth parted. It was the sign he needed to move closer.

With the tip of his index finger, Zane trailed a light, scrolling path along her jaw toward her mouth. "I find I'm having a difficult time keeping my hands to myself. All I want to do is kiss you." He lowered his voice and turned up the seduction. "Touch you." He drew his thumb across her lower lip, smearing the berry-red lipstick there. "Make you mine."

Her breathing resembled an athlete after competition. The ragged, harsh breaths almost made him smile. Good to know he affected her as much as she affected him.

He closed what was left of the distance between them and tilted his head towards hers. Her unique smell filled his nostrils when he inhaled. The light floral scent teased him, and it dawned on him why he'd become dizzy in the diner. A small part of his mind had recalled the fragrance of her skin. That scent had triggered the fleeting images in his head.

When his lips settled on hers, he sighed his satisfaction. It had been too long since they last touched. Their light moans mingled as the kiss drew out longer and became more heated. And like the day in the clearing so long ago, Zane found himself over-eager to sink inside her. To have her shapely thighs cradling his hips. To experience the euphoria of an orgasm of such power that it rocked his world.

Because his urges were animalistic in nature, Zane forced himself to pull back. The space below her ear required his utmost attention, and his lips caressed the sensitive skin there. He could feel her rapid-fire pulse, and he smiled against her throat.

"God, Winnie, you don't know what you do to me," he whispered.

She froze, and it was no guess as to why. Word for word, he'd uttered the exact phrase he'd said the first time they'd made love.

Winnie put her hands between them and eased back. "This is a bad idea."

"Why?" He asked the question, knowing she couldn't reveal the truth. Knowing if she did, she'd unleash a maelstrom she had no way of containing.

"Because I like you too much," she said, a repeat of his earlier words.

Faced with a choice, Zane had no idea which way to go. He could let go of his anger and see where a relationship could lead, or he could exact payback for her duplicitous behavior.

Winnie, the woman who he'd always dreamed of one day marrying and who just confessed to her attraction to him, was also the instigator of a dirty trick played against him. A man didn't get over that easily, if at all.

His gaze dropped to her swollen mouth. Those succulent lips made him want to continue to kiss her for days without end. But he couldn't trust her to be truthful. She was an expert at games and manipulation. Not once, in all the years he'd known her, had she given any indication they'd been together. She had lied by omission the rare times they'd come in contact. And for that, he decided he couldn't forgive.

"Okay."

Her jaw dropped. Her squeaked *"What?"* almost caused him to laugh.

"I said, okay. I get it. We like each other too much to chase this thing between us. With both of us desiring to remain free agents, it would be foolish to start something."

"It would?"

He bit the inside of his cheek to hold back his amusement. "Yep."

Her angry scowl forced him to turn and hide his grin.

"Who said I wanted to be a free agent?" she muttered behind his back.

"Maybe it would be better if someone else trained me."

"Why?"

Zane toyed with a candle holder atop a nearby cabinet. "Because we'd find it difficult to keep our hands off each other."

"Well, I can if you can, Mr. Sex God."

The sarcastic edge in her voice caught his attention. He pivoted back around. With her hands on her hips and a fire flashing in her blue eyes, Winnie was magnificent.

"I'm not sure I can," he admitted truthfully.

He almost swallowed his tongue when she said, "I need you."

Screw it, he was going to cave and give her whatever she wanted. *Any position she wanted for however long she wanted.*

"I need you to go to Egypt with me," she said.

Okay, so that wasn't the *need* he'd been expecting. Zane managed to clear away his muddled sexual thoughts to ask, "What's in Egypt?"

"An Egyptian Uterine amulet that Alastair says can revive my mother."

White-hot rage flooded him. He was a sucker. No doubt about it. In her attempt to manipulate him, she'd almost made Zane believe she wanted him.

He shook his head, moved to the attic window, and stared out toward the glen without speaking. If he shut his eyes, he could recall in technicolored detail the entire few weeks they'd dated. Every moment was now branded in his brain.

God, how he had adored her! The sun had risen and set on all things Winter Thorne. He would've cut off his left nut to have her forever. He snorted. What a blind fool he'd been.

"Zane?"

Her tentative voice caused his heart to contract and harden. He was done playing the fool. "Yes."

"Yes, you'll go?"

"Yes, I'll go." He didn't bother to turn around. "Call my receptionist, Penny, and determine the schedule that suits you."

"Thank you."

Her sweet, choked words would have stirred another person. But they left Zane cold. When the timing was right, he'd switch the tables, and Winnie would see what it was like to lose something she cared about. But in the meantime, he planned to seduce the hell out of her. After all, he had a lot to prove this time around.

7

"*W*hat's the plan, boss?" Penny snapped her gum in rapid-fire succession. "Are you really going to leave the business to go jetting off around the world?"

"I'm going to one location—Egypt. It's a scouting mission to see if we can find an artifact."

"We, as in you and Miss Winter Thorne?" she teased.

"Yes."

"I could go with you and pave the way, book hotels, set up rental cars, that sort of thing."

Penny appeared hopeful.

Zane hated to squelch her excitement, but the situation required him to remain secretive. That meant limiting social interactions with non-magical beings and staying mum on the subject of magical artifacts.

"I need you to hold down the fort here, Pen."

"There's nothing here to hold down but musty, old misfiled papers."

"You can't go," Zane stated, infusing steel into his tone.

Penny ignored his dictate.

"Are you worried I'll screw up your game with Winnie? If anything, I can help."

"I am not worried. Believe me, my *game* will be perfectly fine."

She scoffed before popping her gum again. "Dude, you are so far from having game."

He glared. "You, too? Seriously? What is with the women of this town?"

Penny's eyes flew wide. "Did Winnie reject you?"

"I'm not discussing this," Zane snapped. Since when had he lost control? Why did the women in his world feel it was all right to discuss his romantic life? Was nothing sacred anymore?

"Do you need pointers?"

"No, Pen. *I don't need any damned pointers!* If I want to seduce Winnie Thorne, I can damned well do it without any help."

"Am I interrupting?" Humor laced the voice of the man behind him.

Zane closed his eyes and hung his head. Of *course*, Alastair Thorne would enter the law office at the precise time Zane was discussing the scary man's niece. Such was Zane's luck.

"Mr. Thorne," he said in acknowledgment.

"Mr. Carlyle." Alastair strolled farther into the room and gave his surroundings a cursory glance. "Nice place you have here." The tone stated he meant the exact opposite.

"We're in the takeover process. It needs work."

"Hmm." The noncommittal word expressed Alastair's opinion in spades.

"How can I help you?" Zane asked through gritted teeth.

The other man cast a pointed look in Penny's direction.

"Pen, go grab some lunch and bring me a sandwich on your way back, please," Zane suggested. As a courtesy, he asked Alastair if he would like something. The cold stare he received in return was answer enough. "Okay, then. That should do it, Pen. Be sure to take your full hour."

After his assistant grudgingly took the thirty dollars from his hand and headed out the door, Zane turned to Winnie's uncle. "What you heard, I wasn't planning… that's to say, I didn't…"

One of Alastair's dark, arrogant brows lifted. "I have no problem with you seducing my niece. I *do*, however, have a problem with you breaking her heart." The second brow joined the first, and his dark-blue eyes hardened. "You don't intend to break her heart, do you, boy?"

"Uh…" How would he know if her heart would be broken if he seduced her? In his experience, Winnie didn't have a heart. She was a cold, unfeeling—

"You still with me, son, or did you take a side trip?" Alastair mocked, not bothering to disguise his amusement.

"Yeah, sorry. What can I do for you, Mr. Thorne?"

"I thought we might discuss your journey to Egypt."

"What about it?"

Alastair toyed with a dragonfly paperweight on the corner of Penny's desk. "How much do you know about Isis?"

"The Goddess?"

"The very one."

Zane shrugged. "Some, not much. But I have a laptop and the ability to google."

"The last documented whereabouts of the Uterine amulet you'll be searching for was in Isis's temple. Not the temple in Philae. It's in Saqqara, buried." Alastair set the paperweight down and focused his attention on Zane. "The amulet is made of Jasper and had a Tjet— that's a knot of Isis—engraved on the front side. You'll know it's the one when you feel the power. It's like no other."

"How do you propose we find a buried temple?" Zane asked impatiently. It wasn't as if he had an excavation team at his disposal.

"I expect you to apply what you've learned. There will be signs and symbols that guide you to the temple's location. I'll provide what intel I can find. Then, it is a simple matter of Winnie using her power to clear away the sands and debris."

"If it's so easy, why aren't you going after it?"

"Son, are you *trying* to piss me off?"

Alastair's anger vibrated between them.

"Nope." Zane in no way wanted to upset him. Since finding out Alastair was one of the most powerful men in existence, Zane had developed a healthy respect for the guy. He shook his head and sighed. "I just don't understand why I have to be the one to go when you seem to have a handle on where and what you are after."

The stern expression on the other man's face gave way to a half-smile. "You'll understand soon enough. In the meantime, if you break my niece's heart a second time, I will destroy you." So saying, Alastair slapped Zane on the back and teleported away.

A second time? Alastair had to be mistaken. Winnie hadn't cared about Zane in the least. If she had, she never would've done what she did. Never played him for a fool and laughed behind his back with her family.

In that moment, Zane came close to hating all the Thornes.

With a deep sigh, he lowered his large frame into Penny's office chair. Placing his elbows on the armrest, he steepled his fingers—his standard thinking pose.

That's how Winnie found him when she sailed through his front door. As she cast him a tentative smile, he caught his breath. With her windblown hair and color high on her cheeks, she was the most beautiful woman he'd ever seen.

Without tearing his gaze from hers, Zane stood and ambled to her. He took his time studying her flushed face. With a sweep of one finger, he cleared the unruly hair from where it clung to her left cheek. Dipping his head, he brushed his lips against hers. As her mouth moved in response, he possessed her more fully, sweeping his tongue into the warmth of her mouth. She mewled in response—a soft, sexy sound that shot straight to his 'nads—and dug her fingers into the muscles of his upper arms.

Zane drew back and nipped her lower lip. The dazed, passionate look she sported satisfied him to the extreme. "Ah, Walinda, those delicious lips of yours make me wonder what other wondrous things they can do. My office is empty if you'd like to show me."

The crack of Winnie's palm against his cheek echoed around the reception area. Zane's head snapped to the side from the sheer force. *Holy hell, that woman packed a helluva wallop!* He flexed his jaw and faced her.

"You're an ass," she hissed.

"What did I say? I thought I was paying you a compliment."

"By suggesting I give you a blow job?" she screeched.

He flared his eyes wide. "What? I never suggested such a thing! You have a dirty mind, Wanda."

"It's Winnie, and you know damned well you did."

Her eyes flashed silver; her irises altered by her fury. He'd learned that sort of color change was a witch's tell.

Zane was perverted enough to take pleasure in her anger. In fact, it aroused him to no end. All he wanted to do was get her behind closed doors and ravish her. "Has anyone ever told you that you're stunning in your anger?" he asked huskily.

ZANE'S QUESTION BROUGHT WINNIE UP SHORT. WHAT TYPE OF MAN was he that he found her anger a turn on? And what did it say about her that the idea of him turned on aroused *her*? She was as twisted as he was.

When his hot gaze raked her body, she wanted to jump him. But because her desire for him was mind-melting and nearly over-whelmed her in its intensity, she shoved aside the urge and shifted away. "I'm here to discuss Egypt."

"Of course you are." She heard his heavy sigh behind her. "What's the plan?"

"I figured we would spend one more week in training and then head to Cairo to see what we can find."

"Your uncle paid me a visit. He believes the amulet is located in Saqqara."

Alastair had visited him? When had the two become as thick as thieves? The idea that they might be in cahoots made Winnie uneasy.

She faced him. "Does he know exactly where?"

"He has an idea."

"Tell me."

"Why? So you can run off half-cocked by yourself? It's not happening."

Irritated because Zane had guessed her intent, Winnie shrugged. "It was worth a try."

Fire flared to life in his eyes. "You aren't going to bother denying that was your goal?"

"No."

"I swear to all that's holy, you and I are going to have a day of reckoning very soon, Win."

His tone, the use of the nickname, and his anger all spoke of a deeper meaning. If she didn't know any better, she'd believe he knew about the past. But how could he? She'd done nothing to alter the spell or reverse it.

As Winnie opened her mouth to ask, Penny sailed through the door with a paper bag in hand.

"I got your sandwi—oh! Uh, hey, Ms. Thorne. I thought I'd given the boss enough time, but I can head back out."

"No, Penny. Please enjoy your lunch with Zane. I'll catch him another time," Winnie said with a graceful nod of her head, or what she hoped was one. Appearing cool under Zane's intent regard wasn't easy. She gave him a slight nod. "Zane."

"Wenelle."

She gritted her teeth but didn't correct him. She had no doubt he knew her name. It had become obvious that he was playing a twisted game; one where only he knew the rules.

Winnie had taken two steps toward the exit when the undeniable truth hit her. She spun back around to stare. "You know," she whispered. Her heart hammered at what felt like a thousand beats per minute.

"I know," he agreed, expression stony.

"Can we discuss it?" Not that she wanted to, but they needed to clear the air before their trip. Nothing good would come if they weren't on the same page when they went after the amulet.

"All in good time," he answered silkily.

Winnie cast a nervous glance in Penny's direction. Though her confusion was obvious, Penny wisely kept silent. Something Winnie herself should've done.

Leaving him to stew in his anger didn't sit well. "For what it's worth, I'm sorry."

He snorted his disbelief.

"It's true, Zane." She walked back and placed her palm flat over his heart. The heat building in his body caused her to jerk back. Unsure if his body temperature was normal for a fire-elemental warlock, Winnie backed away. She'd need to discuss this with her father or Alastair. Because if it wasn't the norm, they needed to determine what was the root cause of Zane's overheating and find a way to neutralize it before it caused him—or someone else—injury.

"I'll send you a text with a time and location to discuss it. Be there," he ordered.

She bit her lip and nodded.

She'd barely closed her car door when his message dinged her phone.

6 p.m. at the clearing. You know the place.

Winnie had roughly four hours to kill and didn't think she could stand the wait. Nerves on edge, she cranked her vehicle and headed home.

On the drive, she toyed with leaving the country no less than fifteen different times. Australia was probably the farthest she could go. Since it was on the other side of the planet, they would be experiencing nice weather and not the cold temperatures of winter.

Anything would be better than facing Zane with the truth of her actions.

Despondent, Winnie pulled into the drive of the Thorne estate and berated herself for her foolishness. The fun, flirty side of Zane was gone. In its place was an enraged dupe. His anger was justified, and yet, hers had been at the time, too.

How could she prove she was remorseful?

8

*a*t 5:59 p.m., Winnie almost chickened out for the hundredth time. Closing her eyes, she breathed in and teleported to the glen.

Zane was waiting. He stood staring at the old, gnarled oak on the edge of the clearing. When Zane shifted slightly, Winnie saw what he'd been so intent on: their carved initials. How she'd never noticed them before was beyond her, but the darkness of the grooves said they'd been there for some time.

"Why?" One word, that's all he asked. Yet, the wealth of feeling behind it couldn't be mistaken. He felt betrayed by her actions.

Winnie couldn't blame him.

"You said you wished we'd never gotten together. I was giving you what you wanted."

His head dropped back, and he loosed a long, guttural yell. It screamed of his frustration and pain.

Winnie wanted to go to him. Wanted to hold him and beg his forgiveness. But she didn't know how. Nothing had changed, and she'd done what she thought was best at the time.

"For what it's worth, Zane, I'm sorry."

He stormed to where she stood. "You're sorry? You played God and removed my memories, and you're *sorry?* That's all I get?"

Her own anger came into play. "What more can I do or say? You acted like I was the dirt beneath your feet. You practically called me a whore. And you insulted my family."

"That gave you no right to cast a spell on me!" he snarled. "Do you have any idea how freaked out I was to find myself sitting beneath that damned tree with no recollection as to why I was there?"

Because she was in the wrong, Winnie stayed silent.

"Do you want to know what caused my accident last week?"

She shook her head.

"The memories when they came flooding back," he said, ignoring her desire to remain oblivious. "I was driving to your house when it all returned with a vengeance. A dog ran into the road. Because I was distracted, I wrecked and put my head through the windshield." He gripped her upper arms and shook her. "I would be dead right now had your uncle not come along. *Dead*, Winnie. Process that."

The thought of Zane hurt or dead devastated her. Tears came unbidden and coursed down her cheeks. She closed her eyes and gulped in large quantities of air, unable to breathe freely as the sobs took hold.

"Dammit," he muttered, hauling her into his embrace. "Don't cry, Win."

"I c-can't h-help it."

He shifted to wipe her tears. "Please don't. I can't take it."

"I d-don't want t-to be in a w-world without y-you in it," she croaked out between sobs. "I'm s-sorry."

"Oh, Win." He scooped her into his arms and sat beneath the tree with their initials. "Please don't cry."

She clung to him for all she was worth. She wrapped her arms around his neck and buried her face against his throat. "If I c-could've undone it, I would have. I j-just didn't know how. I didn't want to hurt you f-further."

His arms tightened around her, and for the first time in years, she felt protected and cherished. How long they stayed wrapped together was anyone's guess. All Winnie cared about was being held by Zane.

"Don't hate me. Please," she whispered.

"I could never hate you, Win. But so we are clear, I'm not happy with you right now."

Hot tears pooled and poured from her eyes.

Zane pulled back enough to tenderly wipe the tears from her cheeks. "I think it's my turn to explain my side of this whole fiasco."

"You don't need to, I—"

"I do," he insisted. "From the first moment I saw you, I wanted you beyond reason. When you agreed to go out with me, I was over the moon. But then came my piss-poor performance. You just felt too good in my arms, Win. I couldn't hold back to save my own life in that moment." He made a face. "I wanted it to be earth-shattering for you, but I flubbed it. I followed you to apologize. But I think, by then, you must've started your spell. I made it as far as the edge of the clearing when I got dizzy. Within a few minutes, I'd forgotten why I was there."

"Zane—"

He placed a finger over her lips. "Let me finish. I'm sorry for all the horrible things I said that day. You didn't deserve them. But I didn't deserve what you did either." Zane focused on her and shook his head. "If you ever pull another stunt like that again, I'll wring your neck. Are we clear?"

"I won't. I promise."

"Good." They sat in silence for a few minutes. Zane finally spoke. "I'm a little disappointed you figured out my game. I had more W names ready to go: Winerva, Waverly, Wylda."

Her head came up, and she couldn't stop the bubble of laughter. "You're a jerk."

"Wendolyn, Whitney."

"Stop!" She shook her head and pressed her forehead to his. "I really am sorry."

"It's okay, Wanda. Really."

Winnie rolled her eyes and attempted to climb from his lap.

He anchored her in place with his hands. "Where do you think you're going?"

"I thought we cleared the air," she hedged.

"Oh, no. Not completely. I owe you an orgasm—with interest."

Shock made her face numb. While a good part of her wanted to bump nasties with Zane, the more conservative part applied the brakes. "I don't know if that's a good idea."

He grinned, and she felt it down to her toes. "It's a great idea. I swear I know where the g-spot is located now."

Zane shifted, and Winnie felt the full length of his erection against her.

"Ohmygod!"

His self-assured smile told her that this time around, he intended to make it good for her. When his mouth captured hers, she ceased to think at all.

The kiss was far different from the ones she remembered from when they'd dated. And yet, there was an underlying element that made Winnie believe Zane still found it difficult to hold back. A wild need he conveyed with every touch.

His passion triggered her own. In their crazed desire, they barely dispensed with their clothes. Shirts were ripped open, her bra shoved aside, skirt shimmied up, and panties… well, she had no idea what happened to those. But she didn't find it hard to believe they melted into nothingness from his hot hands.

Zane pulled back, panting. "We need to slow down. I promised it wouldn't be a repeat of eight years ago."

"I'm not opposed to a repeat. I'm just opposed to not getting the big O."

"In that case, let's get that out of the way first."

His head dipped, and he kissed the treasured spot at the apex of her thighs. When he caressed her clit and inserted a finger into her wet core, she cried out.

Zane seemed to find delight in teasing her and bringing her to the brink, only to back away.

She growled her frustration and snared her fingers into his thick, blond hair. "One more time and I'm turning you into a toad!"

His mischievous gaze connected with hers. "Patience is a virtue, Win. Haven't you been told that?"

"Not when torture is involved."

"In that case…"

Zane lowered his head, and Winnie's orgasm followed directly after. Before she could come down from her euphoria, her second orgasm hit.

"Yeah, you've definitely mastered the art of making a woman come," she sighed.

His lips twisted in a semblance of a smile, but it didn't reach his eyes. A tremor of alarm chased down her spine. She couldn't dismiss the feeling that something was still off.

"Zane—"

When he ducked his head and captured her breast, she lost her train of thought.

He lifted his head and blew on the tightened nub. "Don't think, Win. Feel."

Taking his advice, Winnie gave over to the riot of sensations he was causing. And as Zane eased inside her, it was as if he'd come home and Winnie welcomed him with open arms.

9

"*Y*ou're glowing," Autumn stated.

Winnie fought back her grin when she glanced up from rolling out the dough for the next batch of cinnamon rolls. "Am I?"

Spring studied her and nodded. "Yep. Spill."

"There's nothing to spill," Winnie said in a bald-faced lie.

Autumn swirled a small fireball between her fingers. "Liar, liar, should I set your pants on fire?"

Winnie laughed, and her sister extinguished the flame.

"Seriously, who was he, or is there a new and improved vibrator on the market?" Autumn asked as she crossed to make her morning tea.

"I'll never tell. And what are you doing here this early, Tums? Shouldn't you be honeymooning it up or something?" Winnie tried to deflect but just received amused smirks for her effort. Apparently wedded bliss for Autumn meant butting into other people's lives in a convoluted attempt to make everyone as happy as she was with her new husband, Keaton.

"I'm taking Chloe for a pedicure this morning. And you aren't getting out of answering that easily. Shall I run down the list of candidates?"

Winnie shrugged and grinned. "You'll never guess."

"Zane," Spring and Autumn said in unison.

Winnie's head snapped up to stare. "How did you know that?"

Spring snorted. "Oh, please! You act like we don't know how to scry."

"You spied on me?" Winnie's outrage knew no bounds. The idea of her sisters seeing the whole dirty deed made her ill.

"No! Or at least not *during*." Autumn laughed at Winnie's disbelief. "Seriously, we aren't a bunch of pervs. But since you've been training him, it's been more entertaining than Summer and Coop's little romantic dance." Autumn's brow shot up. "You weren't opposed to spying on the two of them."

Winnie glared her disgust. "You need a life."

"And you need to stay on topic. Zane. Sex. You're glowing. Spill."

"Five."

"Five?" Autumn asked in disbelief.

"Five what?" Spring asked.

Their oldest sister snorted. "Seriously, Spring. You need to lose that virginity. Your mind doesn't stay in the gutter long enough to hold a conversation."

"Oh," Spring muttered, embarrassed. An instant later, she gasped. "Oh! Wow! Seriously? Five times?"

Winnie laughed at her youngest sister's dumbfounded expression. "Five times and twelve orgasms."

Autumn paused with her teacup halfway to her lips. "Goddess! No wonder you're lit like a Christmas tree! I take it he learned how to use his equipment in the interim."

"I'm seriously glad he did," Winnie laughed. "Can you imagine if the sex still sucked after all this time?"

"Uh, Winnie…"

The warning note in Spring's tone caused Winnie to abandon her chore and shift her attention to the newcomer.

In the doorway stood a furious Zane.

"Zane!"

"You *told* them? Did the three of you have a nice laugh behind my back?"

"I…" What could she say? She *had* told them, but it wasn't what he thought. "It wasn't like that."

He dropped the bouquet of flowers he held on the ground and wordlessly turned away.

"Zane, wait! Please!"

His long legs ate up the distance to the door, and Winnie ran to catch up.

"Please listen to me," she begged. "It wasn't what you think."

The rage in Zane's face was terrifying, and for the second time in her life, Winnie feared he might strike her. His fist clenched and unclenched as if he contemplated strangling her. "Did you, or did you not, just say 'can you imagine if the sex still sucked after all this time?'"

The tone of his voice and the structuring of his words made her feel like she was in a court of law. "Well, if you're going to get all lawyer-y and shit, yes. But technically, I was bragging about your skill."

"Not from where I was standing," he bit out.

Winnie didn't know how to defend herself and stared at him in helpless frustration. What he'd overheard was damning.

"Well, had you been here two minutes earlier, stud, you'd have heard her going on about the twelve orgasms and five rounds of sex. So, I don't think your prowess is in question," Autumn inserted, coming to Winnie's rescue.

The blush started somewhere around Winnie's toes and quickly colored her entire body. Unable to maintain eye contact, she shifted her gaze to the floor.

Zane's large hand captured hers.

Hope blossomed in her chest, and she lifted her head.

"I only recently told them about erasing your memory and why," she explained. Careful to keep her voice low, she added, "I would never make fun of you like that."

His expression bordered tender. "I'm sorry, Win. I always seem to overreact where you're concerned."

With a squeeze of his hand and a tentative smile, she said, "I know. I have the same problem."

He shot her sisters a pointed look. "If you don't mind, I'd like a little privacy so I can kiss my girlfriend now."

Girlfriend? He viewed her as his girlfriend? Winnie couldn't prevent her wide, happy smile.

"Oh, we don't mind if you kiss her. We had numbered signs made for judging," Autumn quipped and conjured cardboard signs containing the numbers one through ten.

"Hold on," Winnie whispered and teleported the two of them to her bedroom.

"Not fair, Winnie!" Autumn hollered from downstairs. Laughter coated her words.

Zane wrapped an arm around her back and pulled her close. "Much better," he murmured as he dipped his head toward hers. He jerked to a stop right before their lips connected. "Twelve orgasms, Win? Really? I lost track after your seventh."

"Shut up and kiss me." She tugged his head down to hers.

He chuckled and complied with her demand.

She couldn't prevent the throaty moan of pleasure as his hands found their way under her shirt and across her bare skin to cup her breasts.

"We have so much time to make up for," he whispered against her neck.

Winnie didn't disagree.

A knock on her bedroom door stopped them before they got further than heavy petting.

"What?" she snarled. Her tone promised death to anyone on the other side of that wooden panel.

"Wow! After twelve orgasms, you'd think you'd be a little nicer!" Autumn called through the door.

"Bite me!" Winnie snapped.

When Zane bit an exposed portion of her neck, she yelped.

"Sorry, I thought you meant me." His chuckle was low and sexy, warming Winnie from her inside out.

Autumn called out, "Chloe called a meeting of the Witches' Club. She thinks we should all go for pedicures together."

Winnie groaned her frustration as Zane's hands made short work in disposing of her bra and shirt.

"I only need ten minutes to give you numbers thirteen and fourteen," he whispered in her ear. "Think they'll wait?"

"They're going to have to," she panted as his mouth latched onto her breast.

To Autumn, she called, "I'll meet you at the salon. Go ahead and start without me."

Her sister's laughter echoed down the hall.

"You and Winnie seem to have patched up your differences," Coop said with a grin.

Zane looked up from the book he'd been reading. "What makes you say that?"

"Autumn told Keaton you'd popped over this morning with flowers for Winnie."

Zane snorted and turned his attention back to the page in front of him.

Coop tugged the book from his hands. "What game are you playing, cousin?"

"She figured out that I regained my memories. I had to change my strategy."

"You still intend to pay her back for the trick she played?"

"Count on it." Zane snagged his book back.

Censure layered every line of Coop's face. "Don't do it, Zane."

"Why? Because she doesn't deserve it?" Zane sneered. "Can you honestly stand there and tell me you would've forgiven Summer had she pulled a stunt like that?"

Part of him wanted to squirm under his cousin's disappointed gaze, but Zane hadn't gotten over the fact that Winnie had so easily lied—and not just once, but multiple times on a continual basis.

"I would forgive Summer almost anything," Coop said softly.

The words brought Zane up short. "Almost being the key word. What would it take to make your forgiveness impossible?"

"I don't know. But I do know I wouldn't play a game of that nature."

"Really? Because as I seem to recall, you did just that with your little prom stunt."

Coop had the grace to look embarrassed. "Yeah, and look how well that turned out. But the difference is that I wasn't sleeping with her. I was also a stupid kid. You should know better, Zane."

After Coop stormed away, Zane checked the time and closed his book. He had a dinner date to keep with Winnie.

As he showered, he played over her confession in the glen. Her tears had moved him. How could they not? Yet, she could've easily employed them as a means of manipulation.

But damn, the sex was amazing. Each time was better than the last as they explored each other's bodies and learned likes and dislikes. So far, she'd been up for anything. She was a wildcat in bed, and Zane appreciated her enthusiasm. Finding himself aroused by the thought of her special warmth, he adjusted the temperature of his shower to cool himself down.

He fully intended to use her until he'd grown tired of her body. Only then would he confess to payback, right before he burned her and walked away for good. And after he was done with her, she'd be wishing *she* could forget *him*. He intended to make it difficult. For the rest of her life, she'd compare other men to him and find them wanting.

If it bothered him to think of her with another guy, Zane shoved it away. It was inevitable she'd eventually move on. He certainly would the second he was convinced she loved him. His revenge would be complete.

wo days later, Winnie finished bottling her latest batch of pain-relief cream for the local senior center when Autumn entered her workshop.

After a few minutes spent browsing through Winnie's stock, Autumn finally got to the point. "You and Zane are moving too fast."

Winnie shot a questioning look in her direction. "How so?"

"It's only been a week and a half since you've reconnected, but you're basically inseparable. I don't know if that's a good thing, sister."

"You and Keaton didn't move fast? For goodness sake, you married almost immediately."

"But before our fight, we dated ten months and were planning marriage," Autumn defended.

Her sister referred to the fight that had ended her relationship with Keaton and caused a nine-year rift between the two. Winnie had had a front row seat and witnessed a good amount of the heartache Autumn had suffered.

Winnie nodded. "Thornes only love once. We all know that. Once we've found The One, why wait? What makes my relationship different from yours, Tums?"

"I don't like the fact that he played you right after his wreck." Autumn frowned. "I'm not convinced he's forgiven you."

Winnie laughed and wiped her hands free of cream. "He has. We're in a great place."

"Let me put this another way. If the situations were reversed, how easily would you find it to forgive him, sister? Would you accept his apology immediately, or would you want a little payback?"

Unease danced along Winnie's spine, but she shoved it away. "Zane isn't the spiteful type. He's intelligent and logical. He understands it was an impulsive move on my part, and I would've fixed it if I could have."

"Does he?"

Uncertainty gave way to anger, and Winnie stormed to where Autumn rested against her work table. "Stop it! I'm not going to let you disparage him, Tums. I love him, and he loves me."

"Has he told you that?"

The question gave Winnie pause. He hadn't—not yet anyway. But the look in his eyes, the touch of his hands, and the way he catered to all her wants and needs indicated he did.

"He hasn't, has he?" Autumn asked gently.

Tears burned behind Winnie's lids. "Why are you doing this?"

"I don't want you hurt."

"Looks like I'll be hurt either way, doesn't it?" If he didn't return her feelings, then it was going to sting like a bitch.

Her sister wrapped her in a tight embrace. "Don't let this drag out, Winnie. Take it from the voice of experience. You need to find out his motives."

"I trust him," Winnie insisted stubbornly.

Expression grim, Autumn released her. "Fair enough. But I'm going to fry his ass if he's playing you for a fool."

After her sister left, Winnie closed up shop, unable to concentrate on anything but the doubts Autumn had planted in her mind. She'd just shut the door when Alastair appeared, causing her to nearly shed her skin with fright.

66

"For fuck's sake, Uncle! A phone call or warning wouldn't be remiss."

He chuckled. "My apologies for startling you."

"What do you want?"

"When do you leave for Saqqara?"

"Zane is wrapping up a few things today and tomorrow. We intend to leave early Wednesday morning."

Alastair handed her a necklace. "Take this and wear it at all times."

She held it up to the light to admire the gorgeousness of the piece. The multifaceted tanzanite stone reflected hues of deep purple and blue with hints of burgundy. "It's beautiful. But what's this about?"

"I've charmed the stone. It will give us a direct psychic link. If you find yourself in trouble, call to me." He took it from her hand and placed it over her head. "It will act as a homing device should I need to get to you."

"But you can't spy on me?" she asked. The thought of her uncle hearing her with Zane or during any other private moment gave her a serious case of the ickies.

"Child, if I wanted to spy on you, I don't need a charmed crystal to do it." He shoved his hands in the pockets of his black slacks. "With Zhu Lin still on the loose, I feel the need to take precautions."

Zhu Lin.

Winnie had hoped to never hear the name or see the man again. As a member of the Désorceler Society—the organization sworn to bring down witches and warlocks worldwide—Lin retained a single-minded focus to kill or capture every existing Thorne. He'd almost succeeded twice with Autumn. Little Chloe and her friend Derek had been caught in the crossfire and almost died as a result.

"Is there an early warning system if he's close?" she jokingly asked.

Her uncle's lips twisted in a half-smile. "Ah, if only I could create something so useful. Alas, you are going to have to settle for the instant psychic connection the stone brings."

"Thank you, Uncle. I'll be sure to wear it."

"How are things progressing with your young man?" Alastair asked.

She cast him a side glance. "Wonderfully."

"You sound sincere."

"I am."

"Be careful. Not all Carlyles have the same agenda."

"What's that supposed to mean?" she asked, irritated that Alastair was the second person to question Zane's motives in the last half hour.

"It means you trust too easily," he informed her sagely. "Have a care."

"What does everyone know that I don't?"

"When the time comes for you to make a decision about love, whether to walk away or stick it out, weigh all your options carefully. Make sure you have all the facts."

"Has Zane murdered someone or done something unspeakably wrong?" she asked, praying to the Goddess he hadn't.

"No, to the first, and possibly, to the second. In the long run, only you can decide if his actions are wrong since they affect you." In a rare show of warmth, Alastair smiled and tapped her on the nose. "You'll figure it out, child. I'm confident you'll make the right choice. In the meantime, be careful of Lin."

A memory from her youth stirred. One where Alastair would bring her treats and tap her nose. She gazed up at him in wide-eyed wonder. "Did you bring me candy when I was small?" She frowned as she tried to recall more. "When I would play outside... that was you watching over me!"

A bittersweet smile lit his face. "You and your sisters are the children of the woman I love. How could I not watch over you?" He tugged a lock of her hair. "You are almost identical to your mother in looks, you know. She'd be proud of you."

Winnie experienced an urge to hug him, but before she could react, he was gone. She touched the shone around her neck. "Thank you, Uncle Alastair."

"You're welcome, child."

She smiled at their new connection. While she'd never admit it aloud, there was a sense of security in knowing that someone had her back. Her only concern was why people felt the need to warn her about Zane. It was time to do some digging on her own.

ZANE ARRIVED AT THORNE MANOR IN TIME TO HEAR ALASTAIR'S conversation with Winnie. In order to avoid detection, he ducked behind the building to listen.

When Winnie said their relationship was proceeding "wonderfully," Zane experienced a sharp pang of guilt but immediately shoved it aside. He had to keep reminding himself that she deserved whatever she got.

He leaned against the outer wall of her workshop, one foot resting on the cream-colored siding and his arms across his chest. As Winnie walked past, her mind seemingly occupied with her busy thoughts, he spoke. "Hey."

She screamed and shot a forceful blast of air in his direction.

He grunted when his back impacted the wall.

"Zane! Ohmygod! I'm so sorry!" she babbled as she checked him for injuries.

"I shouldn't have surprised you like that," he acknowledged. "I'll know better next time."

She bit her lip, and he suspected it was to keep from laughing.

"Go ahead and laugh. But if you tell anyone you kicked my ass with a blast of cold air, I'll call you a damned liar."

Her amused expression disappeared and was replaced by wariness. "Zane, can I ask you a question?"

"Technically, you just did," he teased and dropped a kiss on her lips.

"I'm serious."

"Too serious." Zane wrapped an arm around her waist and pulled her flush against him. "You don't laugh enough, Win. We need to do something about that."

Despite his best efforts, she didn't melt into him as she had over the last week and instead, remained stiff within his embrace. "Twice today, I had people warn me about you. Is there something you're hiding that I should know about?"

Twice? Alastair was one Zane knew about, but who was the other? Had Coop come forward with what he knew?

"I don't know what anyone could possibly warn you about, except that I'd keep you chained to my bed twenty-four-seven if I had my choice." He flared his eyes wide and leered. "Maybe they're worried you'll never be able to walk properly again."

Winnie studied him in silence.

Maintaining a carefree facade wasn't easy when another person was viewing you with suspicious eyes. He dropped the playfulness and went for earnest.

"Win, I don't know what anyone thinks they know about me. I have nothing to hide. I'm an upstanding citizen. And I want you to the point of insanity." He rubbed his nose against hers in a soft Eskimo kiss. "I hope you never question my sincerity when it comes to how I feel about you." And he did hope that, because while the easy-going persona wasn't hard to pull off, the loving, considerate partner was a bit harder.

"I'm sorry," she said. "I think it makes everyone nervous that we are moving so fast."

How were they moving fast? "Moving fast?"

Winnie beamed up at him and clasped his hand to her heart. "I love you, Zane."

His lungs seized up, and he found it difficult to breathe. This was what he wanted; Winnie to fall in love with him so he could crush her heart. Now that the moment was upon him, he wasn't prepared. Not that he had a problem with his planned revenge, but he thought he might have more time to get his fill of her delectable body. More time to plan the final act.

Her smile dissolved, and she dropped his hand. "I... y-you don't have to say it back. I j-just wanted you to know."

When Zane continued to imitate a stone statue, Winnie pulled back and ducked her head, her disappointment obvious.

He needed to do something, or he'd ruin his well-thought-out retribution.

"I love you too, Win." The lie left his lips before he could stop it.

Her irises shifted from a cloudy blue to the color of the sky on a clear summer day. Her face could scarcely contain her smile, it was so wide. The sight stole his breath away.

"Oh, Zane!"

He caught her as she flung herself into his arms and clung to her for all he was worth. The wild rhythm of his heart had nothing to do with her feelings for him and everything to do with the success of his ploy, *or so he told himself.*

As Winnie drew back, Zane tightened his arms around her. Soon enough, her incredible body would be lost to him, and he needed to take advantage every chance he could.

"Want to teleport us to your bedroom?" he whispered.

"What about dinner?"

"We could order pizza."

"Done."

*T*he next afternoon, they stood together in Thorne Manor's attic.

"Are you ready?" Winnie asked Zane.

Despite his apprehension, he nodded.

"It's not difficult," she laughed. "All you have to do is visualize what you want. You picture it down to the last detail: smell, texture, color. Whatever you imagine, you can conjure."

"Aren't there cosmic consequences? Like I'm stealing someone else's property?"

Winnie frowned.

He could tell she'd never thought about it before. Most likely, because she'd grown up conjuring items, it became second nature to her. But for him, who was learning the process as an adult, he had to wonder where an object came from.

"I don't know. It's always been this way. We buy what we must and conjure our basic needs," she said with a shrug.

"I need to know where it's coming from," he insisted.

"Your power is a gift from the Goddess, Zane. We don't question what she's bestowed upon us. But if it makes you feel better to buy things, then buy them."

"Are you saying you don't grocery shop?" he asked incredulously.

"We don't. We grow our own fruits and vegetables. None of my family are meat eaters. As far as the other items, like I said, we conjure what we need."

"And did you ever stop to think you might be taking food from other people's mouths, Win?" The harshness of his tone wasn't lost on her.

"No, I never did. And I don't intend to start now because that's not how this works."

"How can you be sure?"

"Oh, for the love of the Goddess!" She grabbed her necklace. "Uncle Alastair, I need you."

Within mere seconds, Alastair appeared.

"Is this normal? You can summon another witch at will?" Zane didn't like the idea that someone could pull him from a business meeting or off the toilet if he was otherwise occupied.

"No," Alastair answered for her. "This is a special circumstance. Now, since I see you aren't in danger, does someone want to inform me why I'm here? My steak is getting cold."

Zane turned an accusing glare on Winnie. "I thought you said your family doesn't eat meat." She couldn't even tell the truth for something as innocent as her eating habits?

Again, Alastair answered. "I don't know what the personal preferences are for my nieces, but my brother and I eat meat."

"I didn't ask you!" Zane snapped. Although why exactly he was getting angry was anyone's guess.

Alastair's dark brows rose as his cold, sapphire gaze pinned Zane in place. "Mind your tone, boy, or I'll remove your tongue from your head."

"Zane wants to know where the things we conjure come from. Are we taking them from someone else?" Winnie effectively diverted her uncle's attention with her question.

He frowned and studied the two of them. "No. Why would you believe that?"

"Zane—"

"I—"

"We—"

Alastair held up a hand. "Never mind. By the time either of you can come up with an answer, I'll be dead." He sighed and shook his head. "I cannot believe Preston never addressed this with you children." With his palm face up, Alastair said, "Watch."

The older man slowed down the conjuring process in order for them to see exactly how the object formed in his hand. First was a flash of light, followed by strands of organic matter as it wove together. When the fruit in his hand was a perfect, round orange, Alastair tossed it to Zane.

"All living things are made up of energy. Conjuring is a simple manipulation of that energy," Alastair explained. "Earth signs like Spring or Nash have a greater ability to create and grow, but each of us can feed ourselves when the need arises." He straightened his tie and shirt cuffs. "The lessons Winter has taught you are the exact ones she learned growing up which were passed down from her parents, and their parents before them. It goes back as far as our ancestor, Isis."

Zane flushed. He and Winnie had been a bit preoccupied lately when it came to their lessons. He'd been intent on seduction, and she willingly allowed herself to be seduced.

"Ah." Alastair shook his head and concentrated his attention on Winnie. "You had one job to do, Winter. Teach him to survive if you come up against Lin. If either of you gets hurt, it's on you."

The cold, steely anger Alastair directed toward Winnie set Zane's teeth on edge. "She's done her best."

"At what?" Alastair scoffed. "Certainly not training you as instructed."

"Don't talk about her that way!" For the most part, Zane believed in fairness. He supposed he was defending her because he was the one who distracted her from the task of training him for this mission. He didn't dare imagine it was because he was protecting his mate. Winter Thorne would *not* be his wife.

"Zane, it's all right," she said soft and low as she laid a hand on his forearm.

Instinctively, he jerked away.

Her surprise was evident, but what had him concerned was the speculative look in her uncle's gaze.

Zane forced a smile. "Sorry, Win. When I'm irritable, I don't like to be touched."

She bit her lip and nodded. He could tell she wasn't convinced.

He could've reached for her hand and offered her comfort, but his emotions were all over the place. Why did he still feel the urge to defend her? She didn't deserve his loyalty or help. He avoided Alastair's hawk-eye gaze. That fucker missed nothing, and he scared the hell out of Zane.

"If you'll excuse me, I need a minute."

He made haste for the front door.

"HE'S HIDING SOMETHING," WINNIE FINALLY ACKNOWLEDGED.

"Yes, he is."

"What do you suppose it is?"

"Could be his feelings. Could be he has an ulterior motive. Could be he's been approached or recruited by Lin."

Winnie's head whipped around from where her gaze followed Zane's departure down the stairs.

Her uncle was as serious as she'd ever seen him.

The idea of Zane betraying her nearly drove her to her knees. She sank down into the nearest seat. "Why would he do that? He'd betray his cousins in the process."

"Money, revenge, any number of reasons."

Her head came up to stare. "Revenge?"

"He was furious when you stole his memories, child. Anger of that magnitude doesn't exactly dissipate into thin air."

"But we talked about it. I explained, and he was cool with it," she argued.

"Was he?"

Her stomach hurt at the implication. Why was everyone so centered on the past and Zane's reaction to it? "What would be his end game? I can't see him betraying everyone. It's not something he'd do."

"Would you like me to ask him?"

Winnie noted the sympathy in his expression. Obviously, he was privy to what was happening. "You spied on him, didn't you?"

"I don't trust as easily as most. Not at all, really."

In the face of Alastair's honesty, Winnie felt sadness. What type of existence did he have where no one could be trusted?

"You can trust me," she said.

He inched up his slacks and squatted before her. "Your offer is lovely, child, and not one I'd reject out of hand. My trust issues come from many years of betrayal by those I've loved. Those I thought would always have my back." He rubbed a hand across his eyes and focused on her again. "But if I had the ability to trust, know that I would gladly do so."

Overcome with sadness for him, she closed the distance between them. "I'm sorry, Uncle."

For all of seven seconds, he returned her hug. He cleared his throat as he drew away. "You have nothing to apologize for, Winnie. But I appreciate that you care."

In one graceful movement, he rose to his feet. "I would give you one other warning. Lin always has a gun. Should you encounter him, be cautious and prepared to teleport within seconds of his arrival. If you have to leave your young man, do so."

"No! I won't leave Zane!" She surged up, unable to remain seated.

"You cannot save both yourself and him if it comes down to it, child. Live to fight another day," he warned.

"I won't leave him." She'd as soon rip out her own heart.

"Ask yourself this, would he leave you?"

"He wouldn't. I know he wouldn't," she stated stubbornly.

"Hmm. I wonder."

"Stop it!" she ordered. "Stop making me question his motives. Please," she ended on a pleading note.

"Then be prepared. Lin has many tricks up his sleeve, and he's prepared to use every single one of them."

Alastair held out his palm and conjured her favorite chocolate candy.

She accepted the box with a smile. "What's that for?"

"So you don't think too horribly of me for suggesting your young man might be in the enemy camp."

"I'm learning not everything is black and white. You have your reasons for what you do. And while I may not always like them, I appreciate that you do them for the good of the whole."

A bittersweet half-smile flashed. "Your mother said almost that exact thing to me many years ago. Be careful, child. If it comes down to your safety or the retrieval of the amulet, choose safety first. I'll find another way to save Aurora."

Her mouth dropped open and before she could form a response, Alastair departed.

Winnie sank back down into the chair. The side Alastair had shown her was not one he showed many. Now, she had a new understanding of his actions, and if pressed, she couldn't fault him, knowing she might very well do the same.

"Are you all right?"

The deep baritone of Zane's voice brought her head up.

"Yeah. I think so."

"I'm sorry I bailed, Win. All of this is new and overwhelming at times."

"That's understandable." She rose and placed the unopened box of chocolates on the seat. "But my uncle was right about one thing; I did you a disservice by not training you properly. We need to postpone our departure until you're ready and spend what is left of today on teleporting."

He moved farther into the attic. "That's a tall task."

"You are a Carlyle warlock. You have powers beyond the norm. I'm sure you've noticed how quickly your cousins have picked up everything. To me, you've always been outstanding: athleticism, brains, motivation. You can do this."

A fleeting emotion passed across his countenance before he pasted on a smile. "Your faith in me is humbling."

"But not misplaced. Let's get started."

They worked hard through the late afternoon and into the evening. At times, Zane's temper became frayed. But in the end, Winnie was confident he could hold his own. He had the basics of teleporting from one room to another, of conjuring necessary items, and of casting a spell. Anything more would have to wait until they returned.

"Are we calling it a night?" he asked tiredly.

"We are," she agreed as she closed the grimoire. "Well done."

"Thanks."

When he approached, she caught her breath. She imagined it would always be so, and part of her worried that if he truly had a secret agenda, she'd never recover from the hurt.

"Do you want to come back to my place?" His suggestion was low and smooth, awakening her desire with the single sentence.

"I don't think it would be a good idea."

Startled, he studied her. "What's going on, Win?"

"I'm tired."

"Let's go to bed. I only want to hold you."

She wanted nothing more, but the seed of doubt had been planted firmly in her mind, and she didn't know how to eradicate the weed it had become.

"I really want a little alone time. A hot bath, some wine, a good book," she lied. "Can you understand?"

The hand he'd used to caress her neck dropped to his side. "Sure thing. I'll see you tomorrow."

As he headed to the door, Winnie called to him. "Zane? It's not you. Please don't think it is."

"I'm not an asshole. I get that people need alone time."

She ran to him and hugged him. "Thank you." She hesitated a

moment and nodded toward his hand. "Do you have a ring or something I can borrow?"

"What do you need it for?" he asked as he twisted his school ring off his finger.

"I want to add a protection spell." Lie number two. It was scary how easily they tumbled from her lips.

He handed her his piece of jewelry and kissed the top of her head. "That's sweet, Win. Thanks."

She waited until she was certain he'd gone, then pulled out a black scrying mirror. On it, she placed Zane's ring before she cast a circle of protection. She sat down to wait and watch.

Zane didn't head home. Instead, he headed to a bar in downtown Nashville. As the scene unfolded, the warnings from Alastair and Autumn replayed in her mind. And when Zane kissed the woman he'd bought a drink, Winnie stopped watching.

The pain of his betrayal gutted her deeper than she'd ever imagined it could. She couldn't say she hadn't been warned. Heartsick at her own naiveté, Winnie trudged to her bedroom and allowed herself a good cry.

*Z*ane wasn't a fool. Winnie had no intention of casting a charm spell on his ring. He'd heard her uncle warn her, and without a doubt, the seed of distrust had been planted in Winnie's brain. There was no better time than the present to give her a little payback.

As he left Thorne Manor and sat in his car, he shot a text to a college friend to meet at their old stomping grounds in Nashville. Angelica readily agreed.

They shared a drink, a slow dance, and a smoking-hot kiss.

Or it should've been at any rate. In his younger days, a kiss from Angelica could scorch his lips and make him wild to have her. Tonight, it left him cold. All he could see was Winnie's large, shining eyes gazing up at him with love. So bright. So beautiful.

As he pulled away from Angelica, he knew. *He was in love with Winnie Thorne*—the lying little jade that she was.

"It's not happening is it?" his ex-lover asked.

"I'm sorry, Ang."

"It's not a big deal. I'm sort of seeing someone myself."

"Yeah?" he asked, infusing fake interest in his tone, not surprised she'd figured out the reason for his lack of response.

She smiled and dropped a quick kiss on his lips. "Go back to her, Zane. Grovel if you have to, but if she's the one who holds your heart, who makes you happy, then you have to follow through."

"Once she finds out I came here, it's as good as done."

"How will she know?"

"Trust me. She'll know." If she hadn't been scrying with his ring, she certainly had one of her sisters spying on him.

"I'm sorry."

"I hope you're happy with the new guy."

"Girl."

"What?"

"The someone I'm seeing is female," she said with a laugh and a pat of his cheek. "You've spoiled me for all other men."

Christ, maybe he *did* suck in bed! "Was I that bad?"

Again, she laughed. "No. You were that good. That sweet, too. Most of the others after you were assholes. But then I met Jo, and my world turned around."

"I'm happy for you, Ang. Really."

They made small talk for a little while longer as they shared their second drink.

Three hours later, he found himself parked outside of Winnie's home, staring up at the darkened window of her bedroom. The longer he sat, the more jumbled his thoughts became. Why did he always find himself in the position of apologizing to her for his stupid behavior?

A noise outside the car had him checking the side mirror.

He started and banged his knees on the steering wheel.

Without his assistance, the window powered open.

"Have you come to your senses, son?" Alastair, in a negligent pose, rested back against Zane's car with his arms crossed over his chest and one foot hooked over the other.

"I may have just fucked up."

Alastair snorted and straightened. "Oh, I'd say there was no maybe about it." He shook his head. "I had high hopes there was one smart one in the lot. You Carlyles are a hopelessly dense group. Reactive Neanderthals in my humble opinion."

He placed his elbows on the opening and leaned in to ask softly, "But the question is, what do you intend to do to fix it?"

"What can I do?"

Alastair sighed and straightened. "For starters, you can get your butt to Saqqara and help my niece find the amulet."

"We plan to leave tomorrow…" Zane checked his watch. "Make that later today."

"Boy, if you think she's up in that room or that she waited for you, you are sadly mistaken."

Zane's blood ran cold. "What?"

"She left about two hours ago."

"How could you let her leave?" Zane yelled in his panic. He shoved open the car door and made haste toward the front door of the manor.

"I didn't know she'd gone right away. Do you honestly believe I'd let her run into danger?"

Zane ignored Winnie's uncle and charged up the stairs to her room. Next, he checked the attic.

A sleepy Spring stepped into the hall. "What's going on?"

"Do you know where Winnie went?"

"She isn't in her room?"

"I wouldn't be asking if she were," he ground out.

Spring snapped to wide awake in a split second. "What did you do?"

He waved a dismissive hand. "It doesn't matter. How do we find her?"

Her attention was caught by something beyond his shoulder, and Zane turned to see Alastair moving toward them. In his hand was the necklace Winnie had been wearing earlier.

The older man's face was carved from granite—all cold, hard lines and planes. His anger was a sight to behold. "She took it off! That foolish, foolish girl!"

WINNIE DIDN'T HEAD DIRECTLY TO SAQQARA. A STOP OFF IN MALTA was needed to get her head on straight. Perhaps, if she was extremely lucky, she'd meet a nice, single Maltese man who was the extreme opposite of he-who-shall-no-longer-be-thought-of.

Before she'd left home, she made a study of the airport. She'd sent out a feeler into the ladies' room and teleported just as a flight was arriving, with her passport in one hand and an overnight bag in the other.

She breezed through customs and found an ocean view room at a swanky hotel in St. Paul's Bay. By ten a.m., she was sipping wine on her balcony, gazing out at the aqua waters of the bay.

The sliding door to a neighboring suite opened, and she nearly groaned. She didn't want anyone to witness how low she'd sunk by drinking first thing in the morning. Another thing she could lay at Zane's door.

An olive-skinned man, roughly thirty-five, with black, wavy hair, stepped onto the balcony. He wore only the white hotel robe—unbelted—and a pair of black speedos.

Her wine halted its ascent to her mouth as she took in the view. Holy crap on a cracker! The man was a virtual advertisement for sex.

He bent over the railing and leaned on one arm while he sipped from an espresso cup. If someone wasn't shooting a coffee commercial, they should be.

Winnie sighed at the beauty he presented.

"Why are you sad, pretty lady?"

His voice had a smoky, rich quality. Prior to Zane-the-Asshole, she'd have reveled in its warmth.

She lifted her glass of wine. "Betrayal."

He nodded as if her answer was expected and squinted out over the aqua water. "Some men are fools. They do not treasure what they have."

"You're preaching to the choir, mister," she agreed and downed a third of her wine.

He took a sip of his beverage in silence, and Winnie appreciated he could let her comment go.

After another minute, he asked, "What are your plans for today?"

"I have none," she admitted. Although, if she were smart, she wouldn't tell a stranger she was alone, bitter, and without a plan. But as a witch, she knew she could hold her own.

"May I show you my homeland?"

As she turned over his offer, she questioned, "Homeland? Why are you staying in a hotel if you live here?"

He smiled, a flash of white on his dark features. "I live and work in Italy. I'm home to visit my family." He shrugged, and she was reminded of Autumn's habitual careless gesture. "I find myself with extra time on my hands. Time enough to show a beautiful woman around the island."

"You're a warlock." Winnie wasn't exactly sure how she knew, she just did.

His midnight eyes twinkled as he straightened. "And you are a witch."

"Should I take it as coincidence that we happen to be on the same island, in the same hotel, right next door to each other?"

"The Goddess has always smiled on me and mine. Her kindness is legendary."

"Christ, you could charm the panties off any unsuspecting woman."

He laughed—deep, golden, and delicious.

They stared at one another for another long minute.

"Okay."

The beatific smile he cast her was her reward. "I am Rafe Xuereb."

"Rafe? That's more of an American name than Maltese, isn't it?"

"American mother, Maltese father."

"Ah. I'm Winter Thorne, but my friends call me Winnie."

For a moment, his jovial expression slipped. "You should be careful when using your real name, Winter Thorne. Your family has powerful enemies."

Winnie tilted her head to study him. "Are you one of them?"

"No. But to be on the safe side, let's make up a name should the need arise to introduce you."

"Are you worried about me, Rafe?"

His grin was slow but blinding when in full bloom. "No, *qalbi*. I suspect you can take care of yourself."

She nodded her head in approval. She didn't need an overprotective alpha male on her hands, although she suspected that's exactly what he was.

"Whom shall I be?" she asked ready to become someone else— anyone else—if it provided a distraction from her broken heart.

His lips twitched as he pretended to concentrate. "Helena."

"Oh, I like it! And for the last name?" It amused Winnie that he'd chosen the name of the woman whose diary started her family's search for the artifacts.

"Why not my wife?"

She arched a brow. "That would mean touching and kissing in public."

"Yes."

Rafe's sexy, wicked tone should've inspired an answering effect, yet unexpected tears struck Winnie, and she hurriedly shifted her gaze to the bay. A few hours ago, she'd thought Zane would one day be her husband. Now her love life lay in ruins.

An instant later, she felt the warmth of another person at her side. "I'm sorry, I didn't mean to overstep." Rafe's voice was kind, and the proffered sympathy caused her to blink back her unhappiness.

"It's okay. I'm okay. I just need a few minutes to change." She swallowed hard past the lump in her throat. "That is, if you still want to play tour guide."

"Nothing would make me happier. Finish your wine, put on a bathing suit—preferably something tiny and see-through—and a casual cover up. We will make a day of it."

Winnie turned and got an up-close and personal view of his massive chest along with the abs that went on for days. Mouth too dry to speak, she nodded. Okay, she may be hurting, but she wasn't dead. Maybe he was the type of distraction she needed for today.

"Perhaps by the end of your time here, we can make you forget your foolish man."

"That's what I'm hoping," she returned.

Eyes that held a vast knowledge of the world viewed her solemnly. "It hurts now, but someday, you will feel whole again. I hope, when that day comes, you will call me, Winter Thorne. I promise I will come running."

"Thank you," she whispered, doing her best to keep her emotions in check.

He raised her hand and kissed her knuckles. "Go change. I know a pastizzerija that makes the most mouth-watering pastry you've ever tasted. Do you like tea?"

"I do."

He nodded his approval. "Shall we meet in the lobby in ten minutes?"

An hour and a half later, Winnie and Rafe found a cozy spot on the beach to settle and people-watch as they talked about the island.

She noticed the attention he attracted and smiled.

"What do you find amusing?"

"You're a total chick magnet," she told him with a light laugh.

Rafe shrugged as if it were his due. "It comes with the territory, I'm afraid. Most people don't understand why they are attracted to us."

"Us?"

He rolled on his side and rested his head on his hand. He scooped up a handful of sand and held it over her belly, releasing a small stream in a swirling pattern.

"We are magical beings. People feel the power, the draw, but they don't know what it is. They think it's our attractive bodies or faces. We let them believe it."

"You have it all figured out."

He couldn't hide his slight grimace as he dusted off the sand he'd poured on her stomach. "I don't know about that, but I've been around a long time. I've seen a great many things in my life."

"You sound a bit jaded, Rafe."

He lifted surprised eyes to meet her steady gaze. "I suppose I am to a degree."

"We're a pair, aren't we?"

The soft smile he offered her was his most honest yet. "I'd like us to be."

She didn't protest when he kissed her. In fact, she wrapped her arms around his neck and gave over to his expertise. The kiss was pleasant and warmed her, but his touch didn't contain near the heat of Zane's.

He lifted his head and surveyed her face for her reaction. With a deep, sad sigh, he rolled on his back and tucked an arm behind his head. "I should've remembered when I heard your name."

"What's that?"

Rafe turned his head to face her. "The old saying, Thornes only love once."

She rose on her elbows and stared down at him. "You must know my family well to know that."

"I do," he confirmed. "Your father is a business associate."

"Why have we never met?"

"He has a strict policy of keeping his children away from the Witches' Council."

Her shoulders tensed as she sat up straight. "You're with the WC?"

"I am."

"I'm such a fool!" She rose and dusted the last of the sand from her body.

Rafe stood and reached for her arm. She evaded him and stepped back.

"You have nothing to fear from me," he said.

"Really? Because from where I'm standing, I do." She swore under her breath and paced. "I *knew* it wasn't a coincidence you were next door. How fucking gullible can one woman be?" she muttered.

"Actually, it *is* a coincidence. I am truly here to visit my family. It's been fifty years since I've last been home."

Winnie froze in place. *"Fifty years?"*

Rafe shot her a wry glance.

"How old *are* you?"

"Seventy-two."

She pressed her fingertips to her eye sockets. "I had to pick the one man old enough to be my father. Nice."

In fairness to her, after thirty, warlocks aged at such a slow rate as to not age at all. She should've realized if her initial impression of him was a thirty-five-year-old male, then he'd be an older warlock.

"I don't mind a younger woman," he teased.

"Get a clue, Romeo."

He laughed and wrapped a muscular arm around her waist, hauling her against him. Leaning in close, he whispered in her ear, "I think I'm more than half in love with you, Winter."

She shoved at his overdeveloped chest with a snort. "Well, don't be. I've had enough of the male species in general."

"Get your fucking hands off her!"

Both Rafe and Winnie froze, their eyes locked as they sensed the danger in the air.

"The boyfriend?" he murmured.

"The asshole," she murmured in return.

His eyes crinkled as he fought a laugh. "Shall I smite him?"

"He's a pureblood Carlyle warlock. Do you think you could take him?"

"For you, I would try," Rafe said and dropped a light kiss on her lips.

The growl from behind him was feral in nature.

"If it helps, he's a novice," she added.

"He has anger on his side," he countered as he released her and turned.

Winnie caught her first glimpse of Zane.

Dark circles under his eyes spoke of his lack of sleep. His light-blond hair was mussed from either his hands or the sea breeze. But his expression was pure white-hot rage.

She stepped in front of Rafe and effected a bored tone. "What are you doing here, Zane?"

"Are you kidding me right now? You disappear without a word to anyone and you expect no one to look for you?" he seethed.

Winnie borrowed from Autumn's stock of careless shrugs and offered one up. "I intended to text Spring when I knew she was awake."

"What about me?" he snarled as he stalked forward. "Did you intend to text *me*, Win?"

"No."

He stopped short. His breathing resembled an enraged bull.

Rafe switched places with her. "I think it's obvious she does not want you around."

From the corner of her eye, she noticed the flame come to life and dance in the palm of Zane's hand.

"Zane," she warned. "Not in a public place. Contain it."

He shook his hand and glanced around. A few curious bystanders watched the confrontation from afar.

Rafe snapped his fingers and gestured the gawkers away. "They will remember nothing."

"Damn, that was impressive," Winnie breathed. "You're going to need to show me that little trick."

He grinned at the same time Zane swore.

"A warlock?" Zane asked.

"What gave it away?" Rafe asked dryly.

The old adage "if looks could kill" came to Winnie's mind as Zane glared his fury at Rafe.

"He's awfully territorial of you," Rafe said in a loud aside.

"Because she's my girlfriend," Zane snapped.

"No!" Winnie practically shouted as she rounded on him. "I'm your *nothing*!"

His tone changed. "Winnie—"

"Get lost, Zane. You're not wanted here," she said in a calmer but no less serious voice.

Zane stalked to where she stood. "I'm not leaving until you talk to me."

Rafe heaved a sigh and scrunched up his nose. "I'd hate to do this in a public place, but say the word, *qalbi,* and I will send him to the center of the earth."

"Try it," Zane growled.

The air pulsed and crackled. Alastair and Spring walked through a fold in space.

"Alastair Thorne." Rafe didn't sound happy. "You know magic in public is forbidden. I was about to teach this young puppy the error of his ways. But perhaps now I know why he's undisciplined."

"We're cloaked, Rafe." Alastair said with a smirk. "You'll have to tell the Council they'll have to find another way to crucify me."

Her uncle tossed Winnie the necklace he'd given to her at the Thorne estate. "You forgot something, child."

"I swear I didn't leave it behind on purpose," she said as she slipped it over her head.

"I'd hoped you weren't that foolish. But knowing what you saw, I thought maybe you were reacting badly." He eyed Rafe. "Although, it could still be said you *are* reacting badly." Alastair mock shuddered and straightened his sleeves. "You could've chosen better than an elder on the Council for your revenge fling, dear girl."

"An elder…" Winnie closed her eyes. Yep, just her luck.

"Revenge fling?" Zane didn't bother to keep his voice down. "What the fuck? Is he serious, Win?"

A throbbing began behind her eyelids, and Winnie bent to scoop up her belongings. "Go home. All of you."

"I'm not leav—"

"Leaving." Winnie cut him off and turned her full rage on Zane. "Yeah, I heard you the first time, *asshole.* But I am. Enjoy the beach." She spun on her heel and headed toward the hotel.

"I must follow my heart," she heard Rafe say. "Safe journey!"

A second later, Rafe's large, warm hand settled on her waist. It didn't last long.

13

Chapter Thirteen has been omitted for standard reasons. During this intermission, go ahead and order Spring Magic. Trust me, you don't want to miss the next exciting installment in this series.

14

*Z*ane saw red the instant the handsome warlock placed his hand on Winnie's hip. One second, he had a fragile hold on his temper, and the next, that hold snapped.

He closed the distance between them and ripped Rafe's hand away from Winnie. In one fluid movement, Zane hauled her against him. "If you touch her again, I'll kill you."

Zane didn't expect the impact to his balls. He dropped to the ground at Winnie's feet and struggled against the nausea her forceful blow to his family jewels had wrought.

From his pain-induced haze, he watched as she took Rafe's hand and walked away. He made a mental note to murder the laughing fucker the first chance he got since he couldn't kill Winnie.

Shiny black shoes appeared in his peripheral. "Well, that was impressive."

Alastair Thorne was added to his hit list.

"Shut up!" Zane ground out.

He thought he heard tittering from Spring. Christ, he was starting to hate this family.

Alastair placed a hand on his shoulder and blasted him with his healing magic. A favor for which, Zane grudgingly scratched a line through the man's name on his mental murder list.

"Thanks."

"Don't mention it. But if you ever tell me to shut up again, I will obliterate you. I'm putting your lapse in judgment down to the pain my niece inflicted."

"Understood."

Alastair nodded toward the hotel. "Now, get in there and break that up. But try to keep your head, son."

Zane dusted off the sand from his left side and headed toward the hotel.

"THINK HE'LL WIN HER BACK?" ALASTAIR ASKED SPRING AS THEY watched Zane jog toward the hotel.

"I'm not sure what he did, but Winnie's pissed."

"He played her for a fool and kissed another woman," Alastair explained.

"What is with those idiot Carlyle men?" Spring muttered, gaining his undivided attention.

He looked down into her beautiful, young face. "Trouble in paradise, child?"

"No. Because I'm not stupid enough to fall in love with one."

Fighting the urge to laugh, he nodded solemnly. "Aren't you the logical one?"

"I hope Winnie holds out. At this point, I'm voting for the hot islander."

"Don't. He's bad news."

Spring cast him a sharp glance. "Is she in danger?"

This time Alastair smiled his humor. Everyone seriously underestimated this lovely girl. But she was the sharpest tack in the Thorne box. "No. I just don't like rule followers."

Her thousand-watt smile almost blinded him. "I like you, Uncle Alastair. I really do."

He grunted and pulled her into a one-armed hug. "Don't let

anyone know I did a nice thing, okay. I don't want to tarnish my reputation as an unfeeling bastard."

She laughed, and the musical sound was like clear bells on a summer day.

"Do we stay and referee or do we go home?" she asked.

"I think Winnie can handle the two of them. Let's watch how this unfolds from home. Unless you'd care to spend a few days in the sun."

"A vacation does sound nice," she murmured with a longing look at the ocean.

"A vacation it is." He handed her his wallet, and nodded toward the hotel. "A suite for each of us. Let Carlyle figure out his own arrangements. I'll be back after I make arrange for your mother's care with Summer."

"Top of the line?"

"Of course! Anything less would be uncivilized for a Thorne."

Her laughter made him smile. She was a breath of fresh air on an otherwise dreary day.

WINNIE AND RAFE SETTLED POOLSIDE AND WERE JOINED A SHORT while later by her sister, bearing a tray of fruity drinks.

"We intend to sightsee this afternoon. Do you care to join us?" Rafe asked Spring.

She shot an inquiring look at Winnie.

"I don't mind if you want to go," Winnie said as she took a drink from the tray Spring held. "It's up to you. Rafe has promised an amazing time."

"What about Zane?" Spring asked quietly.

"His wants don't weigh into this, sister."

"Can we talk privately for a minute?"

Rafe rose in one swift, graceful movement. "I have phone calls to make." He checked his watch. "Would you like to meet up again in about one hour?"

"That works."

He gave a slight nod. "Until then, ladies."

Both sisters admired his backside as he strode away.

"You sure know how to pick hot men," Spring sighed.

Winnie snorted a laugh and sipped her drink.

"Are you truly through with Zane, Winnie?"

"Yes."

"When he showed up last night and found you missing, he was frantic."

Unable to picture Zane in a frantic state, Winnie rolled her eyes. "Right."

"You weren't there. You didn't see him. He tore through the house like it was on fire."

Winnie sat upright and placed a leg on either side of her lounger. "You know what, Spring, *I don't care*. He left me—after telling me he loved me—and went into the arms of another woman. He's a liar and a player."

"That's not what happened," Zane's deep voice said from behind her.

She didn't bother to turn. "Go peddle your lies elsewhere, Zane. I don't believe you anymore."

"Win, you have to give me a chance to explain."

The imploring note in his voice tore at Winnie's heart, but she shut down that avenue of feeling. She met Spring's concerned gaze and shook her head. "You don't have to worry for me, sister. I'm perfectly fine." Her insides tightened in response to her own fib.

Spring shifted forward to touch her hand. "Do you want me to stay?"

"Not unless you want to."

Her sister's troubled green gaze shot to Zane. Whatever she saw in his face must have persuaded her to give them privacy. Spring patted Winnie's hand and left without a backward glance.

When he settled on Spring's empty chair, Winnie laughed harshly. "You certainly have her fooled."

"I didn't feel like your initial explanation in the glen was enough," Zane stated. "I was hurt by what you had done. Angry that I almost died. But there you stood, all tears and apologies, and it wasn't enough, Win. It didn't erase eight years of trickery."

"So you had the idea to pay me back. To sleep with me, make me fall for you, and then break my heart." She didn't need to ask; his motives were crystal clear.

"Yes."

Hearing him admit it somehow hurt worse. Not that Winnie wanted Zane to lie or deny what he'd planned, but the raw honesty stung. She cleared her throat. "Well, you can congratulate yourself on a well-executed plan."

"That's just the thing, Win, I can't." He sat forward. "I made a terrible mistake. I fell in love with you."

It was a mistake to love her? "Wow."

"I do love you," Zane insisted, misunderstanding her disbelief.

She twisted to face him. "You don't. Love isn't about one-upmanship. It isn't about payback or bitterness or whatever the hell else is going on in your sick, twisted mind." She inhaled a steadying breath. "It's about setting aside hurt and learning to see things from the other person's perspective. It's about forgiveness and understanding. About making sure your mate's needs are met by putting them first. You're too selfish to understand this."

"I'm not."

"You *are*. I should've remembered that lesson from our first time in the clearing." She gathered her beach wrap around her and tied it at her hip. "I'm sorry I did what I did. I've said as much. But that gave you no right to purposely try to destroy my sense of self. To trick me into loving you, and then stomp on that love by cheating on me."

"I didn't cheat, Win."

Finally, her fury kicked in. With it, so did the wind. Black storm clouds rolled in at such a high rate of speed, people scattered like ants. "You did. I saw you," she snarled.

Lightning struck two hundred feet away. Still, Zane and Winnie stayed visually locked onto one another.

"You spied on me when I left last night," he stated flatly.

She gave a sharp nod. "I did."

"You saw me drive to Nashville, have a drink with an old lover, and share a lukewarm kiss."

"Since I wasn't in your shoes, I couldn't tell you how *lukewarm* it was, but it looked pretty heated from my viewpoint."

"Then you would've seen and heard the rest."

She rose to her feet. "No. Witnessing your initial behavior was enough, thank you."

He stood and towered over her. "She isn't you, Win. Her kiss didn't move me in the least. But I'm grateful for it."

She couldn't believe her ears. Couldn't believe how he justified his outrageous behavior and expected her to be understanding and forgiving. "Well, bully for you, Zane. I'm so happy that cheating with another woman provided you with whatever you were looking for."

Unable to bear another second of his presence, Winnie turned away.

"You misunderstand me. I'm grateful for the kiss because it proved to me no other woman makes me feel the way that you do. It made me realize how much I love you. How much I want our relationship to be real."

Without facing him, she said, "Too bad for you. Our relationship is as dead as my feelings for you."

"I don't believe you. You don't mean that," he protested.

"I honestly don't care what you believe, Zane. But I'm trying to enjoy a much-needed vacation. I'd thank you to get lost."

He surged forward and reached for her arm. "I don't believe you because your emotions are evident in the very air around us. The storm, the wind, the bending trees. That's all you, Win. And if the magic is that strong, then the emotion behind it must be stronger."

The wind picked up to tropical storm force gale. The pool furniture around them crashed together. "What do you want from me, Zane? What? *Tell me*. You want me to say I'm sorry for my actions? I already did that, but I'll say it again. I'm sorry I stole your memories. You want me to love you? I did that, too. But the man I fell in love with wasn't you. It was only someone you pretended to be. There is nothing left."

The air stilled around them.

"I have nothing left," she whispered. "If you ever had even a small ounce of affection for me, one kind thought, you'd leave me alone. I'm empty."

"Win." His voice was achingly sweet. Longing and regret weighed heavily in that one word.

But she couldn't trust him. Couldn't trust from one moment to the next what he was planning. Couldn't trust that his temper wouldn't send him over the edge of reason. Zane's affection, if he truly cared, was unstable at best, and Winnie couldn't live that way.

She liked the consistency of everyday life. Liked waking in the mornings, manually making baked goods for her family, and then spending the rest of her day tinkering in her workshop. Liked dinner or a movie with a lover who would spend the entire night in her bed and who woke her with the gentlest of touches to make love again. She wasn't lying when she said she loved who he had pretended to be. That was the Zane she wanted. *The man who didn't exist.*

As Winnie's energy drained away, her hold on the storm clouds eased. Blue skies returned. She looked around at the damage she'd wrought. "This is what you do to me, Zane. This is destructive and ugly. I don't want that in my life."

"We don't have to be that way," he protested. He smoothed back her wind-blown hair and pressed his forehead to hers. "Please, Win. Please give me another chance."

She shoved him in the pool.

15

*A*s Zane stomped and sloshed his way toward the elevator, the metal doors parted. Spring exited in front of the Maltese warlock. When she saw Zane, her hand flew up to hide her smile. The older man's mocking gaze scanned him from head to toe.

Zane narrowed his eyes and glared his anger. He could feel the water starting to evaporate into steam as his body warmed in its fiery fury. "Not one *fucking* word," he warned, his tone low and lethal.

Rafe bowed and with swirling gesture of his arm, the dumb prick gestured to the empty elevator, unaware he was two seconds away from dying a painful death at Zane's hands.

The doors dinged and closed before Zane could catch them.

He could feel his lip curl into a snarl and struggled to stave off the growl of frustration. One check of the mirrored doors showed his resemblance to a soaked and rabid mongrel.

As he dripped water on the tile, the doors swished open to reveal a cool and collected Winnie. With her black hair swept up in a high-sitting ponytail and dark liner to emphasize her sultry blue eyes, she stole his breath away. Yet, she stepped around him with her nose in the air as if he were a steaming pile of dog dung.

Before he could stop himself, his hand shot out to stop her

progress. "This isn't over between us, Win. I don't care what you do. This…" Zane gestured back and forth between their bodies. "… isn't over."

A calculating gleam entered her storm-colored eyes, and she shifted her gaze to Rafe. A half-smile shaped her berry lips. When she leaned in, Zane got a whiff of her seductive floral scent.

"Tonight, when you're lying in bed alone, I want you to think about how it felt for me to see you kiss your girlfriend, Zane."

His heart stopped. Her meaning was crystal clear. She intended to take Rafe for a lover.

"Don't do it, Winnie," he rasped out. "Not if you care about him even the smallest bit."

"Oh, I think he can hold his own against you, newbie," she mocked. "In fact, I'm counting on it. I'm counting on him being better in all ways."

He lost his mind. One minute he had a grip on his reality. The next, he had her up against the wall in his suite, kissing the living hell out of her. He didn't have time to appreciate his teleport skill or worry that he might have left witnesses to his disappearing act. All he could concentrate on was Winnie.

Zane ignored her soft mewl of protest and ravaged her mouth. Because while he would never resort to taking her against her will, he had no problem reminding her what she craved most about their lovemaking. He felt the movement of her knee and countered by shifting his hips sideways. Her hands gripped his hair and tugged, but despite the burning scalp and potential bald spot, he continued to kiss her. Part of him feared losing half of his tongue should she take it in her head to bite him. She didn't. She gave as good as she got; her tongue tangoed with his, sucking and drawing in an angry duel.

Soon enough, the fingers woven tightly through his hair eased, and Winnie's sexy little moans were pleasure filled. When she softened against him, he unbuttoned her lacy, white shirt and parted it, pulling back slightly to admire the expanse of skin in her white push-up.

Their eyes connected. Her irises were the color of dark, churning waters before a thunderstorm. *The color of her passion.*

Zane leaned in to capture her lips for a second soul-shattering kiss and bumped his nose against the drywall.

He spun in a circle. No Winnie.

His grin came unbidden. She was wily, his Winnie. But their kiss proved she was far from over him—as did her running. She could bluff a good game, but she wouldn't sleep with Rafe. Not when she desired Zane.

With a snap of his fingers, he was once again dry and decked out in a clean outfit. He could thank Winnie's relentless training for his newfound abilities.

From his balcony, he observed Winnie from where she walked beside Rafe and Spring. As if she were unable to resist, she glanced back and up toward his room. Her mouth tightened in irritation as Zane waved and blew a kiss.

He intended to enjoy seducing her back to his side. Call it arrogance on his part, but he believed she'd come around. After all, Thornes only loved once.

"You have your work cut out for you, son." Alastair's voice beside him nearly caused him a heart attack.

"Jesus, man! A warning of some kind might be nice."

Deep, dark laughter echoed around his suite. "Where's the fun in that?"

"You stuck around."

"I'm invested in how this turns out."

Zane eyed him. "How so?"

"She's my niece, boy. If you think I'm going to allow her to be hurt by you or anyone else, you're sadly mistaken."

Zane turned back to watch Winnie's retreat. He waited a long moment, then said, "She won't be. Not by me. I admit I was an ass. But I love her and want her to be happy. Preferably with me."

"We will put down your kiss with the lovely Angelica as a lapse in judgment. *This time.*" Alastair moved to stand in front of him. "But know this, if you *ever* pull something like that on Winter again,

I will remove your balls and serve them to you on a silver platter. Are we clear?"

The promise of retribution was in Alastair's hard stare.

"Crystal."

"Good. Now, what's your plan for getting rid of that waste of space she's hanging out with?"

"I thought I'd find out from Winnie's sisters what might soften her attitude."

Winnie's uncle held up his palm. A small booklet appeared.

"What's this?" Zane asked as he accepted the gift.

"I did the work for you."

He stared at Alastair in open-mouthed wonder. "How the hell did you know this would be my plan?"

"The ability to stay five steps ahead of others is my special talent."

"You're a scary bastard, Alastair Thorne. I want you to know that."

The other man's lips tilted up in his amusement. "Believe it, son."

He clapped a heavy hand on Zane's back and left him to work out his seduction alone.

LATER THAT EVENING, AS WINNIE OPENED THE DOOR TO HER SUITE, she came up short. On every available surface was an item she adored: a small, potted gardenia tree, the finest English chocolates, a framed letter that stated a donation had been made in her name to a favorite charity, and much more.

As she moved from one item to the next, warmth gathered in her chest, melting the coldness.

"Do you like it?"

Zane's deep, smooth voice didn't startle her. Once she saw the gifts, she expected he was lurking about.

With deep regret, Winnie did what was necessary. She threw the box of chocolates on the ground and smashed them. The tree went into the trash, and the letter she removed from its frame and shredded into tiny pieces. Systematically, she worked her way around the room, and with each thing she destroyed, she maintained eye contact with Zane.

He rubbed a hand over his mouth, and she suspected it was to hide a smile. Dammit! He'd predicted she'd destroy his gifts.

Heat crawled up her neck as he continued to stare.

"What are you still doing here?" she asked.

"I had time to kill before we headed to Egypt."

Egypt.

Colorful swear words rolled off her tongue. For the short time she'd been wallowing in grief caused by the demise of their relationship, she'd forgotten about the amulet.

He shoved away from the wall and ambled to where she stood.

"How was your day, Win? Did you enjoy the sights?" Love, or something like it, along genuine interest, was infused into his questions.

Had he touched her, made a move on her in any way, Winnie would've been able to snarl and snap her way out of the situation. But he didn't. Instead, he gazed down at her as if she held all his heart could ever desire. And wasn't that worse?

She lifted her chin and put on a superior air she didn't feel. "Rafe was the perfect tour guide."

A shadow darkened his gaze. "I'm glad you had a good time. Would you join me for dinner tonight?" He held up a hand. "Before you say no, think about it. We need to discuss our upcoming trip and make arrangements."

"Not dinner," she blurted. Dinner with Zane would bring to the forefront of her mind the times he'd wined and dined her, along with all the delicious lovemaking afterwards. "I'll meet you at ten tomorrow for coffee."

He didn't try to hide his disappointment. "Where?"

"There's a great little café Rafe took me to this morning. It's only a few blocks away."

Zane's mouth tightened. He nodded once and abruptly turned to leave.

Winnie's conscience got the best of her. "Zane."

He paused in his retreat.

"This isn't payback. The café serves great coffee and pastries."

"That's fine, Win," he said gruffly without sparing her a glance. "I'll meet you in the lobby at ten. Enjoy the rest of your day."

After he left, Winnie played back their conversation. Yes, she'd been more than a little confrontational, but he had to understand, she wasn't going to be a pushover. He'd hurt her, and if she let him back in, chances were he'd hurt her again. She wasn't as forgiving as her sisters, Autumn and Summer. She didn't have it in her to overlook the poor choices Zane made because he was angry. Logic dictated that he'd do something similar if he was upset with her again. And he would definitely become angry with her again because he felt things with a stronger intensity than most.

Deep down, he hadn't forgiven her for her mistake, and there was no way to rectify it at this late date. Her sincere, tearful apology hadn't moved him. He'd set out to exact his revenge at the expense of her heart, her self-worth, and her peace of mind. With surprising ease, he succeeded.

Winnie wasn't likely to put herself in the position to be hurt again. The one thing she needed to do at her first opportunity was to check the Thorne grimoire for a spell to break her bond with Zane. She'd be damned if she'd go her whole life loving the one man who wasn't worthy of her love.

Dry-eyed and resolved, she conjured a bottle of wine and stepped out on her balcony. Next door, Rafe lounged in a chair.

"*Qalbi.* I see that you're upset."

"The expected visit from Zane."

"Do you wish to talk about it?"

"No."

"He's insane for you."

She closed her eyes and rested her head back against the top of the seat.

"Would you care for company?"

Winnie smiled without opening her eyes. "Aren't you company of a sort? You're only eight feet away."

"I meant company of another nature." The suggestive tone left her in little doubt about what type of company he had in mind.

Before she'd hooked up with Zane, this man's voice alone would've had her aroused. The raspy, knowing quality had that effect on women. She'd seen it in the short time they'd been acquainted. Hell, it halfway turned her on now. But she was heart-weary and couldn't drum up the energy for another romance this soon.

"You tempt me, Rafe. You truly do. But I'll have to pass."

"He's volatile. Be careful."

She opened her eyes and stared at him across the distance. "Thanks for caring."

"I find myself liking you more than I should."

"Why?"

"All you need do is look in the mirror, *qalbi*. But it's also more than that. You are beautiful on the inside as well. A rare combination in women."

She grinned. "You say the nicest things."

One shoulder lifted in an air of careless dismissal. "I mean them." He gained his feet and toasted her with his cup. "I'll leave you to your quiet."

"Thanks for today."

"It was entirely my pleasure."

16

*T*he bright morning sun, diffused by the white curtain, eventually penetrated Winnie's fog of sleep. Zane's unique scent of hot chocolate and cinnamon filled her nostrils. With a gesture born of instinct, she reached for him. When her hand came in contact with his chest, she smiled.

"Zane," she murmured.

His palm settled over the back of her hand, and one finger stroked along the vein located there. She loved waking this way. Loved knowing—*wait a minute!*

Her eyes flew wide.

Zane lay beside to her with his pale-blond head next to hers on the pillow. His mussed hair said he'd been there awhile, but he didn't look tired. In fact, he looked fresh and yummy.

A spark of awareness flared to life inside Winnie. One that brought her mind around to other, more intimate, things. She sucked in a breath and did a quick scan of his body. He was fully dressed. She breathed a sigh of relief that she hadn't slept with him—or at least, she hadn't had sex with him. Still, it bothered her that in her drunken, wine-induced state from last night, he'd been able to sneak into her bed without waking her.

For reasons unbeknownst to her, she didn't pull away now. Perhaps she should put it down to early morning brain fog. Their eyes connected and held. His chocolate gaze was adoring. Maybe that's why she hadn't freaked out. How did one reject puppy-dog eyes?

"What are you doing here?"

He raised her hand to his lips and kissed her knuckles. "I was worried about you."

She frowned and lifted her head to peek over his shoulder. The clock showed ten minutes to eleven. "Holy crap!"

"Yeah, when you didn't meet me in the lobby, I panicked and teleported."

"What if I'd had company?"

His eyes cooled. "I'd have dealt with that if it happened. My main concern was your welfare. This place isn't warded, and there's a crazy man on the loose who has a hard-on for destroying your family." He tightened his hold on her fingers. "Something you seemed to have forgotten when you took off alone."

Winnie jerked her hand away and sat up to massage her temples. "I don't intend to live my life afraid of Zhu Lin, Zane."

"No one expects you to, Win. But precautions wouldn't be remiss."

"Thanks for checking," she said grudgingly. "I need a shower first, then I'll meet you in the lobby in fifteen."

"I could conjure us food here," he offered as he sat up next to her and hugged his knees.

She could've told him at least ten reasons why that idea was terrible, why spending time with him was dangerous to her resolve. Any answer on her part was aborted by a knock on the balcony door. Rafe waited on the other side with two to-go cups of coffee.

"That fucker needs a clue," Zane growled.

"No, *he* doesn't, but *you* seem to," she retorted as she padded to the door.

In response, he lay back down and crossed his arms behind his head. One brow lifted in challenge. The sexual pheromones he exuded had Winnie considering forgetting her late-morning visitor and jumping Zane's bones. She didn't think he'd be opposed to the idea based on the grin directed toward her.

With a regretful internal sigh, Winnie opened the door to Rafe. "Good morning." She took one of the proffered cups from him and kissed his smooth-shaven cheek. "Thanks for the coffee."

"You're welcome, *qalbi*. I see you have company. Should I leave you alone?"

Zane cut through her "no" with his "yes."

Without bothering to spare Zane a glance, Winnie smiled at Rafe and repeated, "No." She took a long sip of her coffee and groaned her appreciation. "Zane was just leaving."

"No, Zane wasn't," the man in question retorted.

"We could always enjoy our coffee on the deck, like yesterday morning," Rafe suggested.

Zane jackknifed into a sitting position. "I'll say one thing for you, asshole. You sure work fast."

Rafe shot him a slow, mocking smile. "With someone as lovely as Helena, one would be a fool not to."

"Helena?"

"*Qalbi*, I'm hurt. You didn't tell him we were married?" Rafe winked down at her.

"You'd better be joking, you knob," Zane snarled. "Win?"

She rolled her eyes. "When would we have had time to get married, Zane? And for that matter, do you honestly believe I'd be wasting my honeymoon sleeping in a separate suite?"

"Shall we take our coffee outside?" Rafe placed a hand on the swell of her hip.

There was an explosion of movement behind her right before the hand touching her was ripped away. Zane's muscled arm wrapped around her waist and pulled her back against him.

"The only reason I'm not turning you into a human torch is because Winnie seems to like your smarmy ass. But if you touch her again, all bets are off," Zane warned.

Winnie could feel his body tremble from his anger where it

pressed against her. The heat radiating from his front to her back was enough to scorch her. She stroked a hand along his arm.

"Zane, you need to simmer down and control your power. Please," she added softly.

His other arm came around her, and he buried his nose in her neck. She could feel his calming inhale.

"I'm sorry, Win," Zane murmured.

His lips brushed the tender flesh below her ear. Desire, unbidden and embarrassing in its intensity, rushed through her, setting her lady bits ablaze.

As abruptly as he'd grabbed her, Zane released her body and snagged her cup of coffee. He downed half the container before he returned it.

Had he just played her again? Goddess, she was feeling as dumb as a rock.

ZANE ALMOST LAUGHED AT WINNIE'S STUNNED EXPRESSION AND THE calculating gleam in Rafe's eye. He'd made his point perfectly clear. Winnie was Zane's, and if the poaching bastard wished to keep his limbs intact, he'd keep them to himself.

While he was at it, Zane decided Winnie needed a robe to cover her tank top and boy shorts. He didn't care for the way Rafe's eyes were repeatedly drawn to her braless breasts. He conjured one and draped it over her front.

"Why don't you wait outside, Ray? Winnie and I need to chat a sec."

"Rafe," Winnie corrected on a hard note, struggling to untangle herself from where he'd tied the bow in back.

"Ray, Rafe, Randy—who cares?"

"*I* care. Stop being an ass, Zane."

He patted her cheek. "You're adorable when you're mad, Win."

Winnie growled, and both men stepped back.

"I should go," Rafe said. "I don't care to be witness to murder. But if you need help disposing of the body, I know people."

If the guy hadn't been after Zane's woman, Zane might've liked him. As it was, he didn't find Rafe the least bit amusing. "That line was probably original in nineteen forty-something when you were first born. But it's been around the block a few times. Not dissimilar to yourself, I suppose."

"What is *wrong* with you?" Winnie shouted and shoved at his chest. She'd succeeded in dislodging the thick robe he'd used to cover her.

Zane was dog enough to enjoy the picture she presented with her pale, flashing eyes and her hands on her hips.

Rafe surprised him when he laughed. "I'd love to stay and see the fireworks, but I have an appointment." He bent to whisper something to Winnie and chuckled when she blushed. "Take care, *qalbi*. I hope to see you again someday soon."

For a split second, Rafe's expression turned forbidding. "Remember what I said about using your own name here. Be careful, Winter Thorne."

"Thank you, Rafe." She reached up to caress his cheek. "I'll remember."

The man's face softened as he gazed down upon her loveliness. "Good."

Zane felt a moment of unease press on his chest. These two had formed a bond of sorts. He prayed it was only friendship.

After Rafe left, Winnie turned on Zane and punched him in the arm. "You were a complete jerk!"

"Your point?"

"Why?"

"Ah, Win, if you don't know by now..." he said with a shake of his head.

"I've come to the conclusion that you are a mental case, do you know that?"

He straightened and frowned. What about him came across as crazy?

She wasted no time clueing him in.

"One minute you are out to exact revenge against me. The next you are swearing your undying love. Then, the very *next* minute, you're kissing another woman. And thirty-seconds after *that*, you are snapping and snarling at any man who looks sideways at me." Winnie inhaled a deep breath. "You're crazy."

She wasn't wrong. Zane *was* crazy. Crazy for her. He told her as much. "It's you, Win. I'm mad about you."

"I told you yesterday; I'm not doing this. What I thought we had is—in reality—a game to you. And what you seem to believe we have is all in your head." She held up a hand when he stepped toward her. "I don't want a relationship built on lies and anger, Zane. I told you yesterday. I don't want you."

"What can I do to prove to you that I'm serious? That I love you?"

The eyes she turned on him were filled with sadness and resignation. "Nothing, because I'll never believe you."

If she'd plunged a dagger into his heart, Zane might have found it less painful. As it was, his heart spasmed in his chest and found it difficult to maintain its rhythm.

"All relationships have rough patches, Win. Please don't give up on ours."

"What is it you miss, Zane? Tell me? The sex? You can get that anywhere. The blind devotion? I imagine you can find that, too. The thrill of getting away with cheating behind my back? Yeah, there's a sucker born every minute. You'll have no trouble finding a woman like that."

The injustice of her accusations caused his anger to take hold. "Stop it! I didn't cheat on you, Win. Not once."

"You're a damned liar! I saw you with her. Drinking, dancing, kissing. *I saw you!*"

The small sob she let loose hurt his heart. "It was staged for your benefit," he confessed. "I knew you took my ring to scry. I can't deny wanting to hurt you for what you did. But the moment my lips touched hers, I knew, Win. There isn't another woman alive who matches me as perfectly as you. I love you."

She shook her head.

TM CROMER

"I do, Win. I love you. And I will find a way to prove it to you every single day of our lives." He cupped her pale, tear-filled face. "I love you. *You*, Winter Thorne. Only you. If you believe nothing else, I need you to know that much."

Her next words were spoken so low, Zane strained to hear.

"I need you to go, Zane."

Sure the sound of his cracking heart had to be heard throughout the hotel, Zane pressed a fist to his chest. "Please, Win." He wasn't above begging. "Please."

"I need you to go," she said again, her voice stronger; her resolve firmer.

With no energy left to drag his feet out of the room, Zane took the path of least resistance and teleported to the one place he'd always found comfort. The clearing between their homes.

It was still dark, and a light rain sprinkled to the ground. He didn't care. He sat beneath the old oak with his and Winnie's initials and stared at nothing. If the moisture on his cheeks had little to do with the rain, no one was around to see.

He'd taken a gamble, and he'd lost the most precious thing in his world.

17

*A*fter Zane had disappeared, Winnie sprawled on the bed and stared at the rotating ceiling fan. She swiped at the tears leaking from the corner of her eyes. She *would not* cry! Crying should be reserved for real situations: real love and real relationships. Not falsehoods and games. Those things to which she refused to fall emotional hostage. She was a Thorne, and Thornes were made of stronger stuff. And if she kept telling herself that enough, she'd eventually believe it. Continuing on in this vein wasn't conducive to getting over him. If he repeatedly showed up at every turn, he would lay waste to her emotions.

Mind made up, she headed for the shower. As she lathered her hair and luxuriated under the steaming spray, she recalled how happy she'd been to wake and find Zane in her bed. No other man had ever made her feel that way, yet she wanted someone who could. Truth be told, she wanted someone to truly love her in the way her Uncle Alastair loved her mother: so strongly that he would bend time and space, manipulate people to do his bidding, and destroy anyone who got in his path to save her. His love for Aurora was single-minded and spanned decades.

Rafe had potential. But rebounding within a day of her breakup was stupid on every level. Perhaps down the road, when her life was back on track, and her mother had awakened from the stasis state, Winnie could explore a relationship with him. She mentally dismissed the age difference. It didn't matter between witches and warlocks. Their life expectancy was easily two to three times that of a non-magical human.

Winnie stepped from the shower and dried off. She snapped her fingers to style her hair. Nothing happened. With a frown, she snapped twice more in succession. Aghast, she stared at her fingers. She fought to center herself, held out her palm, and tried to conjure another cup of coffee. Nothing.

Alarm swelled in her mind, nearly sending her into a panic. Magic on the fritz? It just didn't happen—and definitely not to a Thorne. For a split second, she wondered if Zane was playing games and had cast a spell. Winnie dismissed it. He wouldn't take that risk —or at least she didn't believe so. As much as she'd like to believe she knew him, she didn't. But as he'd said, enemies were on the loose. She only prayed he didn't hate her enough to make her vulnerable.

Tucking the towel tightly around her, she wrapped her palm around the pendant Alastair had insisted she wear. "Uncle Alastair, I need you."

On my way.

Winnie took clean clothing from the stash she'd conjured the day before and quickly dressed as she ran over different scenarios as to why her magic might not be working.

The knock on her suite door came two minutes later. That had to be a record for her uncle. Usually, his appearances were instantaneous. The door had cracked open only six inches when she realized her mistake; *she'd never checked who was on the other side!*

Winnie was thrown back as the door was forced inward. A dark-haired Asian man stepped over the threshold as if he owned the place. Behind him were at least a half-dozen men dressed in black.

Zhu Lin.

Winnie tried to keep her terror at bay. With no magic, she had no way of fighting him.

"Who are you?" she demanded in hopes of bluffing her way out. She certainly wasn't teleporting anytime soon. But perhaps if she could convince him he had an everyday mortal, he'd depart.

"I should think you'd know who I am, Winter Thorne."

"You're mistaken. I'm just a guest here. I don't know who... what did you say the name was again?"

He sneered as his icy green eyes swept the length of her body. "Nice try. But you are the spitting image of your mother."

She wrapped a hand around her necklace and prayed the physic connection the stone provided would continue to work. *Stay away. Lin is here.*

Teleport now!

Can't. Magic is gone.

Winnie had no way of knowing if Alastair received her last transmission.

"What did you do to the room?" she asked. "How did you neutralize my magic?"

"I see you've given up the pretense." Lin casually strolled toward her. "It's not difficult to do if you have the right resources."

Winnie lifted her chin and stared down her nose at him. "What do you want?"

He tilted his head and narrowed his eyes as if she were a novelty to him. A fleeting glimpse of humanity flickered to life in his eyes before he ruthlessly suppressed it. His eerily pale-green gaze returned to cold.

Without answering, he glanced to one of his men and lifted his brows.

"All clear," his minion said in his heavily accented voice.

Lin nodded and returned his attention to her. "Since your family is exceedingly difficult to kill, I've decided to take you hostage."

Oddly enough, once murder was taken off the table, her nerves settled. She laughed, sat on a nearby chair, and crossed her legs. "What's the long-term goal for taking me hostage?"

"Unless I miss my guess, I believe your uncle Alastair will gladly give himself in exchange for you." Lin rested on the armchair beside her and picked up a strand of her damp hair to run through his fingers.

She wanted to smack his hand away but refrained. "You're wrong. Alastair only cares about himself." Winnie sent a silent apology through the tanzanite stone.

Lin laughed. "Am I? I doubt it."

She didn't doubt her uncle would stage a rescue. She only hoped no one was hurt in the process. The last time Lin had made an appearance, there was an all-out battle in the city park of Leiper's Fork. Had her father and Alastair not joined forces with Coop, Spring, and herself, the situation might've ended in more casualties.

"What happens to me when he laughs in your face?" Her plan was to keep him talking as long as necessary. If he didn't shoot her or drag her from the room, she might be able to stall long enough for reinforcements to arrive.

Lin frowned and dropped her hair. "I will be forced to kill you, pretty Winter Rose."

Her heart rate kicked up at the death threat.

"Winter Rose?" she asked curious despite herself about how he knew her middle name.

"I have a dossier on all your family members. But your name fits you. You are like the most delicate bloom. Beautiful in every way, but with long, wicked thorns."

Well, he wasn't wrong. She did have her thorny side. And she intended to prick him with it the first chance she got. "Who would've thought you were poetic, Mr. Lin?"

He smiled with genuine amusement. "I hope your uncle decides to sacrifice himself for you. I'd hate to kill you."

"Well, like you said, we are exceedingly difficult to kill. You tried twice with my sister."

Mentioning Autumn was a mistake. Lin's face hardened to stone, and all warmth left his eyes. If she'd thought his expression cold before, it was nothing compared to the arctic quality of his countenance now. Her spine tingled from the dangerous currents in the air.

"She stole from me."

In for a penny, in for a pound. Winnie scrunched up her nose and squinted. "Stole from you? *Really*, Zhu? May I call you Zhu? I feel like we should be on a first name basis." She didn't wait for his answer. "Don't you think that's stretching it to say she stole from you? I mean, the Chintamani Stone belongs to no one person. And you can have it back when we are done with it. I'll personally see to it if you let me go."

"Come. We've delayed long enough," he said and jerked her to her feet.

Time for a new tactic.

"Please don't do this." Winnie placed a hand over his heart. "You don't need to. I'll help you in any way I can. There's no love lost between me and my uncle."

He ran a hand along her scalp as if to caress her. When his fingers tightened in the strands at the base of her neck and jerked her head back near to breaking, she realized her mistake.

"Don't play the whore with me, Winter Rose. I would give you to these men without reservation."

"I wasn't," she replied, careful to keep her tone neutral and alarm from her voice. She suspected he would respect her level-headedness over trembling fear. "I was only trying to get you to see reason. My apologies for offending you, sir."

His gaze dropped to her lips and lingered.

To hide her revulsion, she dropped her gaze to the floor.

"Come," he repeated gruffly.

With a rough shove, he propelled her toward the front door.

The air moved, and the smell of the salty sea air drifted to her.

She heard a whine and the first body drop. Three more men went down in rapid succession.

A hard, wiry arm wrapped around her throat. Winnie was spun around and placed in front of Lin. A human shield.

"You are not who I was expecting, Mr. Xuereb."

"But you aren't surprised to see me, Lin. I wonder why that is?"

"My spies told me you were here. I knew you'd return home eventually." A gun appeared in his left hand, aimed directly at Winnie's temple. "As for finding you co-mingling with the Thornes, that is an added bonus."

Winnie's eyes sought backup behind Rafe. He was still outnumbered three to one. Or three to two if she was counted, but honestly, she was useless other than as a pawn for Lin to use against Rafe.

"I wouldn't kill her. You'll have every Thorne, Gillespie, Fennell, and Carlyle on your ass. She's connected."

Winnie didn't have time to express her surprise that Rafe knew her family tree. Lin shoved her in Rafe's direction and fired. She waited for the pain, but when none came, she rounded on Lin.

Time had frozen, a bullet hung in the air inches from the nine millimeter Lin had fired. Moving quickly, she tackled Rafe to the ground and snatched his gun from where it landed. She whipped around just as time corrected itself and snapped back into place. A single round was all she managed before hell broke loose. Her shot hit Lin's guard in the right shoulder.

The slider behind her shattered, and a container clanked across the tile.

Lin met her eyes across the distance, sketched a half-bow, and rushed out the hallway door with his minions fast on his heels.

The container never released its toxic nerve gas, or tear gas, or whatever the hell it was supposed to hold, and Winnie lowered the arm she'd flung over her nose and mouth.

She started to shake. Now that she was coming down from the adrenaline rush, her knees felt too weak to support her. She sank onto the edge of the bed.

Gentle hands reached for her and removed the gun from her hand. Rafe smoothed back her hair and took stock. "*Qalbi*, are you hurt?"

"No," she finally answered.

A tall, rugged man entered the opening between the balcony and her bedroom. He ran a cursory glance over her and nodded.

Winnie was certain her eyes had to be deceiving her. Disbelief clouded her brain. The thick, dark-brown beard that covered the bottom half of his face was new, but he looked remarkably like he had the last time she'd seen him: vital and powerful. It was easy to see why her Aunt GiGi had loved him.

"Uncle Ryker?"

"She's unhurt," he said into the Bluetooth device in his right ear. "The suite is clear."

Rafe helped her to her feet.

Winnie breezed past him and halted in front of GiGi's husband, who had been in the wind for the better part of fifteen years or more. "Thank you."

He opened his arms.

Winnie flew into his embrace as if she were still a child and he could soothe all her hurts. Tears burned behind her lids and slid down her cheeks. She hadn't realized how much she'd missed him until this exact moment.

"None of us knew what had happened to you," she choked out. "Aunt GiGi—"

"It's okay, love," he said, cutting off her mention of GiGi.

Glass crunched, signaling another person's entry into the room.

"How does it look that you made it here before me, Ryker?" Alastair complained good-naturedly.

"Like you're a slacker?" Ryker retorted.

The two men grinned and clasped hands.

Alastair surveyed Winnie where she stayed tucked against Ryker's side. "Are you okay, child?"

"I think so. I was a bit freaked out when I realized my magic had been neutralized."

"I've been there. I can imagine what you went through." He tapped her nose. "But you handled it beautifully. Thank you for making sure I didn't walk into a trap."

High praise, indeed.

Winnie finally remembered her sister had been staying over and grew frantic. "Where's Spring?"

"I sent her home the second you relayed to me there was a problem. She should be secure in the Manor, but if you want to message her, you can."

"Did Lin ward the whole hotel against magic or only my room?" she asked as she found the strength to pull away from her uncle and stand on her own.

Rafe answered. "From what we can tell, only this room."

One thing bothered her: that someone still had the kind of power to perform magic even when a room was warded. She needed to know who that person was and what abilities they possessed. "Who froze time?"

All the men looked at her as if she'd lost her mind.

"What?" she asked nervously.

"Winnie, *you* were the one who created the time shift," Rafe said. His troubled expression unnerved her.

"But I didn't," she denied. "I heard the shot and waited for the impact of the bullet. When I turned, everyone was frozen in place. It wasn't me. As far as I know, only Summer can do that, and it's accidental at best." She sat heavily on the bed. "My magic was gone, remember?"

"Your sister?" Ryker stepped in close and addressed Alastair. He was careful to keep his voice low enough that Winnie could barely make out what he was saying. "With the exception of Preston, she's the only other witch I know who can. She must've been scrying when this all went down."

"That's the most likely scenario," Alastair agreed.

With a sharp glance around the room, Ryker leaned down and kissed Winnie on the crown of her head. "Take care of yourself, kid."

"You're not leaving?" she cried, heartbroken at the thought of their reunion, however impromptu, cut short.

"Yes. But I'll be back in touch soon. I promise."

He was gone before she could form a protest.

"Where is the Carlyle boy?" Alastair wanted to know.

"I sent him away this morning."

Rafe's head came up from where he'd been fidgeting with his smartphone. "Sent him away? For good?"

"For now," she returned.

Her uncle studied her silently. Alastair's expression was bland, but Winnie could almost see the wheels spinning in his brain.

"Where is he?" he asked again. This time, there was more menace in his tone.

Winnie was left to wonder what he believed he knew. "Has Zane done something?"

"That depends," Alastair said silkily. "He was ordered to protect you."

"Ordered. Pfft." Winnie's irritation spiked. "He's a newbie, Uncle. What could he possibly do to protect me?"

"He's six-feet-three, and you're all of five-feet-seven. In a situation like this, where your magic was neutralized, he can physically fight."

"Zane would've gotten himself shot based on his inability to hold his temper. I did better without him here."

"Did you?" Alastair crossed his arms and tilted his head. "Correct me if I'm wrong, but had another witch—or warlock—not altered time, you would not be breathing right now."

He wasn't wrong.

Winnie intended to give her savior a big smacking kiss when she found him or her. "Don't be angry with Zane, Uncle. I'm the one who got ugly and sent him away."

When Alastair changed tactics by shifting to kind and caring, it threw her. "He's a Carlyle, dear girl. Remember, he can't help being a stubborn ass. Try to bear that in mind when you deal with him in the future, okay? It will save you both heartache."

*W*innie said her goodbyes to Rafe thirty minutes later. It was time to get back to the safety of Thorne Manor and plan out the recovery of the amulet.

"If you are ever back in my neck of the woods…" He smiled and drew her into his warm embrace.

"Same goes," she said as she squeezed him tight. "Be careful. I don't think Lin was too happy that you disrupted his little plan."

"Same goes," he repeated and kissed her forehead. As he pulled away, he caressed the line of her jaw. "I would be devastated to learn something had happened to you."

Alastair approached and shot Rafe a disapproving scowl.

"No Zane?" Winnie asked her uncle. They hadn't been able to reach him since the incident with Lin had gone down. Worry, dark and ugly, wormed its way into her thoughts. "Why do you suppose he isn't answering his phone? I know he was upset with me, but I doubt he'd purposely hold out, knowing what had gone down."

"I don't know, child. Once we get back to Thorne Manor, we can search for him on the off chance he hasn't returned. Your sister is scrying as we speak."

"You don't think Lin captured him, do you?" Her worry kicked up into the alarmed zone.

"I couldn't say for sure." Alastair laid a comforting hand on her shoulder. "But we'll find him."

Winnie nodded, slightly reassured by his confidence. She returned her gaze to Rafe. "I think I'm going to miss you most of all, Scarecrow."

His lips twisted in a half-smile at the Wizard of Oz quote. "Time to click your heels together, Dorothy." Rafe squeezed her hand. "Goodbye."

In a flash of warmth, Winnie and Alastair teleported home. When they arrived in the living room of the manor, a shout went up, and her family piled into the room.

Winnie glanced around at all the beloved faces: her dad, Aunt GiGi, Summer, and Spring. For the short time she'd faced down Lin, she'd been heartbroken at the thought that she hadn't said goodbye. They'd never know how much she loved them. She hugged each in turn.

"Has anyone found Zane?" Winnie asked.

"No. Coop and Keaton are out looking for him," Spring said. "Autumn is upstairs scrying right now."

"Did anyone check the clearing?"

"I'll go," Alastair said, and teleported out.

Her father hugged her a second time, holding on a little longer than necessary. "GiGi told us what happened," Preston said.

She turned to her aunt. "Uncle Ryker was there, but I guess you know that."

"I do." GiGi smiled through her tears. "I'm glad he helped you, dear girl."

"He said he thought you might have been the one to save me by suspending time. I didn't know you could do that."

"I can, but I didn't. The room was warded against magic."

"I don't understand. Then who saved me?" Winnie asked. "Summer?"

Summer shook her blonde head. "Not me. I was at my animal

clinic. Holly was with me, so even if she had the same ability, which none of us is sure she does, it couldn't have been her."

Winnie was at a loss. For the moment, the mystery of the time suspension would have to wait. "We need to find Zane. I'll head upstair—"

Alastair arrived with a rumpled Zane in tow.

Winnie took one look into Zane's tortured dark eyes and ran to him. With his hard, tight arms around her, they fell to their knees.

"God, Win! I had no idea!"

"It's okay," she assured him. She shoved aside her resolve to keep her distance, if only for the time being. The feeling of being loved, even if it wasn't real, was too much to resist.

"I should've been there. I should've—"

"You'd have only gotten hurt. Lin was out to cause havoc."

"I'm sorry, babe."

"It's okay," Winnie said again. "Really." She pulled back and studied him. "Where have you been? The glen?"

"I went straight there after... I needed to clear my head."

She nodded and smoothed the wrinkled material of his shirt. Having never seen him rumpled before, she was taken aback. "What happened to you? You're a mess."

A telling glance was shared between Zane and Alastair.

Winnie whipped her head in her uncle's direction. "Did you hurt him?"

"Not really. I may have given him a bit of an attitude adjustment when I found him, but he's unhurt." Alastair's bored, arrogant tone grated on her nerves.

"You had no right!" She stood and charged to where he rested a shoulder against the wall.

"Didn't I?" he asked as he straightened. He leaned in as if to impart a secret. "Know that I have no problem meting out justice, child. As I see it, he deserved a thrashing and more."

"Butt out of my love life, Uncle," she snapped.

A self-satisfied smile transformed his face and left Winnie befuddled.

Warm arms encircled her from behind. "It's okay, Win. I'm fine. None of that's important right now."

She closed her eyes, leaned back against Zane's chest, and centered herself, struggling not to blow the roof off the manor.

Autumn chose that moment to rush down the stairs. "Winnie!"

Winnie pulled away from Zane to embrace her sister. "I'm okay, Tums."

"Lin! I almost had a heart attack when I saw he showed up."

"You saw?" Winnie frowned. "You were spying?"

Her sister gave her a sheepish look and uttered one word, "Hallmark."

"My life isn't a made-for-TV movie, Tums!"

"I don't know, the hottie who saved you made the perfect hero."

"Hottie?" Zane thundered. "You ran right to that Italian playboy after I left?"

"Maltese," Winnie corrected. "And no. He charged in when Lin arrived. He saved me, Zane, and I owe him."

"I don't want you to be indebted to that asshat," he growled.

Autumn laughed and gave a sharp clap of her hands. "See? This is what I'm talking about. Drama, drama, drama. It's good stuff."

Winnie sighed her exasperation.

Zane wasn't so nice and swore a blue streak. He glared down at Winnie. "Do you think we can have this conversation in private. I'm tired of being your sisters' personal amusement source."

"That's just mean spirited of you, Studly," Autumn stated.

"Bite me," he snarled.

Her sister cocked her head to the side as if contemplating his seriousness. "You know, I'd always believed you were the nice one. Always calm in the face of every situation. Who knew you were so volatile?"

"The woman I love was in danger from a psycho who likes to kill witches. I wasn't there to save her. So yeah, I think I have the right to be a little upset, Autumn," Zane stated somewhat calmer.

"Don't forget the hot Maltese," Autumn taunted.

Zane's jaw tightened, and the muscle there started to tick.

Winnie was sure he would snap and murder her sister at any second. She ran her fingertips along his clenched jaw. "Zane."

The uncertain gaze he turned on her nearly broke Winnie's heart. "I'm home, and I'm fine."

He closed his eyes and rested his forehead against hers.

ZANE WAS UNABLE TO SPEAK. HE'D ALMOST LOST WINNIE WHILE HE was wallowing in his pain earlier today. Pain he'd caused himself by his stupid revenge scheme. Why Winnie was reassuring him now was beyond his ability to comprehend, but she was, and he loved her all the more for it.

He hated that they had an audience for this, but then again, he didn't intend to rock the boat. For whatever reason, Winnie seemed to have released her anger toward his past actions. Maybe it was only temporary, but he'd take it.

"Can we go somewhere to talk?" he finally managed to ask.

"Nothing has changed," she whispered. "I can't allow myself to love you, Zane."

When he drew back and opened his eyes, they were alone in the room. Zane supposed he should be grateful the Thornes allowed him the courtesy of being rejected and crushed in private. Yet somehow, it didn't make Winnie's rejection any easier.

"But you do anyway. I know you do, Win. I can feel it as sure as I'm standing here."

"Even if I do, it makes no difference. Autumn wasn't wrong— you *are* volatile."

"I'm not—or not normally. I swear it. You've seen me at my worst, but you have to admit; there have been extenuating circumstances."

"And should things get worse instead of better? How do you plan to react then, Zane?"

He threw up his hands and turned away. How could he convince her the man whose terrifyingly erratic behavior she'd witnessed up to this point wasn't him? It was some crazy, out of control, version of himself who was spawned in his rage over being duped.

"I don't think you should go to Egypt with me, Zane."

He closed his eyes and shook his head in frustration.

Winnie's warm palm settled on his mid-back. "I'm not trying to be hateful. I just think it's better for all involved if we cut the ties now."

"I promised to help you find the amulet. Your mother's welfare trumps my feelings, Win." Zane pivoted around and gently clasped her hand before she could drop it. He kissed her fingertips and released her. "I'll be a wreck until you return, wondering and worrying if Lin would show up and nab you at any second. It couldn't hurt to have me there."

Her unhappy look said it could hurt, but she didn't object. "I need a day or two to recover. Then we can head over."

"Don't go without me, Win. Please. I'll go insane with worry."

Winnie nodded. "I won't."

"Promise?"

"Promise."

Because he wanted to touch her, to sweep her into his arms and never let her go, Zane stepped back. "You have my number."

"Electronics don't work in the clearing. The Stones," she said by way of explanation due to their inability to reach him earlier.

His cousin, Keaton, had explained about the massive ancient stones hidden below ground that rose up when all the witches had performed a healing ceremony for Autumn last month. Zane had yet to see them, but he had no doubt their power could easily interfere with cell phone reception.

"I'll be at home. You know what my room looks like, so if you need to teleport…"

She snorted and looked away.

"What?"

"I won't be teleporting into your room, Zane. Goddess knows, I don't want to catch you in the act with another woman."

Self-disgust and irritation flared to life inside him. "Jesus, Win. How many times can I apologize for the set-up?"

"I'm sorry. I didn't mean to be catty or spiteful," she said quietly in an about-face. "I'll call you tomorrow to schedule a time. Now if you don't mind, I need some sleep."

Zane was loathe to leave it like this. His instinct screamed to push until she relented and understood how much he loved her. But logic told him she wouldn't be moved, and compassion encouraged him to retreat to allow her the time she needed to rest after her ordeal.

But what he couldn't do was leave without touching her one last time. He approached as if he were dealing with one of his family's skittish horses. "Win?"

She lifted her head. Sure enough, Zane saw the same wild look in her eye as an untrained mare. Winnie wanted to trust, but a stronger urge to bolt remained.

Zane held out a hand and lightly stroked the smooth column of Winnie's bare neck. "I'm glad you're okay. The idea of you hurt, or worse…" He closed his eyes and shook his head. "Please don't take off by yourself again, not until Lin is stopped."

"That I can promise."

For a long moment, they stared into each other's eyes. Zane had so many things he longed to say but didn't know how, and from the solemn, watchful look on Winnie's face, she felt the same.

His gaze dropped to her berry bright lips. No makeup, and still she was stunning. He gave in to the urge to taste her. She met him halfway.

The kiss was life affirming and passionate. Wrapped up inside it was all the words they wanted to speak, but couldn't.

Zane ended the kiss and inched away. His thumb caressed her swollen lower lip. "I've always loved you, Win. From the first time I saw you in the glen playing with your sisters, I knew you were my soulmate." He trailed his fingers over the beautiful skin of her face. "I carved our initials in the old oak by the clearing after our first date. Did you know that? And even after you'd taken my memory,

I'd see you in town on occasion and think I wanted to know you better. I dreamed of the day I would ask you out. But somehow, the timing was off and you'd walk away before I could screw up my courage. That should tell you why I reacted badly." He dropped his hand. "My feelings will never change, babe. If you never give me another chance, I'll understand. But more than anything in this world, I wish you would."

Zane left by way of the front door. He could teleport, but he wanted the time to walk and clear his head. He'd just cleared the porch when the sound of running feet on wood caught his attention.

"Zane!"

Swinging back around, he held out his arms. "Take the leap, Win. I'll catch you." Indecision was written in every line of her body. He saw the moment she made her decision and sighed his relief.

Winnie flung herself off the porch, and true to his word, Zane caught her mid-air. She wrapped her legs around his waist, and he cupped her bottom to hold her against him.

"I love you, too," she choked out.

The sting of his salty tears burned behind his lids. "I'm so glad," he said gruffly. "I don't know what I would've done without you in my life."

Without another word, he teleported them to her room.

19

*A*lastair swiped his palm over the scrying mirror and lifted the object representing Winnie from atop the glass. "Okay, children, show's over. Let them have their privacy."

"Aww, Uncle Alastair, you're ruining our fun," Autumn complained with a huff.

"What, are you eight?" he asked with a raised brow.

Autumn laughed and kissed his cheek. "Fine. But just so you know, I am dubbing you Spoiler of Fun."

"I'm pretty sure I dubbed Summer that a few months back," Coop said with a laugh, wrapping his arms around his girlfriend from behind and hugging her to his chest.

"Shut it!" Summer warned with a blush.

Alastair fought back a smile. Seeing his daughter happy made him ecstatic—on the inside. Not that he'd ever allow his emotions to shine through. He'd been conditioned well while being held prisoner in Lin's dungeon.

"I have to head out and make an appearance at the department or Lil will kill me. She's been on my ass about the upcoming election," Coop said, referring to the woman who essentially ran the sheriff's office single-handedly.

Alastair remembered her well from when he was young. Lil had been a firecracker then, and it seemed she continued to burn brightly.

After Coop left, Alastair faced his daughter and two nieces. "We need to come up with a foolproof plan to stop Lin and his minions. I have a spy in his camp, who tells me Lin's gearing up for another big move. My man also stated Lin is keeping things tight to his chest and not giving details."

"That makes you nervous?" Spring asked.

Alastair lifted his brows. "You need to ask?"

"Sorry."

He clasped his hands behind his back and strolled to the attic window to overlook the expanse of Thorne land. Longing struck. Or perhaps it was more like homesickness. He'd grown up running wild across those rolling hills. Scraped his knee more times than he could count climbing the large rock formation on the north side of the property. But Alastair had ceded the property and the manor to his brother Preston in exchange for his daughter's care.

Alastair picked up Summer's worried reflection in the glass. Goddess, she was lovely. All wild blonde hair and bright blue eyes, and more powerful than any of them had imagined. He did smile then. Summer had no idea what she could do. As a witch who could manipulate time, it made her more powerful than even he or Preston, and probably equally powerful to his sister GiGi.

Summer's spells went wild because she had too much power to contain. Only she didn't know that. But she would. Once Aurora was awake, Alastair could spend more time on training his daughter properly. The way she should have been trained to begin with.

But in the meantime, he needed to find a way to destroy Lin. That bastard had powerful magic on his side if he could neutralize Winnie so effortlessly. Winnie, who was a force of nature in her own right.

"Who's your inside man?" Autumn asked.

"I believe you referred to him as Ollie," Alastair told her. His lips twitched at her outrage.

"Jolly Ollie?"

"Who's Jolly Ollie?" Summer asked.

"It's for the best that you don't know." Alastair smoothed his shirt cuffs and straightened his cufflinks.

"I know."

All eyes turned to Spring.

"Who?" Autumn asked.

"It's obvious if you think about it. Who used to transform into various characters to amuse us as kids?"

"Uncle Ryker?" Summer frowned. "Why do you think it's him?"

Spring's beatific smile bloomed. "He's the only person Uncle Alastair would trust."

Alastair couldn't stop the grin. "You're too smart for your own good, child."

"I'm confused," Autumn said. "I thought he'd disappeared for good. Have you been in touch with him all this time?"

"I have," Alastair confirmed. "He works as a spy for the Witches' Council. They've been after Lin a long time." Alastair straightened his pink tie and shrugged. "If he slips me information here or there, well, let's just say, he's not hurting anyone."

"Does anyone find it odd that Autumn dubbed him Jolly Ollie and his middle name is Jolyon?" Spring laughed.

"No! Is it really?" Summer laughed in turn.

Spring nodded. "Yep. Check the family tree in the back of our grimoire."

"Can we get back on track, ladies?" Alastair sighed. "Lin is a real threat."

"Don't you think I know that better than anyone," Autumn retorted irritably.

When she rubbed her flat abdomen, Alastair smiled for a second time. "When are you due?"

Autumn's head came up at the same time her sisters gasped. "How did you guess?"

"I've been around pregnant women before, child. I think I can tell when one is expecting," he said dryly.

"You're pregnant and didn't tell us?" Summer demanded, even as she tempered her indignation with a hug for Autumn.

"You should tell them," Alastair said. He referred to her previous miscarriage. Other than Alastair, not another living soul, outside GiGi, had known she'd lost Keaton's first child. He'd known because he kept his pulse on the happenings of the family, and not always in an above-board way. If he had to dabble in a little dark magic now and again, he justified it as the means to an end.

Alastair waited as Autumn told the others the details of her miscarriage from nearly ten years before. She went on to express her worries that she might not be able to carry to full term since she'd believed she would never be able to conceive again. The women talked in hushed tones as Alastair returned to the attic window to stare down over the glen.

He noted the lone black-haired woman wandering around, enjoying the day.

Alastair cast a glance behind him. All three women were wrapped up in the baby discussion. Without a by-your-leave, he tele-ported to the clearing.

"Hello, Beloved One."

"Hello, Exalted One," he returned the greeting to Isis, as was their custom. "To what do I owe the pleasure of your visit?"

She smiled as if he amused her. "Do I need a reason?"

"No. But you don't cross through the veil without a reason, not in my experience, anyway."

She shrugged. Alastair recognized the movement. The interesting thing about genetics was that simple movements or gestures, along with looks and temperament, could be inherited. The careless shrug was a signature move of Isis that Autumn had perfected without knowing from whence it came.

When Isis remained silent, Alastair leaned back against the closest tree and crossed his arms. There was no rushing her.

"What did you do with the poison we drew from Autumn?" he asked, curious about the fact that she'd removed the urn in exchange for returning his niece to the fold.

"Nothing… yet. But I have plans for it. The exchange was a fair one by the laws of the Gods."

His lips twitched. His ancestor was a wily one. Perhaps it was where he had acquired the trait.

"How is Autumn?"

"She's good. I believe she's worried about the birth of her babe though."

Isis shook her head. "Oh, the young. How they always have to question a gift."

"Indeed."

Her laugh was clear and beautiful as it rang out. "You are my favorite," she confessed. "Of all my children throughout time, you've always been my favorite."

He smiled and bowed his head in acknowledgment. "I'm honored."

"As you should be," she quipped. "I've decided Lin's life shall be the exchange for that which you desire."

Alastair straightened. "How am I supposed to get him to this clearing unharmed?"

Isis shrugged again, but this time Alastair didn't find it as endearing. "You'll find a way. And if you don't, your love is lost to you."

Was she being a jealous shrew?

"No," she answered his unspoken question with a sharp look. "You know better than to question me."

Alastair tempered his thoughts and apologized. "Forgive me, Exalted One. My response was due to the unpleasant surprise."

A crafty smile flitted across her stunning face. "You are forgiven. *But*, I shall have a second payment for your disloyal thought."

"Of course. What do you ask of me?"

Isis crossed to where he stood. She studied him from beneath thick, black lashes and pursed her lips as if contemplating his question, when in fact, he suspected she'd already planned what to ask.

"Quentin."

Alastair's heart dropped into his stomach. "Excuse me?"

"I want Quentin to be my consort."

"No."

Her face hardened to displeased, and thunder rumbled. "You would dare defy me?"

"Not if I could help it. But I won't put my happiness above my daughter's. Holly loves him. Ask of me something else."

Isis played the waiting game. They stared into each other's eyes, each expecting the other to relent and speak first. She surprised him when she did. "You know I could take him for my own and still deny you your own happiness?"

Alastair hid his alarm and gave her a nod. "I do."

"Good. I find it admirable that you should care so much for your child. I will ask for a different payment. One to be determined."

"Thank you," he said.

"Now, I must run. I've been here too long." She touched his cheek, and Alastair felt the warmth of magic from her cool fingertips; a complete contradiction to his way of thinking. "Never doubt you shall succeed, Alastair Thorne." She leaned in as if to impart a secret. "I'm on your side."

"Thank you," he said again, this time with feeling.

"Tell your niece not to question my gift. She was completely healed during her stasis and shall bear a fine, healthy son."

"Your wish is my command," he replied, causing her to laugh.

"Yes, see that it remains so."

20

*W*hen Winnie awoke, the light outside had faded to dark. A strong, muscled arm was wrapped around her stomach.

Zane.

He'd taken a wrecking ball to her objections. She was either a fool for love or a sucker for punishment. Neither description sat well with her.

"I can feel you thinking, Win," Zane murmured, his nose buried in her hair. "Don't. Just feel. Know that this is right."

"I'm an imbecile."

He sighed and rose up on one elbow. She turned onto her back to gaze up into his warm, chocolatey eyes.

"You're not. You never were, and you never will be," he told her. "You may be an optimist, but there's nothing wrong with that."

"Did you love her?"

He frowned. "Who?"

"The woman you were kissing."

Zane closed his eyes, grimaced, and shook his head. "Christ, Win. I can't apologize enough for that jackass move. I swear, it was all staged."

"No, I don't mean do you love her now. I meant, did you love her before, when you were dating?"

"I cared about her, but did I love her? No, never." He leaned forward and placed a soft, lingering kiss on her mouth. "I've only ever loved you."

"That day in the clearing, when we first... I'm sorry for being honest."

He groaned and dropped back on the bed. "Stop! Please, just stop."

"I—"

Zane rolled atop her and settled his hips between her parted thighs. "Babe, you have nothing to apologize for, and we've said all we are going to say about the past. We are going to leave it where it belongs." He smoothed back her mussy hair. "Agreed?"

"If you've really forgiven me, then we are agreed."

"I've really forgiven you."

"Okay, in that case, we have a few days to make up for," she said with a wicked grin.

He sighed his happiness and rubbed his budding erection against her. "Thank the Goddess! I thought you'd never ask."

"I'm not asking; I'm stating."

"Sounds a bit demanding to me. Is this going to set the precedent for our entire relationship?"

"You bet!"

He laughed and skimmed his fingers across her lower belly. "Works for me!"

Her stomach chose that moment to protest and make known its hunger.

Zane squinted down at her. "I'm not getting lucky until you're fed, am I?"

"I'm sorry. For a second, I forgot I hadn't eaten in a while."

"Fair enough." He stood and hauled her to her feet. "Will pancakes work?"

She glanced at the wall clock. "Where are we going to find pancakes at nine o'clock at night?"

"Never you mind. Just know, I've got you covered."

After they'd dressed, she said, "Lead on, kind sir."

He clasped her hand and tugged her downstairs to the kitchen.

Winnie was surprised to see all four of her sisters gathered there. "What's going on?"

"In a word? Alastair," Holly said and pulled a face.

Holly was never thrilled to have to cater to her father's whims.

"Has something happened?" Zane asked as he went about searching the fridge for pancake supplies.

"He mentioned moving up the timeline for collecting all the objects," Summer said. "He thinks Lin is planning something big, although we don't know what yet."

"Then why are we borrowing trouble?" Zane asked.

"That's the question of the hour," Holly sighed. "But I can't hang around much longer. I need to get back to the sanctuary."

Summer reached across to pat her twin's hand. "Coop is there. He'll let me know if anything comes up. I say we eat pancakes and then turn on the blender for some margarita madness."

Zane poured the first of the batter onto the wide griddle. He then proceeded to create six more perfectly rounded pancakes.

Winnie smiled at his foresight in making a double batch of batter.

When he caught her eye and winked, she joined him at the stove. "What can I do to help?"

"Set the table and then put out the maple syrup and butter."

After that was done, she brought the first plate of pancakes to the table. "Dig in, ladies!"

"What about you?" Autumn asked, forking two pancakes onto her own plate.

"I'll wait on the second batch. Go ahead."

As everyone ate, Summer relayed the news of Autumn's pregnancy. The sisters all babbled at once, unable to contain their joy.

"Oh, Tums," Winnie cried. "I can't wait for a baby to spoil."

"We could have one of our own for you to spoil," Zane said.

All five females whipped around to stare at him with various degrees of disbelief.

138

. . .

ZANE LAUGHED AT THE SHOCK ON WINNIE'S FACE. HE DIDN'T KNOW where his comment had come from, but the more he thought about it, the more he loved the idea of Winnie round with his child.

She'd waddle and complain about not being able to see her feet, but secretly she'd love every second of her pregnancy. And of course, he'd rub her back and feet whenever she needed him to.

"I think we're moving a bit fast, don't you?" she managed to choke out.

It had never occurred to him to ask if she wanted children, but now he found himself wondering if she did.

"Don't you want kids, Win?"

"I do, but not until after the marriage vows."

Autumn laughed. "How antiquated."

"But you're not opposed to practicing beforehand?" he asked Winnie with a smirk. He'd never seen her skin turn such a shade of pink before, and it thrilled him. "Why, Winter Thorne, are you embarrassed?"

"You're such a jerk!"

Zane threw down his spatula and gathered her close, humming and waltzing her around the limited space of the kitchen. "But you love me anyway," he said with confidence.

She snorted and lifted her chin.

He buried his face against her neck, kissed the soft skin lightly, then blew a raspberry against a ticklish spot. Her giggles pleased him.

"You're burning our pancakes, you fool!" Autumn complained.

With a snap of his fingers, the pancakes were on the platter in the center of the wood table and the burner was off.

"Damn, son! You developed magical skills!" Autumn crowed.

Winnie beamed like a proud parent.

"I owe it all to my teacher. She's amazing." He dipped her backward and lowered his voice so only Winnie could hear. "What about it, Win? Do you want to have my baby? We can get to work now."

He meant it to be teasing, or so he told himself, but Winnie's look of indecision cut him to the quick.

"It's okay, babe. You can wipe off that look of panic." Did his tone hold a hard edge? He straightened and tried to rein in his disappointment.

"We're moving too fast," she whispered in turn. "Someday, I'll want it all, Zane. Just not today. Please understand."

He'd be an asshole not to. "I do. I'm not sure what came over me. I'm pretty sure I channeled your sister's hormones."

"Do you two think you could speak loud enough for the rest of us to hear? I'm getting an ache in my neck from straining to eavesdrop," Summer complained.

Winnie laughed and leaned in close to Zane. "*That* is the baggage I come with. Be sure you can survive it before you commit."

"Keep it up, sister, and we'll spill the beans on the fact that you cloaked yourself and spied on Zane in the locker room shower," Autumn said.

Zane's head whipped in Autumn's direction. "What?"

Winnie conjured a nerf football and chucked it at Summer's head. "You weren't supposed to tell anyone!"

"I only told Autumn!" Summer argued with a laugh as she conjured a super soaker water gun.

Before Zane could blink, all the Thornes were armed with super soakers. Delighted, he laughed and stood back to observe. Squeals and screams nearly pierced his ears as sister shot sister and ran for cover. The house became a full-fledged war zone. Periodically, someone would shout *"Watch out! That's priceless!"* or *"Oh, Dad is going to kill you!"* but it never slowed their game.

Winnie ran back into the kitchen, with her hair dripping wet, laughing like a loon. When she caught her breath, she placed her back against the wall and gave him some sort of special ops-type of signal.

If Zane hadn't already fallen in love, this moment would've cemented it. He conjured his own water gun and fell into line beside her. "Just so I have this straight, you spied on me in the shower while we were in high school?"

A blush flared to life in her face. "My sisters have big mouths."

"Don't feel bad. If the situations were reversed, I'd totally spy on you."

Winnie giggled then screamed as he soaked the front of her shirt. Her nipples shot to attention from the icy water he'd conjured for his gun. The damp material outlined every curve and made his mouth salivate.

But the water war wasn't done, so Zane stole a kiss and laughed. "Payback," he said before he darted around the corner.

"What's with you and payback?" she hollered.

He popped his head back into the kitchen to answer, but got a face-full of water.

"Gotcha!" she cried before teleporting.

Yep, Zane was crazy about her.

21

"*W*in, my darling, my sweetness, my snook'ems… we need to get going," Zane tried to tease Winnie awake.

She groaned and rolled away from him. "I'm sleeping."

He propped his head up on his elbow and traced circles on her sleek, bare back. "It's time to wake up, babe." Leaning forward, he rained kisses along her left shoulder and collarbone then nuzzled her ear.

With a groan, Winnie flopped on her back and let the sheet fall to her waist. A mischievous smirk played about her berry-red lips, but she kept her eyes closed. "I'm sleeping," she murmured.

Bending, he captured her areola in his mouth and sucked. "Do I need to bring out the big guns to wake you up?"

"Mmhmm," she agreed; her smile widening.

Slowly, Zane trailed a hand down the smooth curve of her side, dragging the sheet as he went. "Three rounds of sex last night weren't enough for you?"

"True confession time: I'm a nymphomaniac."

He hid his own smile against her belly. "Good to know. I guess it's a good thing I'm a dog and can't get enough of your incredible body." He kissed his way south.

She gasped as his tongue swiped across her already wet folds and dug her fingers into his hair. "The Goddess definitely had foresight in matching us."

"Mmhmm," he agreed and got busy making her scream.

On the crest of her second orgasm, he rose up and eased into her opening. Their gazes met and held. Her eyes were filled with equal parts want and love. Zane knew, down in the deepest region of his soul, he would never get enough of that particular expression of hers. He could easily spend his life like this and never get tired of pleasuring her.

"I love you, Winter Thorne," he said huskily. "You are my reason for breathing."

Tears filled her eyes and escaped down her temples. She appeared to be too overcome to speak and pulled his head down to kiss him. Her arms tightened around his neck when he tried to draw back to look down into her face. "I love you, too, Zane," she whispered.

Once the words left her lips, Zane could no longer hold back. His hips pumped in a wild rhythm to match the rapid beating of his heart. Winnie's pleasure-filled gasps and pants drove him on.

The moment he felt her walls contract around him, milking him, Zane picked up his pace. Within a minute, his cry mingled with hers.

Taking care to stay connected, he pulled her atop him and gripped her ass for one final thrust. "That's the baby maker right there," he stated.

She laughed and dropped a kiss on his chin. "That's the fourth time you've said that in two days."

"Maybe we'll have quadruplets," he teased with a grin.

"Bite your tongue, man! I've never agreed to babies of any sort."

With a light slap to her butt cheek, he sat up and buried his face in the valley of her breasts. "Do you know how beautiful you'd look? Your belly swollen with our baby? He'd be adorable like you, with an IQ like mine."

Winnie pulled his hair in a not-so-gentle move to see his face.

"*Your* IQ? What's wrong with mine?" she demanded. "I'll have you know—"

He chuckled and kissed her. "You're so easy, Win."

"Sex is beside the point," she said, as she shoved him flat. "I'm not letting you out of this bed until you say I'm smarter than you."

Zane cupped the breasts above him and drew his thumb over her perky nipples. "If you haven't figured out that that's my plan..." He lifted a brow and grinned.

She rocked her hips, and his dick went back on high alert, ready for action. "I'm going to have fun making you cave."

"No, *I'm* going to have fun with you making me cave."

A sharp rap on the door interrupted their play.

"You've had two days to hide out and do the dirty, kids. Alastair has decreed it's time to get your asses in gear," Autumn's muffled voice came to them through the old wood door.

"Go away, Tums, or I'm never making you cinnamon rolls again."

"Sheesh, you don't have to get bitchy!" Autumn exclaimed. "You'd think with all the banging going on in this room, ol' Studly would be keeping you happy."

Zane couldn't hold back his amusement. The Weird Season Sisters, as the town had labeled the Thornes many years ago, should have their own reality television show. There was never a dull moment in their household.

AN HOUR LATER, HAND-IN-HAND, WINNIE AND ZANE EMERGED FROM her room, sated, showered, and ready to take on the world.

As they joined her family around the breakfast table, Winnie experienced a sense of peace. It was as if this moment had been fated, and she was where she was meant to be, with whom she was meant to be. She watched as Zane laughed and joked with the three of her four siblings who were present. Zane had an easy-going way about him that attracted others without trying. He was fun and flirty without crossing a line.

As if he sensed her regard, he glanced in her direction and winked.

Winnie's smile was a natural reaction to his charm. He held the same allure now as he had eight years before. She could spend every waking moment with him and never be bored. Never grow tired of the sameness that came with the routine of marriage and constantly being together.

And when he turned his twinkling chocolate eyes on her, she felt like she was the only woman in his universe.

"Winnie?"

Autumn's questioning tone caught Winnie's attention.

"I'm sorry, Tums. I wasn't paying attention."

"Oh, I think we all know where your mind was," Autumn laughed.

Heat crept up her neck, and she shot a furtive glance in Zane's direction. But his expression didn't mock her. Instead, he held her gaze and smiled softly.

"Your sisters were discussing the amulet. Autumn discovered an old, hand-drawn layout of Isis's temple in Saqqara. I think it could be useful in addition to the aerial images Alastair sent over."

"Do you think we'll feel the draw of the object like you did with the Chintamani Stone?" Winnie asked Autumn.

"It would be awesome if you did. It could save you a lot of time searching, and help you to get in and out before Lin is alerted to your presence in Egypt."

Zane straightened. "Think he'll know to look there?"

It was Summer who answered. "I get the feeling he has spies watching us."

"I agree," Winnie said. "As a matter of fact, Lin said as much. He knew we were in Malta. Although, I'm surprised he came after me instead of going after Alastair directly. Lin wants him in a bad way."

"He's the one who got away," Spring said. "Lin is honor-bound to capture or kill Uncle Alastair." She rose to prepare another cup of tea. "However, I think Lin intends to use us to get to him. Lin's family died because of the witches' war. In some large part, I believe he blames that solely on our family and on Alastair in particular. If he can hurt Alastair through us and eventually take out the strongest of our clan, yeah, I think he'll go that route."

Zane didn't look thrilled with Spring's assessment of the situation. "Win, you can't go to Saqqara. I'll find the amulet for you, but I want you out of harm's reach."

"I don't think I'm safe anywhere if we are being honest. Lin almost kidnapped Chloe in the park and nearly killed her, Derek, and Autumn in the process."

Frustration apparent, Zane stood and paced the small kitchen. "Then you'll stay here, on the Thorne estate, until he's neutralized, or preferably dead."

"You have to know that's not realistic, Zane." Winnie stood and walked to him. She placed a palm flat over his heart. "I have to work. There are deliveries to make and ship. The elderly residents at senior living centers around the country rely on my creams for their joints."

His dark, tortured gaze met hers. "I can't lose you, Win."

"You won't," she assured him. "We have Isis on our side. Look what she did for my sister."

Zane wasn't appeased, but he didn't comment. In place of frustrated words, he drew her into his embrace and laid his cheek atop of her head. Their embrace was interrupted by a sniffle.

All eyes turned to Autumn who sat waving her hands rapidly in front of her face. "Don't mind me. Pregnancy hormones."

Winnie parted from Zane to hug her sister. "I know I said it before, but I'm so happy for you, Tums."

"Thanks, sister. Do you think your man could make us more of those delicious pancakes? I think I'm going to need a plate of bacon to go with it."

All the sisters gasped.

"What's wrong?" Zane asked, confusion on his handsome face.

Winnie was unable to take her incredulous gaze from Autumn. "Win?"

"We don't eat meat, remember? Autumn especially doesn't care for it since she witnessed a pig being slaughtered as a kid."

Autumn moaned and placed a hand over her mouth.

"You might not want to talk about the ugly side of pig farming," Spring laughed. "I don't think Autumn's morning sickness can handle it."

"Morning sickness? But it's afternoon," Zane said.

All the women looked at him with varying degrees of amusement.

"Have you never known a pregnant woman, Zane?"

"Not one who discussed the process."

"Mmm, well, I hate to break it to you, babe, but *morning* sickness can be any time of the day."

"Can someone just make me some damned pancakes and bacon?" Autumn groused.

Zane's lips twitched. "I've got you covered." In addition to pancakes, he conjured a plate of perfectly cooked bacon and placed it before Autumn. "This is so you don't have to smell the grease."

"Thank you!"

"So, back to our quest. I'm thinking the best time to go to Saqqara will be tomorrow or the next day at the latest," Winnie said. "If what Alastair believes about Lin gearing up is true, then we need to get in and out as quickly as possible."

"I still don't like the idea of you going, but I agree with the timing," Zane said. "It's better to try to get in and sneak under Lin's radar. I can clear my schedule for the next two days."

Winnie nodded decisively. "Then it's settled. We go tomorrow."

22

"*R*eady?"

Zane was always up for anything Winnie had in mind, but for this particular endeavor, he was a bundle of nerves. "Sure."

Winnie laughed and gave him a quick hug. "Don't freak out. Everything will be fine."

"How do you stay so optimistic all the time?"

"I don't. But I refuse to borrow trouble."

He studied her for a moment, taking in the beauty that represented her. Not just the physical, but the spiritual as well. Winnie had a heart of gold and a positive attitude that was contagious.

"Zane?"

"I'm just taking a second to appreciate how much I adore you, babe."

A wide, happy smile graced her features. "The feeling's mutual."

"Let's do this thing."

Winnie wrapped her arms around Zane's neck as his arms came around her middle. "Hold on tight."

"Always."

Zane's cells heated in what he now knew to be the precursor to a teleport, and his grip involuntarily tightened on Winnie. Before the point of burning, his body cooled marginally, indicating they'd arrived. Would he ever get used to the instant jump through space?

"You can let go now," she laughed.

"Maybe I don't want to," he returned.

Her bright blue eyes took on a wickedly delighted light. Before she could form a comeback, they were interrupted.

"Ah, *qalbi,* my heart is broken."

"Oh, hell no," Zane muttered as he spun around to discover Winnie's Maltese admirer.

Zane's *"What the hell are you doing here?"* was cut off by Winnie's cry of *"Rafe!"*

She abandoned Zane to hug the other guy, effectively sparking Zane's jealousy.

"How did you know we were going to be here?" she asked.

"Exactly what I'd like to know," Zane growled.

"Still the asshole, I see," Rafe grinned at Zane. "Honestly, I don't know what she sees in you."

"I'm going to kill him before this is over, Win. I swear to the Goddess!" When Winnie bit her lip against her laughter, Zane rolled his eyes. "What about this situation do you find funny?"

"Who wouldn't want two hot-ass guys fighting over her?" Winnie grinned.

Zane ignored her to glare at Rafe. "What are you doing here?"

"The same as you, I suspect. The Council wants to get its hands on the amulet before Alastair."

"Rafe, I need that necklace to save my mother," Winnie said softly.

"It's too powerful for Alastair to possess. Even without it, he is near unstoppable with his abilities."

"What if I have him promise to turn it over to the Council when he is finished?"

Had Zane been in Rafe's place, he'd have promised Winnie anything. But the unfeeling bastard shook his head.

"If I go against the Council, I lose my job, Winter."

TM CROMER

Rafe's hard tone left little doubt as to where his loyalties lay.

Zane's heart hurt for Winnie. She was going to be forced to take a stand against the Witches' Council. According to what he'd learned in the short time since he'd realized he was a warlock, it never ended well for the witch or warlock who went toe-to-toe with those bastards. The WC's word was law.

Zane clasped Winnie's hand and gave it a light squeeze. "No one is asking you to go against the Council. But if you don't happen to find it, what can they really do?" He was careful to keep his tone neutral, as if he were discussing legal negotiations. Zane found that neutrality went over better during high-stress situations.

Rafe's troubled gaze connected with his before shifting to Winnie. "I suppose if I can't find it, I can't find it. And I suppose, if someone else were to turn the amulet in as an act of good faith, it would go a long way to satisfying the Council."

Winnie's hand tightened in Zane's. "Thank you, Rafe. I promise, the moment we are done with it, I'll turn it over."

"Just remember that when the time comes and Alastair Thorne is digging in his heels."

"He'll do as I ask."

Rafe sighed, nodded, and slowly spun about, taking in the wide expanse of sand. "Does anyone have an idea as to where we start? I only received general coordinates of the original temple, which I assume, is beneath us."

"Correct," Zane said. Three minutes later, he'd conjured what he needed to stake off the temple. He, along with Winnie and Rafe, measured off the rooms and marked the outline. Two hours later, they were close to finishing the perimeter of the original building, along with all the rooms of the temple and its adjoining outbuildings.

Winnie straightened from her current position and frowned. "Do either of you feel that?" she asked.

"Feel what?" Rafe crossed to her side. "I don't feel anything."

But Zane, only ten feet away, felt the zing along his nerve endings. "Yes. What is it?"

"I think it's the amulet."

150

Rafe knelt and placed his hand flat on the ground. "What are you experiencing?"

"It's like an energy pulse that's pulling me to this area," Winnie explained as she crossed to the northernmost part of the grid. "I'm drawn to the power."

Zane joined her, and his body's system went haywire. The "pull" Winnie felt was overpowering to Zane. He had the desire to get on his hands and knees to start digging like a wild dog to find the source.

"The legend must hold true," Rafe mused as he walked up to them.

"What legend is that?" Zane asked.

"As with the Chintamani Stone, only a couple in love can find Isis's Uterine Amulet."

Zane grunted his disgust at his own naiveté. "You never would've found it on your own. You've planted a magical tracker on Winnie."

"*What?*" Winnie cast betrayed eyes on Rafe. "Is that true?"

Rafe's grimace answered her question. "Ah, *qalbi*. I'm sorry."

"What happens now?" Zane asked although he suspected he already knew. Rafe intended to call in reinforcements and take the artifact into his possession.

No sooner had Zane thought it when he saw the black SUVs in the distance. As the half-dozen vehicles raced in their direction, a cloud formed behind the vehicles, blocking out the horizon.

The wind kicked up, and with it, the sand lifted to swirl around the three of them. A furious Winnie shoved at Rafe's chest. "What is it about me that shouts 'Let's play Winnie for a fool'?"

The sand particles stung where they connected with skin, and Zane lifted his hands to protect his face and eyes.

"Win!" His call was lost to the wind.

"I am sick to death of people mistaking me for gullible. You were supposed to be my friend, Rafe!" she shouted over the howling wind. "My friend! Do you realize what you've done?"

Zane absently noted that while sand, pieces of plant, and slivers of broken pottery swirled around Winnie, she maintained a protective pocket of air around her. Neither Rafe, nor himself, were as lucky. Zane felt the sharp sting of a pottery shard cut open his forearm, and he winced at the pain.

"Winnie!" he yelled again as he fought his way against the tropical-storm-force winds to reach her. "Winnie, stop!"

Rafe's face lost its tan as he stared at Winnie. Could be, for the first time, he realized the power of a Thorne witch. Zane almost felt sorry for the bastard. Having experienced what Winnie could do—eight years of it without even knowing—Zane could've told Rafe that she was more powerful than she seemed.

He managed to get close enough to wrap his arms around her. "Babe, stop!"

The air went still. "Call them off, Rafe," she ordered. "Call them off, or I flip their SUVs."

Rafe frowned and glanced over his shoulder. "Those aren't anyone I'm associated with."

The three of them exchanged glances and came to the same conclusion.

"Lin," they stated in stereo.

"We need to teleport. Now!" Rafe said. He grabbed each of their hands. But nothing happened. "He's commissioned Blockers."

"What the hell are Blockers?" Zane asked.

"What the hell does it sound like?" Rafe snapped. "They're witches and warlocks who have the ability to block others from teleporting."

"What if the three of us work together? Maybe we can overpower them." Winnie asked as she eyed the distance between them and the oncoming enemy.

"Pick a place," Rafe said.

"Poolside in Malta?" Winnie suggested gripping Zane's hand tighter.

"Works for me," Zane agreed.

"On three," Rafe stated. "One... two... three."

Again, they were grounded.

Winnie released Zane's hand and grasped her necklace. "Uncle Alastair, if you can hear me, we're under attack in Saqqara. We can't teleport out, and I don't know if anyone can teleport in."

Her worried expression wasn't reassuring either Zane or Rafe.

Zane made a decision. He grabbed Winnie's hand and tugged her into a run. "Head for the pyramid," he shouted as he pointed toward two triangular formations in the distance.

The first structure was roughly seventy yards from the temple ruins. Odds were, they wouldn't make it, but it was worth a try.

WITH EACH LABORED BREATH WINNIE TOOK, SHE MENTALLY CURSED herself for not sticking to a daily exercise routine. She also silently scolded herself for not anticipating the Blockers. But really, who the hell could've possibly known those type of witches existed? With the exception of her hotel room the one time, Winnie had had no experience with this type of thing. Their only hope would be to outrun the area spelled by the Blockers.

When the stitch in her side made taking another step impossible, she tugged out of Zane's grasp. She wasn't going to make it, but Zane and Rafe might stand a chance. "I can't," she panted. "Go on... without me."

"Fuck no! That's not happening, Win."

"I can't... run... anymore."

Without a by-your-leave or warning of any kind, Zane heaved her up onto his shoulder in a classic fireman's hold and hauled ass toward the pyramid. She rose up and pushed her hair out of her eyes to see Rafe keeping time. The SUVs were closing in fast and almost upon them.

They weren't going to make it!

Winnie threw up her arms and said, "Goddess hear my plea and assist us in our time of need." She called her air element and pulled from the earth to create a solid wall of dirt.

They all heard the impact as the lead SUVs crashed. But the other four vehicles circled around her makeshift wall.

Winnie lifted her joined fists and separated them in a sharp gesture. "Hole!"

A crack appeared in the ground behind them, and the crevice was large enough to catch the wheels of vehicle three. Four, five and six continued without slowing.

Internally, Winnie gathered her strength for a hurricane-force blast.

Zane stumbled in that moment.

They went down in a tangle of body parts, taking Rafe out in the process.

As the three of them scrambled to their feet, the remaining SUVs circled and closed in around them. They were trapped.

Winnie lifted her hands for another attempt to save them, but the cocking of a weapon from behind caught her attention.

"Winter Rose."

Lin's smarmy, smug face appeared in her peripheral as he exited his vehicle.

Zane and Rafe closed rank around her in a misguided attempt to protect her. She could've told them not to bother. Lin would cut through them in nothing flat.

She turned her hands over and lifted her palms toward the sky. A thick mist descended outside the air bubble she'd created around their small group.

A shot rang out. Rafe grunted and dropped to the ground.

"Disperse the mist, or I'll open fire on your lover, Winter Rose," Lin commanded. "You already know you cannot teleport."

The uniform clicking of men positioning their guns echoed around them.

Fire flared to life and danced across Zane's fingertips. "It's your call, Win. Chances are, he intends to kill us anyway."

"Last chance, Ms. Thorne," Lin said sharply.

Winnie had never been so torn. Zane was probably right, but if she could spare him, she'd gladly give herself over to Lin.

"I have one condition," she called out.

"I don't think you're in a position to negotiate," Lin returned.

"I believe I am. You see, you can probably gun us down, but not before Zane can barbecue your ass. So, I repeat. I have one condition."

"I'm listening."

"Win," Zane whispered urgently. "Don't you dare give yourself in exchange for me. Don't you do it."

As she remained locked on Zane's worried face, she raised her voice to say, "Zane and Rafe go free."

"No," Lin said without inflection, as if deciding whether to have strawberry or grape jam on his toast.

"Did you miss the part where she said I'd set fire to your ass, Lin?" Zane called out.

"One life in exchange for yours, Winter Rose. Not both."

She closed her eyes.

"Save Rafe, Win. I'm not leaving you."

"Don't be a martyr, asshole," Rafe panted from where he knelt on the ground. "I'm as good as dead anyway. Lin laces his bullets with poison, as your girlfriend is well aware."

"Time's up, Winter Rose. Make your choice," Lin said, almost kindly.

"Zane," she called. "I want you to release Zane."

"No!" Zane shouted and threw a line of fire toward the direction of Lin's voice.

Screams of pain could be heard, but none of them reflected the arrogant voice of Lin.

Zane had missed him.

"Fire!" Lin ordered.

Time froze as the reports of the rifles sounded. The hail of bullets hung in the air around them. Taking advantage of the spare seconds, Winnie had the presence of mind to drag Zane down and shove Rafe flat as she hit the dirt. With a prayer to the Goddess, she swirled her hands up and about, creating a cyclone above their heads and whisking away the bullets.

It was all she could manage before time rebounded with a pop.

"Nice work, babe." Zane praised, careful to keep his voice low.

155

He threw another line of flames toward the SUV on his left and urged them to army crawl in the opposite direction toward the gap between the vehicles. "What about you, hero? What's your superpower?"

"He can't use magic in his condition," Winnie whispered. "His ramped up cells will make the poison work that much faster. It's the same reason I can't heal him with my magic; I could become infected."

"Fuck."

"Yep."

"I can try to hold them off, *qalbi*," Rafe offered.

"No, we're all getting out of this. Keep moving."

Rafe grunted. "Is she always this bossy?" he asked Zane.

"Yep. You dodged a bullet when she fell in love with me, man," Zane tossed back.

"Good one," Rafe muttered.

Inappropriate laughter bubbled up, and Winnie fought to suppress the accompanying giggle.

"Give yourself up, child."

The thought screamed through her mind, and Winnie clutched her head against the pain the sudden psychic onslaught brought.

"Give yourself up to Lin. I will come for you."

Alastair. Her uncle had to be utilizing strong magic in order to break through the blockers.

"He'll kill them, Uncle."

"He will if you don't surrender. If you do, he'll likely keep them alive to control you."

"We are almost to the pyramid."

"He has more men arriving momentarily. You are cut off."

Winnie halted her forward movement. "Zane, stop."

"Win? We don't have time."

"Alastair said we're trapped. Lin has reinforcements."

"Christ! Does he have a way out?" Zane asked, voice low.

"No. He suggested we surrender."

"Are you kidding me right now? That lunatic will shoot us for sport, Winnie."

"Alastair is coming. I just need to keep you both alive until he does."

"What about you, Winter? Who will keep you alive?" Rafe asked gravely.

Winnie crouched and slowed the cyclone marginally. "I have a plan for that too." She withdrew three vials from her pocket. "Thank you, Goddess," she whispered fervently for the sudden appearance of the serum and handed a container to each man. "Drink this and bury your container in the sand." She uncapped hers and downed it.

23

"*L*in?" Winnie shouted out. "I've changed my mind. I'd like to surrender, but I still have that condition."

The gunfire ceased, and she slowed the cyclone to a tropical-speed wind.

"You still here, Zhu?" she called. Couldn't hurt to appear friendly by using his first name, she reasoned.

"I'm here, Ms. Thorne."

Ms. Thorne. That meant Lin wasn't a happy man. And rightfully so. She'd taken out three vehicles while Zane burned a handful of his men.

"I want you to spare Zane," she shouted across the distance.

"Stand and clear the mist."

Winnie did as Lin ordered.

Then she got her first glimpse of him and gasped. She didn't know how he did it, but not a single black hair of the thick, slicked-back mass was out of place. Winnie doubted she looked as neat. With an involuntary glance down at her shirt, she swiped at the sand and dirt there.

From the corner of her eye, she noticed two men utilizing magic

158

to heal the others of their team. Taking stock of Lin's numbers, she changed tactics.

"Okay, so hi!" she said cheerfully. "I figure we can start again. I think we got off on the wrong foot."

Zane snorted at her feet and slowly rose. He held out a helping hand to Rafe.

"Is that so, Winter Rose?" Lin asked as he strolled in her direction. A simple hand gesture on Lin's part had most of his army closing in behind her.

Winnie held up a hand, and Zane's flame flared back to life.

"Far enough, Zhu. I need some assurances first."

A crafty smile spread over Lin's countenance. "I assure you I will not kill him."

"Nor will your men," she clarified.

"Nor will my men."

"I want your word."

"Are you questioning my honor, Ms. Thorne?" His tone had turned dangerous.

Winnie stepped toward Lin. "No. I know if you give me your word, you'll keep it. It's why I asked for it."

"Smart girl." Alastair praised through their private connection.

A light entered Lin's pale green eyes, and to Winnie, it looked like respect.

"I give you my word."

"Thank you. Now, if you'll remove the block for the two of them to teleport, I'd be much obliged."

"That will not be possible." Lin strolled forward and wrapped his hands lightly around her throat.

Zane growled behind them, but Winnie held up a hand for him to stay where he was. The last thing she needed was for him to take it into his head to attack Lin for touching her.

"He's uncivilized, Winter Rose. Not the man for you." Lin told her as he stroked the column of her throat.

"And you are?" she asked casually.

"I could be."

"Somehow, I suspect if I take you up on your offer, you'll be disappointed in me."

Lin dropped his arm to his side and smiled. "You are correct. Come."

Winnie stood her ground. "What about Zane and Rafe?"

His cold gaze swept past her to focus on the men in question. "Bring them," Lin ordered.

Zane and Rafe were forced into one vehicle while she was escorted to another. They all drove the short distance to the temple ruins and parked outside the border of the grid they'd set up.

"I want the amulet. You and your lover will get it for me."

She snorted in her self-disgust. "You never had any intention of killing him outright, did you? Not until you got what you wanted."

"I was testing your abilities," Lin confirmed.

"What if I wasn't as powerful as you'd originally thought?"

"I would have mourned your loss."

"Doubtful."

"No, when the time comes, I will mourn you."

Winnie stared into the soul of the man. "I was told the Désorceler Society no longer exists except for you. You don't have to continue down this path."

"This has always been a much bigger movement than you or your family will ever understand."

"Explain it to me. Help me understand," she urged.

He studied her for a long moment.

During that time, Winnie was careful to appear sincere—which she was. If she could find a way to end the war between Lin and her family, she would.

To her surprise, he launched an explanation.

"We have common ancestors, you and I."

Her lower jaw hit her chest.

Lin chuckled and tapped it closed. "I'm not the long-lost bastard of any of your close ancestors. But I descend from the line of Isis's sister, Serqet. She fell from grace, and her powers were stripped from her. On that day, she swore revenge against her sister.

"You see, Isis was the cause of my ancestor's misfortunes. Had she not interfered when Serqet set out to punish another, the war between our families would not exist."

"At some point, you have to let bygones be bygones, Zhu. I mean, if we're cousins, I'm willing to forgive and forget. Just let us go and—"

"Enough. I gave you the courtesy of an explanation. You turn it into a joke."

"My life is no joking matter," she countered earnestly. "Nor are the lives of Rafe and Zane. Neither are related to Isis, by the way."

"They are the casualties of war."

"Casualties? You gave me your word that you wouldn't kill them!"

"I will stick by my word."

Winnie knew Lin would find a way around his promise, his slip of the tongue proved as much. She only hoped she was able to stall long enough for reinforcements to arrive.

"Pardon me if I'm starting to have reservations about your sincerity. You've mentioned my death and the deaths of Zane and Rafe. That's not instilling confidence."

He cocked his dark head to the side and narrowed his eyes as if he were trying to understand her reasoning. Or perhaps he was waiting for her to comprehend what he was saying.

When it dawned on her, she could've smacked herself in the head.

"You're a warlock." She studied him. It was the only explanation that made sense. He didn't age like a mere mortal. "A warlock *without* powers."

Lin's eyes crinkled, and he applauded. "Very astute, Winter Rose. But I do have power, as you will soon find out. It may not be natural born, but it is useful to me all the same." He signaled someone over her shoulder, and the door opened behind her.

As Winnie exited the SUV, her eyes connected with Jolly Ollie—aka Uncle Ryker—who tried to convey a silent message. She'd almost failed to recognize him in his magical disguise. Had Alastair not given her a photo of Ryker in disguise with the aerial photos of the ruins, Winnie wouldn't have recognized him at all.

With an infinitesimal bob of her lowered head, Winnie acknowledged him without appearing obvious. She needed to be on alert for when their chance to escape arrived.

"Winter Rose."

Lin's commanding voice stopped her in her tracks. She faced him, brows raised.

"I will need a promise from *you* now."

"And what's that?"

"You will be my bride."

Despite the dire situation, Winnie doubled over as laughter took hold.

Lin's tone was pure ice when he said, "I do not understand what you find humorous."

A glance around showed the shocked faces of his minions. Even Zane, Rafe, and Ryker were stunned by her hilarity.

"Sorry. I was picturing family gatherings. Can you imagine how well it would go over when I brought you home?" The picture she painted brought on more giggles she found too difficult to contain. "Alastair's face would be priceless."

"Don't enrage the enemy, child."

Alastair's sharp warning along with the silence of those around her finally sank in and helped Winnie to contain herself. She wiped the moisture from her eyes and cleared her throat. "Sorry," she repeated, trying to affect a contrite façade.

Winnie made it three feet when it occurred to her to question why Lin wanted to marry her. She turned to him again. "Uh, I'm not trying to be ungrateful for your interest and all, Zhu, but do you care to tell me why you're hell-bent on matrimony?"

"You are a Thorne. Descended from Isis."

"That's been established, but how does that work for you?"

"You will be my unending source of power, Winter Rose."

She went cold. *Now* she understood. Lin intended to tap into her magical energy for his own personal battery source. He'd be unstoppable.

"I'm gonna have to decline your kind offer, Zhu," she said with a mock-regretful sigh. "I've a whole host of candidates ahead of you."

Zane's groan indicated she'd misstepped. Lin wouldn't bat an eye about removing the competition—*starting with Zane.* Panic curled in her chest and tried to choke off her airway. She worked to remain calm in the face of her error.

Lin surprised her when he smiled. He seemed amused instead of angered. Was she that predictable? If she lived through this little adventure, she definitely needed to up her game.

"Shall we retrieve the amulet before your reinforcements arrive?"

"I don't have reinforcements coming." She waved to Zane and Rafe. "As you can see, this was the extent of my little army. It's embarrassing when compared to the scale of yours."

Winnie met Zane's incredulous gaze and almost laughed again. His expression clearly indicated that he thought she was the perfect candidate for a mental health evaluation. Perhaps he was right. How she maintained her calm in the face of certain death was beyond her own comprehension.

"You've stalled long enough. The amulet, Winter Rose. Now."

Alastair's voice sounded in her head. *"Give him what he asks for, Winter."*

"No."

All heads turned in her direction. The entire group was stunned stupid. She imagined she could feel Alastair's shock as well.

"I don't mean to be difficult, Zhu, but I need that amulet to bring my mother out of stasis."

A fleeting glimpse of emotion came and went from Lin's face. Did she imagine his flash of regret?

"Let me put this another way. The amulet or your lover's life. You choose."

There *was* no choice. Zane was healthy and alive. Her mother was not.

On leaden feet, she trudged to where Zane stood. For a long moment, they stared at one another. No words were necessary. They both knew this was the end, one way or another.

Suddenly, his mouth twisted in a sweet smile. "I love you, Winter Thorne. You take that with you wherever you go."

Dear Goddess! He intended to make the choice for her!

"Zane," she choked out.

He reached to comfort her but received a rifle butt to the back of his skull.

Winnie screamed as he crumpled. "You didn't have to do that," she snarled at the guard. Rage curled her fists. The air current changed, and the temperature dropped to freezing. Winnie drew her element to her and directed a forceful, icy blast toward the guard.

He flew forty feet and landed with a hard thud.

She spun wildly about ready to take on any and all who challenged her. The mass of men stepped back, fearful of her anger.

"Anyone else looks at him sideways, and I'll cut you in half," she promised. Fury vibrated in her voice and made clear her intent should another hair on Zane's head be harmed.

Satisfied she'd gotten her point across, she knelt and cradled his head. When she felt for the bump, her fingers came away sticky. Tears poured from her eyes, and she swiped at them impatiently. Warming her cells from the nucleus, she concentrated all her healing energy toward the wound on Zane's scalp.

Winnie sighed her relief when his eyes fluttered open. "Welcome back, my darling man."

He groaned and shut his eyes. "Well, this is embarrassing. I mean, all the movie heroes can take a gun butt to the head and remain standing."

"You may not be a movie hero, but you're *my* hero, Zane."

"I think your new beau might object," he murmured.

She leaned in and whispered for his ears alone. "My new beau can go fuck himself."

"That's my vicious sweetheart," he said approvingly. "Is this going according to your plan? Because I'm here to tell ya, I would've been happy had you eliminated the head wound on my part."

She gazed down into his beloved face and gave him a warm smile. "Sometimes we need to improvise."

"Good to know. Does burying my head in your ample bosom fit in there somewhere?"

"After. Can you stand?"

"I'm right as rain thanks to you. I was just enjoying being held against your chest."

Winnie bit her lip to stave off her giggle. Their whole conversation was inappropriate in light of the danger, but it was so Zane.

She smoothed his mussed, blond hair back from his face. "I love you, Zane Carlyle."

"I love you too, Willow."

She dropped his head in the sand and stood.

"Way to spoil a touching moment, babe," Zane groused as he rose to his feet.

"He's trying to keep your anger simmering. Seems he's realized you're stronger when you're emotional," Alastair informed her. *"Smart boy."*

Winnie strode to the area where she felt the amulet's pull the strongest. "How do we determine where to dig?" she asked Zane.

"The rope indicates where the original wall *should* be located. Granted, we are going off of an old sketch, so it might not be accurate, but the aerial photos seem to suggest we're correct. We could conjure equipment to help with that. They pinpoint the depth and width of a wall's location using GPS, radar, and a magnetometer if necessary."

"Conjure your tools, Mr. Carlyle."

"I will when you send Rafe to safety," Zane said, surprising Winnie. "The poor bastard is turning gray."

"Mr. Xuereb is not your concern. Conjure your tools."

"I only see one tool here," Zane snapped. "In case you're not familiar with the term, that's you."

"I would shoot you in the leg to gain your compliance, but then I'd have to kill my beautiful fiancée since she'd call on her power to destroy us all. So, I will do this a different way." Lin pointed his weapon at Winnie and chambered a bullet for effect. *"Conjure the tools."*

24

*Z*ane had little-to-no doubt that Lin would shoot Winnie. The man was deranged and on a mission. And while Zane hadn't been privy to their conversation in the SUV, he had a good grasp on the situation based on Lin's marriage declaration.

How Lin intended to channel Winnie's magic was a mystery, but Zane would be damned if he was going to let that happen. A glance around showed him just how damned. Nineteen guards, minus the one Winnie had thrown halfway across the desert.

Zane made a mental note not to piss her off in the future, and also to kiss the hell out of her for showing restraint when she'd been angry with him in the past. She was one badass chick.

He made eye contact with Winnie, and at her slight nod, he conjured the tools he needed to verify the ruin walls beneath them. With Winnie's help and a watchful eye on Rafe, whose condition seemed to be deteriorating, Zane prepped the area and calibrated the equipment.

They adjusted some of the grid lines according to the readouts.

"This spot is my best guess," he told Lin. "The amulet's energy is the strongest in this antechamber."

"Start digging," Lin ordered.

"Rafe needs attention, and we need water." Zane hoped his tone conveyed his firm resolve. He was done taking orders until Lin compromised on medical care for Rafe. If her friend died, Winnie would never forgive herself.

"There is nothing to be done for him. Continue with your task."

"Zhu, please."

Winnie's soft, pleading tone did what Zane's obstinate tone couldn't; it softened Lin's stance.

At Lin's nod, Winnie conjured a case of water. "I think your men must be thirsty by now, too."

One by one, she handed out water. When she came to a short, oriental man with smiling eyes, she tripped. The man caught her instinctively and cast a worried glance in Lin's direction. From Zane's position, he noticed what Lin couldn't; Winnie slipped a vial into the man's hand. It matched the one she'd given to him and Rafe earlier.

Although Zane hadn't studied the photo of Winnie's uncle in great detail, he assumed the Asian man had to be Ryker. He sent up a silent thank you to the Goddess. Maybe they had a chance of surviving yet.

"What can I do to ease your suffering?" Zane asked Rafe.

"Not much. The blood flow has stopped."

"You look the color of death, man. Is it the poison or blood loss?"

"A little of both, I would imagine." Rafe lowered his voice. "Whatever Winnie gave me has slowed the progress."

Zane uncapped a water bottle and handed it to him. "What do you suppose it was?"

"If I had to guess, some type of serum to counteract the poison. Lin is coming this way. Act like an asshole."

"That shouldn't be hard to do based on your continued flirtation with my woman." Zane winked and stood to face the approaching Lin.

Lin glanced between each man as if to gauge the sincerity of their animosity toward one another. "You should be dead by now," he told Rafe. "Curious."

"Yeah, I guess I'm lucky I'm such a healthy specimen."

With that comment, Rafe clarified for Zane that, in another place and time, the two of them could've been friends. Once the suave, debonair act was gone, Rafe became a man's man; a witty, everyday sort of guy.

Lin glanced over his shoulder to where Winnie was examining the equipment readings then returned his cold gaze to them. "You'll both be dead soon enough."

"Winnie's not going to like that you didn't keep your promise," Zane warned mockingly.

"Your break is over. Start digging."

"It's sweltering, and we need a tent over the site. I'm going to conjure one for Winnie's benefit." Zane wasn't asking; he was telling. If the fucker wanted to shoot him for seeing to Winnie's needs, let him. "I'm also going to make shade for Rafe."

Lin sneered. "You would see to the comfort of the competition for your woman? You are pathetic."

"It's called compassion, asshat. You should try it on sometime."

Zane never saw Lin strike. One minute he was upright, the next, Lin's foot had connected with Zane's solar plexus. The impact sent Zane into the dirt, gasping for breath. Christ, he hadn't realized a blow could hurt so fucking bad. He wanted to throw up from the pain.

"Next time, I will shoot you in the head," Lin said dispassionately.

Winnie was at Zane's side in seconds.

The air temperature dropped, and black clouds rolled in. Lightning struck, and a thunderous boom shook the ground. The wind picked up, and with it, a sandstorm started. Winnie's black hair whipped about her head, and color flooded her cheeks. The blue of her irises became nearly translucent. She'd never looked more beautiful than in her rage.

"What is *wrong* with you?" she shouted at Lin over the gathering elements.

When Lin pointed his gun at Winnie, Zane almost had a heart attack.

Zane forced himself to a kneeling position and hugged her to him despite the pain in his middle. "It's okay, babe," he hollered. "It's okay."

"I'll fucking kill the next person who touches him," Winnie warned. "Just try me, Lin." She fisted her hand, and the gun in Lin's hand was no more. She'd thrown it to kingdom come with the force of the wind.

Lin backed away with a look of smug satisfaction.

As abruptly as the storm started, it ended.

"Let me look at you," Winnie said as she peeled up Zane's shirt to expose his abs. Her breath hissed out when she saw the angry mark across his stomach. "Are you hurt?"

"My pride. That fucker is quick." He leaned in and lowered his voice. "You need to stop reacting when they attack me, Win."

Her dark head came up. "Why?"

"I think they're testing your powers."

"Lin said that earlier. You think this is one continual test?"

"Yep."

"My reaction is instinctive, Zane. I can't stand by and watch you be hurt."

She frowned and grabbed her head.

"Win? Are you okay?"

She glanced back at Lin who had moved to talk to his head minion. "Yes. Alastair is inside my head. He's yelling at me for losing my shit."

"He thinks Lin is testing you, too?"

"Yeah."

"What's his plan for extraction?"

Winnie shrugged and offered him water from her bottle. "He hasn't said. Either there's no plan, or he doesn't trust me with the details." She winced. "Okay, so there's a plan in the works, but no details yet."

"Alastair seems pissed from this end," Zane chuckled.

Winnie cut him with a look. "Let's get this over with. I'm losing my patience with the lot of you."

As Zane shifted to rise, he gasped. "Shit. I think he may have broken my rib."

Winnie probed along his ribcage. Zane was unable to prevent the second sharp inhale when she touched his lower left side.

"I think you're right," she murmured. "Stay still."

A purple arc of light left her fingertips and warmed the area of his abdomen almost to the point of painful. When she was done, she pulled back. "How do you feel?"

Zane shifted from left to right and probed the impacted area. "Good as new, babe. Let's see to your other admirer's comfort."

They joined Rafe, and Winnie conjured a small canvas tent above him, along with a cooler of drinks—inspected by one of Lin's men for weapons.

As they positioned themselves to create a tent over the dig, Zane asked Winnie, "How in the hell did you stop time before?"

"That wasn't me."

"If not you, then who?"

"I don't know. But it wasn't me."

Zane didn't have any more time to dwell on who might've assisted them, because Lin was fast approaching.

"Tell Alastair, I prefer this plan of his to end with me alive, okay?" Zane said hurriedly. When he noticed her tears forming, he smiled. "Don't get all emotional on me, Wynona. I need you to stay focused."

Winnie sputtered a laugh and brushed the dampness from her eyes. "I'm going to part the sand with the wind. Tell me where you think we should start."

Zane gestured toward the north corner of the room. "There. That's the spot where we felt the energy the strongest earlier."

"Okay, come hold my hand to amplify my power."

He complied. Like a dual teleport, he could feel his cells warm. His body fired instantly. But the difference ended there. In performing magic of this magnitude, Zane's cells amped up to almost burning. The hair on his arms stood at attention, and the connection with Winnie felt almost spiritual in nature.

As he watched, a type of mini tornado formed, and Zane experienced a moment of unease. Winnie sensed his misgiving and squeezed his hand tighter. Her control was incredible. She was able to utilize the funnel cloud to rock back and forth over the antechamber. Sand and rock were lifted and deposited along the outside edge of the grid.

The process took time, and Zane was grateful for the tent to shield him from the sun's intensity. Still, the heat was getting to him, both internally and externally.

"Picture a chilly breeze, Zane," Winnie suggested, sensing his distress for a second time. "You can have it circle us and cool us down."

"It won't interrupt what you're doing?"

"Not at all."

Zane did as she suggested and imagined their home in the early morning hours on a fall day. The air around them picked up and dropped by a good twenty to thirty degrees.

Again, Winnie squeezed his hand. "Well, done."

"You should be getting close to the top of the chamber, Win."

"Yes, I'm starting to feel some resistance. What do I need to do after the sand is removed?"

"I'll evaluate what we have once you reach the ceiling, if there is one left intact. I suspect there isn't. The resistance you're experiencing could be that we've hit part of a wall. If that's the case, you'll need to shift focus and spend a little more time using your handy-dandy tornado to remove the sand."

Winnie nodded and left to check on Rafe while Zane examined the structure she had uncovered.

Winnie knelt beside Rafe where he sat. "How are you?"

"Achy, but not dead, thanks to you."

"Don't thank me yet. I still have to get us out of this mess."

Rafe's smile was warm, considering the incredible pain he was suffering. "I have faith in you, *qalbi*. You are a force unto yourself." His smile dropped. "But if it comes to saving me or saving yourself, you leave me to my fate. Do you understand?"

"I can't do that, Rafe."

"You can, and you will. You take Zane and get out."

"Lin will surely kill you if that happens."

"Perhaps."

Her heart contracted at his bravery. "Don't ask me to do that, Rafe. You've become dear to me in the short time we've known each other."

His dark eyes ate up her face. "You are one of the most incredible women I've ever known. And believe me, I've known a few. And for that reason, I want you to get out of this mess unscathed."

"If something happens to you, I won't be unscathed. I'll be heartbroken."

"It is a nice thought that I might be mourned by you."

"You'd be mourned, *if* you were going to die, which you aren't. Not on my watch."

"*Qalbi*, listen to me, even a Thorne can only do so much."

"Well, I haven't met a Thorne who couldn't move mountains when push came to shove." She checked his wound and felt his pulse. "You're going to make it."

"I'm more than half in love with you, Winter Thorne."

"I'm more than half in love with you, Rafe Xuereb."

"Hey!" Zane protested softly as he walked up to their tent. "None of that. Stop poaching my woman, Xuereb."

Winnie appreciated that the men had put their animosity aside to deal with their common enemy.

Alastair's voice rang through her mind. *"Tell that Maltese pleasure-seeker that I said to stop preying on children. It's creepy."*

"I will *not* say that! And I'm not a child," Winnie returned hotly. A blush swept up her neck when she registered the stares of Zane and Rafe. "Sorry. My uncle is in my head."

Zane grinned. "He's on my side. I can tell."

"Feel free to tell that buffoon, if anything happens to you before I can get to you, he will suffer a slow and painful death at my hands."

"I won't say that either. Where's our backup?"

"Did he just diss me?" Zane demanded.

Ryker strolled by. "Keep your voices down. Lin is already suspicious that Alastair hasn't made an attempt to save you," he said in passing.

"My bad."

Alastair's use of the modern idiom nearly set Winnie off into uncontrollable laughter. As it was, she had to bury her face into the collar of her shirt to hide her amusement.

"Lin's Blockers are making a stealthy arrival impossible. We can't even teleport into the temple's grid. An approach by car would be seen."

"You're not coming," Winnie stated flatly.

"We are, child. I promise."

Zane interrupted Winnie's psychic connection with Alastair. "Lin is heading this way. We need to get back to work."

"Go. I'm okay," Rafe urged.

Once Winnie and Zane returned to the antechamber dig, they spent time discussing the best way to uncover the remaining area. Surprisingly, the section of the antechamber that hosted the amulet's location was intact.

The opening was large enough for Zane to drop down. "I found it, Win!"

Excitement bubbled in Winnie's chest. But before she could reach in to assist Zane back above ground, Lin clapped a bracelet around her wrist.

"Hand up the amulet, Mr. Carlyle," he ordered.

That's when Winnie understood what the bastard intended.

"Don't do it Zane!" she yelled. "Try to teleport."

Zane stared at her in confusion. "Win—"

"Go, Zane! Teleport!"

"If you do, I will kill her," Lin warned. He held up her newly shackled arm. "She's powerless."

Indecision was written on Zane's face.

"He doesn't intend to kill me," she cried. She could tell Zane didn't understand the significance of the object in his hand and how it would overpower the Blocker's ability. "The amulet, Zane! You can go!"

Understanding dawned, and Zane tightened his fist around the necklace. He closed his eyes and shook his head. "I can't leave you, Win."

Frustrated tears flooded her eyes and raced down her cheeks. He'd never understand that one way or another, they were about to be separated.

"Zane, he intends to bury you alive. You need to go."

Lin backhanded her across the face, knocking her to the ground. For a wiry man, he had the devil's own strength. Winnie could almost feel the bruise forming. But not one to let something as simple as a blow to the face stop her, Winnie launched herself at Lin's leg and sunk her teeth into the meat of his thigh, ripping with all her might.

A fist connected with her temple followed by a swift kick to her ribs.

"Stop!" Zane bellowed.

The air went still.

"I'll give you the amulet. Stop hitting her, you bastard."

Lin gestured to one of the guards. "Bring him over."

Rafe was dragged to the opening and unceremoniously dropped eleven feet into the room. Zane was quick to break his fall.

"Toss up the amulet, Mr. Carlyle, or I will have you watch as my men take turns beating Ms. Thorne."

Winnie shook her head. "Go," she mouthed.

Her captor fisted his hand in her hair and hauled her to her feet. Still, she never broke eye contact with Zane. The sharp edge of a knife was placed against her throat. Winnie never flinched.

"Go!" she ordered aloud.

The blade nicked her neck. She wanted to scream from the pain of the blade but remained silent, refusing to give Lin the satisfaction.

An ungodly bellow from Zane caused the hair on her arms to stand at attention.

"Go!" Winnie yelled louder.

The second slice of her skin was longer and deeper. This time, she couldn't hold back her scream.

Zane became an enraged animal and surged toward the opening. How he expected to get back above ground without assistance was anyone's guess.

With the last of his energy, Rafe snatched the amulet from Zane's hand and tossed it to Lin. "Don't hurt her anymore."

"You dumbass!" Zane turned on Rafe. "You've killed all three of us."

"No," Rafe said softly. "Just you and me as he intended all along."

Zane's head swung around at the roaring sound above him.

In helpless horror, Winnie watched as Lin used her power to dump the excavated dirt back into the hole. She dove for the opening. Rough hands pulled her back, but she fought like a woman possessed. All the kicking, clawing, and punching did her no good. Her last vision was of Zane bending over and using his body as a protective umbrella for Rafe. "No! No!" she screamed. "Zane!"

25

*Z*ane braced for the impact of the debris as he huddled protectively over Rafe. When nothing crashed upon him, he slowly straightened and glanced around.

Thorne Manor.

How the hell had he come to be here? He glanced down at Rafe who sat half reclined with his back against the base of the sofa. A flash of white teeth in a sea of tanned skin showed the man's amusement.

"I don't understand," Zane said. Again, he looked around. "Where's Winnie?"

Rafe's face turned serious. "Lin has her. This…" He waved his hand around to indicate their teleport to safety. "…was a result of the amulet and what I suspect was Alastair's doing."

Alastair strolled into the room. "Slick move on your part, Xuereb."

"What move? What did he do?" Zane's head was reeling.

"A slight of hand," Alastair explained. "He swapped the Uterine amulet for another he found at the ruins."

"Noticed that, did you?" Rafe laughed.

Alastair extended a hand down to help him up. "Indeed." Alastair addressed Zane, "The magic of the amulet countered that of the Blockers. It's what Winter was trying to tell you."

"What about Winnie? How the hell are you all so casual right now?" Zane's hands curled into balls as he forced down the flame threatening to flare to life inside him. "That bastard sliced her throat."

"He knew exactly where to nick her that wouldn't inflict damage. It only looked like it. And he *will* pay. When the time is right and my niece is safely back in the family fold, I will hunt Lin down," Alastair stated coldly.

"Where will he take her? That damned monastery where he held Autumn prisoner?" Zane wrapped one of Rafe's arms over his shoulder and helped him toward the staircase.

Alastair shook his head and led the way up the stairs to the attic. "No. We compromised his sanctuary. It's doubtful he'll return there."

When they entered the room, Zane's mouth dropped. What had previously been the training area for Winnie and Autumn to teach the Carlyles how to hone their gifts now resembled a full-scale military war room. There were charts, maps, and electronic equipment with tables and chairs enough for everyone in both families, all present and accounted for except Winnie and Ryker.

"Go see Preston. He'll fill you in," Alastair told Zane. To Rafe, he said, "Come with me. My sister will fix you up. Thanks to Winter's fast thinking, you should recover."

Without further ado, Zane joined Preston where the older man had set up a scrying mirror in the corner of the room.

"Glad to see you made it out safely, son," Preston said gruffly as he clasped Zane on the back.

"I'm so sorry, Mr. Thorne," Zane choked out. The trials of the day had caught up to him. "I couldn't…"

"She's not dead, Zane. And she won't be. Lin seems to have taken a liking to her. That will work in our favor. My daughter's quick on her feet, and when the time is right, she'll be ready to fight or flee. My brother-in-law is with her, too."

"I never saw any of this coming," Zane said. Raw emotion made his voice hoarse. Glancing down, he watched as Lin sealed Winnie's wounds with a touch of his finger before shoving her into an SUV. "He's harnessed her power with that bracelet."

"Yes. But he won't be able to sustain it."

"What do you mean?"

"What do you know about our family's history, son?"

"Not much. Only the little bit Winnie, Coop, and Keaton have relayed."

"Thornes are direct descendants of a goddess named Isis. She was the daughter of Ra and was powerful beyond belief. And still is from where she resides in the Otherworld."

Zane ran a hand through his hair, shaking loose the sand that had settled there during Winnie's sandstorm. "How does this play into what's going on with Lin?"

"Lin's line is from Serqet, sister to Isis."

"Shouldn't he have magical abilities if he descends from a goddess?" Zane asked, confused.

"Serqet misused her power and was stripped of her gifts, then she was cast out into the desert," Preston explained. "She became lovers with the man who found her and bore him children. Zhu Lin is of that line. Serqet's lover was a non-magical human. And although any descendants would retain the longevity of life like a standard witch or warlock, they don't have the power we have."

"The history lesson is all well and good, but how does that affect the here and now?"

"Lin believes, because his genetics are those of a warlock, he should be able to steal the magical energy of those around him and utilize it on behalf of the Désorceler Society he's been rebuilding."

"How do you know all this?"

"Because he tried it once before—with my wife," Preston revealed quietly. "The Fennell line is pure, but it isn't as strong as our line. Or yours, for that matter."

Zane considered himself quick on the uptake, but for the life of him, he couldn't sort through this mess. "I thought Aurora had been shot by Lin?"

"She was," Alastair said from behind him. "In a misguided attempt to save my life."

"She did save your life, brother," Preston snapped.

"Yes. But she need not have. Had you not allowed her there that day…" Alastair curbed his angry outburst. "My apologies. None of that is important right now. Saving your daughter is."

"When this is over, you and I are going to have a discussion in regards to how blasé you are about throwing my children into dangerous situations," Preston promised his brother.

Zane waved an impatient hand. "Can we get back to the part where Lin is trying to harness Winnie's magic? She's not a damn nuclear power plant. What can he really hope to gain?"

"He has already gained it," Alastair said as he moved a palm over top of the mirror. "See that? If you look closely, you'll see more graying of his temple."

The mirror replayed the scene when Lin had hauled a hysterical Winnie away as the antechamber collapsed under the weight of the sand and debris Lin had directed toward the room. Sure enough, a thick white streak formed along Lin's left temple where only a smidgeon of gray existed previously.

"What Preston was trying to say, is that because Lin isn't a Thorne, he won't be able to contain the power if it builds to full force within him. It will take its toll on his body. He'll age rapidly, and his spells will go awry."

"He doesn't strike me as a fool. Surely he's done his research?" Zane protested.

Alastair shrugged. "Oh, I have no doubt he intends to only steal a little at a time, but he'll give into the dark temptation to draw more and more power as time goes on. It will become a disease to him."

"But we don't have time for him to self-implode," Zane argued. "Anything could happen to Winnie by then."

"We'll get her back." Alastair's gaze connected with his brother's. A type of silent communication happened between the men.

These warlocks, along with Lin, all played a game with much higher stakes.

From his vantage point, Zane felt as if he was missing a larger piece of the puzzle. Without it, he had no chance of seeing the whole picture.

WINNIE PACED HER OPULENT CAGE. PERIODICALLY, SHE'D SMASH A Ming vase against the silk papered wall to leave Lin in little doubt of her fury. If he intended to pen her up like an animal, she'd give in to the urge to act like one. She hoped he cringed every time she shattered one of his priceless pieces.

As she stared at the fragments littering the floor, an idea struck There was little doubt the cameras in the corners of the room tracked her every movement, but she could be covert and crafty if the need arose—as it now had.

What little power she had left, Winnie channeled. She surreptitiously touched her pocket to feel for the large shard she'd transferred. When the time was right, she intended to gut Lin like a pig. If she died in the process, what difference did it make? Zane was lost to her.

Her rage had kept the grief at bay, but inch by inch, the reality that Lin had buried Zane alive crept in. There was no way either Zane or Rafe could've escaped the cave-in. Lin had made sure of that. After he'd ushered her to the vehicle and healed her neck, he'd made her sit and watch for nearly two hours. No movement. No Zane breaking through the debris.

Without oxygen in that little chamber, Zane didn't stand a chance. And while Rafe was experienced enough to create an air bubble, it wouldn't have lasted long in his condition. Any magic he performed would accelerate the poison in his system and effectively leach the life from him.

Desolation swamped her. Except for taking Lin's life, Winnie's own life meant nothing anymore, and the only thing keeping her upright was her need for revenge.

Her hand went to her throat and cradled the tanzanite pendant there.

"Uncle Alastair? Are you there?"

"I'm here, child."

She sighed her relief. *"Bind my powers."*

"What?"

"I've had time to think about it. If you bind my powers, Lin doesn't have anything to draw on."

"Clever girl!"

Winnie didn't have it in her to bask in the praise. She was wallowing in the misery of Zane's death. A harsh sob wracked her body. *"When the area around the temple clears of Lin's men, will you recover Zane's body for me?"*

The door to her room opened before Alastair could answer. Lin crossed the threshold and took in the ruination of the bedroom.

"I expected better from you, Winter Rose." Disapproval and anger vibrated in Lin's tone.

"And I wish you would drop dead, but hey, we can't all get what we want."

His pale eyes hardened. "You would be well advised to keep a civil tongue in your head."

"And you'd be well advised to go to the devil."

In a flash, he was across the room. The flat of his palm connected with her cheek and made a loud clapping sound. Burning heat infused her abused cheek, and she involuntarily touched the skin there.

An ugly kernel of rebellion rose up within her soul and found its way to the surface. Looking him square in the eye, Winnie spit in his face.

White-hot rage radiated off Lin. His hand closed around her throat and pinned her to the wall. Winnie clawed at his wrist for all she was worth. But he had the additional boost of her magic to give him strength.

As her airway was cut off, she registered the cold fury of his gaze. Behind those pale eyes also lurked a simmering excitement. *He was getting off on hurting her!*

She wasn't escaping death. It was written there in his eyes. She scrambled for the sharp shard in her pocket, but she was too late. As blackness encroached on her peripheral vision, she gave over to the darkness and slumped. Perhaps, if the Goddess was kind, Winnie would see Zane in the afterlife.

———————

ZHU LIN LOOKED DOWN ON THE BODY AT HIS FEET, DISGUSTED HE'D let his anger get the better of him. Yes, he liked inflicting pain. The feeling of total control was heady. Yet, he'd made a misstep. Even now, he could feel the magic ebbing from him. In strangling Winter, he'd cost himself her power.

Furious with himself and with her, he delivered a final kick to her still form. Without a backward glance, he left her where she lay.

"He's killing her! Do something!" Zane shouted and slammed his fist against the wood slats of the attic wall. "What the fuck are you waiting for? All of you together have to be stronger than the Blockers."

The moment Zane saw the resignation in Winnie's gaze, and the realization that death awaited her, he dropped to his knees. As if he were physically connected to Winnie, Zane's own breathing became labored.

After her body ceased to move, Lin released her to crumple to the floor.

Silence reigned. Not a person in the room who'd witnessed Lin's brutal attack could move. A keening wail echoed in the rafters above.

Zane wasn't aware the horrific sound came from him. Not until Spring's arms encircled him did he realize he'd become like a wild animal mourning the loss of its mate.

"Ohmygod!" Rafe whispered in horror.

Zane's gaze connected with Preston's dead-eyed stare.

Without conscious thought, Zane conjured an automatic weapon and three magazines of bullets. Closing his eyes, calling up Winnie's beautiful, still face, he fired up his cells. If he couldn't break through the Blockers, he'd kill himself trying.

"Stop him!" a male voice yelled.

They were too late.

Zane appeared in the oversized bedroom where Winnie's body had been left, gun in hand and finger on the trigger. Not a single soul remained in the room. With a quick turn of the lock, he ran to Winnie's prone form.

"Oh, God, Win! I'm so sorry!" He cradled her deathly pale face between his palms as tears poured from his eyes. "I'm so sorry!"

He ran a hand along her throat and felt for a pulse. It was faint, but there all the same. Feeling for her breastbone, he shifted a few inches lower and started chest compressions. "Stay with me, babe. Please, please, stay with me."

Zane gently shifted her head, pinched her nose, and breathed into her mouth. Her chest hardly moved. Placing his hands around her throat, in the same exact pattern of the bruises, he pulled the magic from deep within. He visualized a healing energy flowing to her, pictured the reduction of swelling and an open airway. In his mind's eye, he pictured the air flowing into her lungs and out again.

Against Zane's hand, Winnie's pulse quickened. "Come back to me, Win," he choked out. "Please, come back to me."

The slap of soles against the bamboo floor echoed down the hallway, indicating Lin or one of his men was almost to the door.

Zane shifted positions and propped his weapon on top of the bed to sight down the barrel. With one hand, he reached back and clasped Winnie's. He pushed more healing energy into her. "I'm going to need you to wake up now, babe."

The air crackled around him—a clear indication of multiple teleports arriving at once.

Knox, Alastair, and Preston materialized without fanfare.

Preston knelt by his daughter and bowed his head in relief when he felt her pulse. "You foolish boy! I don't know how to thank you," he said gruffly to Zane.

"Go to work on that bracelet, son," Alastair directed Knox and took up a position next to Zane. "That was foolhardy, boy. Brave as hell, but foolhardy." Respect shone bright in his gaze as he studied Zane. "You might be the perfect match for her after all."

"I hope so because she isn't getting rid of me."

Alastair's sudden smile radiated that he was pleased as punch, although for the life of him, Zane couldn't understand why.

The door flew open, cutting off any further conversation. But the man who'd burst through the door wasn't Lin. Instead, Ryker arrived in the guise of Jolly Ollie. He tossed a key to Alastair, who in turn tossed it to Knox.

"I owe you, Jolly," Alastair told him.

"I'll put it on your tab. The Blockers are out of commission, but I don't know for how long. You need to get your asses moving."

"What about you?"

"Well, I don't think Lin is going to be too thrilled with me once he sees the security cameras. So, I'll be heading out with you if that's okay," Ryker said with a grin.

"The Council is going to be so mad at you," Alastair mocked.

Zane was speechless at the easy rapport between the two men. He'd understood from Winnie that Ryker was estranged from Alastair's sister, GiGi. Zane had assumed the two men would be at odds. Yet here they stood, joking as if they were the best of friends.

"How is she?" Ryker asked, his tone shifting to concerned.

"Alive, thanks to the hothead here." Alastair gave a short nod in Zane's direction.

Zane cast one last wary glance at the door and moved to kneel at Winnie's side. As he joined her, her eyes fluttered open and widened in reaction to seeing him there.

"Zane! You're alive?" she croaked. Her wild eyes flew around the room, taking in all the occupants. Confusion clouded her face. "H-how?"

"It's not important, Win," he said softly. "I'm taking you home."

Zane scooped Winnie up into his embrace, and her arms crept up around his neck. For a long moment, their gazes connected; each relaying what they couldn't verbalize. Tears gathered in her sweet blue eyes. In an involuntary movement, his arms tightened around her.

"Hold on tight, my love."

With a single thought, he'd teleported the two of them to her bedroom at Thorne Manor. Within minutes, he heard the excited voices of her sisters float down from the attic where the rumble of Preston's deep voice relayed what Zane assumed was the rescue details to the others.

"How did you find me?" she asked hoarsely.

"Don't try to talk." He placed a fingertip on her lips. "Alastair and Preston never lost sight of you. They have a whole war room up there, complete with computers, maps, and all. You should know, I find your family scary as hell."

She tried to laugh, but instead she winced and clutched her throat with a shaky hand.

"I'm going to get your aunt. I'm afraid my impromptu healing of your throat was based on pure instinct on my part. I don't know if I did it right."

Winnie's jaw dropped. "*You* healed me?"

"Don't act so surprised. I am good for some things."

Their eyes met, and all the things they needed to say were in the tender look they shared.

"Thanks for saving me," she whispered.

"Thanks for not leaving me to try to live without you," he whispered past the lump in his throat. "I love you, Win. Don't ever scare me like that again, okay?"

She blinked back tears. "I'll try not to."

Zane scrubbed his eyes with the heels of his hands in his own attempt to dispel the gathering moisture there. "I appreciate that. Be right back."

After he stepped into the hallway and closed the door, Zane leaned back against the wall and tried to gather himself. The day's events caught up in a flash, and he didn't know how to process what had gone down.

Nausea churned in his gut and burned the back of his throat. He'd barely made it to the bathroom to toss his cookies. He sat for a time, trying to regain his composure. As he rose on shaky legs, he spotted Knox in the doorway. Wordlessly, Zane rinsed his mouth and splashed water on his hot face.

"You okay, man?" his cousin asked.

Zane shrugged. "I don't know. I don't have time to wonder. I need to get GiGi to help Winnie."

"She's already seen to her. Why don't you have a seat for a minute? Collect yourself."

While Zane didn't sit, he did lean back against the vanity and closed his eyes. "I almost lost her," he rasped out.

"But you didn't. You saved her," Knox reminded him softly.

Zane rubbed his knuckles between his brows in a vain attempt to ease the headache building there. "I want him dead so bad, I can taste it." He didn't need to clarify to whom he referred. "He strangled her right before my eyes, and there wasn't a damned thing I could do about it. I couldn't get to her in time." Zane took a deep, ragged breath. "All I knew when I teleported was that I wanted to riddle that fucker with bullets. I wanted to see him gasping for his last breath on the floor."

Knox remained silent, and Zane met his cousin's thoughtful gaze. "I've never wanted to hurt someone the way I wanted to hurt him, Knox. That's not me. You know me. I release spiders into the wild. How did I come to love one woman so much that I can't see reason? How can she do this to me without even trying?" Zane shook his head and stared at the grain pattern on the wood floor. "My business is suffering. I'm a mental and physical wreck. I can't continue on this way. I wonder if it's all worth it, ya know?"

A soft gasp brought his head up. Winnie stood behind Knox in the doorway, with her fingertips pressed to her lips. Hurt shone from her eyes, darkening them to gray.

"Ah, Christ, Win! It's not like it sounded." He looked to his cousin for support.

"I'll leave you two alone to talk," Knox said.

After Knox left, Winnie came farther into the room. "Throughout all this—the stolen memories, the accident, the trick you played, my trip to Malta, and the retrieval of the amulet—you haven't really had time to process. Neither have I. It's been one drama after another with us, hasn't it?" She smiled softly: a haunting, bittersweet twist of her lips.

"I don't need time, Win. I love you."

"I know you do. I love you, too. But maybe a little time apart couldn't hurt. It would give us a chance to center ourselves and get our heads in the right place."

"Babe, I don't need time apart. I swear it," he argued, desperate not to lose her.

"But I do. I thought I was going to die tonight, Zane. I saw it in Lin's hate-filled eyes." She took a deep breath and rubbed her throat. "If I live to be a hundred, I'll never forget the feel of his hand crushing my windpipe."

He started forward, but she held up a hand.

"No, let me finish. I thought you were dead, and I was ready to meet you in the Otherworld. It's why I didn't fight. I'm ashamed that I gave up so easily."

Silent tears poured from Winnie's eyes, and Zane couldn't not comfort her.

"Oh, babe." He gently drew her into the circle of his arms and rested his cheek on top of her glossy black hair. "You have nothing to be ashamed of. When I thought you were dead..." He swallowed hard. "I practically went on a suicide mission when I teleported to that room. No plan, no backup."

"That's exactly what I mean. We are reactive without any thought to our own personal safety. Look at what I did in the desert.

"Why is it a bad thing to love one another so much?"

"I want time to find me again, Zane," she said, so softly he almost didn't hear.

"What does that mean?"

Winnie extracted herself from his embrace. "Just give me a few weeks to recover, okay? If, after that time, we both want to pursue a relationship, then we can move forward."

Denial, hot and fierce, flooded his brain. "No! No, Win. How I feel about you is never going to change. Don't ask me to walk away. I can't."

"I'm not asking you to walk away. I'm telling you, *I'm* walking away. For now."

"This is fucking stupid!"

"Why?" she demanded, her anger coming into play. "Why is it stupid? These last weeks have been a whirlwind. And you said it yourself, you're a wreck. How do you even know it's me you want?"

"Is it Rafe? You want to be with him?" Zane didn't know where the question came from. He only knew he was hurting from her latest rejection.

Acute disappointment flooded her countenance. Large, sorrowful eyes stared up at him from her pale face. "Go home, Zane. Be with your family, take care of your business, find your new normal, and I'll do the same. In three weeks, if you find our relationship is 'worth it', then we can move forward from there."

27

*W*innie drank her supper that evening. She was starting on her second bottle of wine when Alastair entered the tiny kitchen.

"What did the boy wonder do this time, child?"

Wine burned her nose as she snorted her bitter laughter. "Oh, shit, that stings."

His amused sapphire eyes watched her from where he perched on the table's edge across from her. Within seconds, a glass of brandy appeared in his hand. "No one should drown their sorrows alone."

"Are you here to offer me some type of stupid, sage advice?" she asked.

"No. I'm here to see if you want me to let him live another day."

A half-smile twisted her lips. "I'm the one who sent him away."

Surprise lit his face. "Why?"

"It's all happened too fast. He doesn't know if he's coming or going. And I feel like I'm in too deep and care too much for someone who isn't sure he wants me."

"Ah, well *that* I can understand," he murmured and swirled the liquid in his glass.

"You can?"

Alastair nodded. "Your mother and I fought the day she was shot. Earlier that morning, she had told me that she wasn't sure a life with me was what she wanted anymore."

"Why?"

He glanced up and shrugged. "She missed her children. She claimed that you were all of an age where you needed her to guide you. Aurora was bitter that GiGi was your North Star."

"I'm sorry."

"So am I. If she hadn't been with me that day, she'd still be here for you."

"No, she wouldn't," Winnie said.

His head came up more fully, and he pinned her with a stare. "What do you mean?"

"Zhu Lin wanted her for himself. He intended to tap into her magic the same way he tapped into mine. I think his intent was to kill you, and maybe eventually my father. Then the path to Mom would've been clear for Lin."

Alastair's icy countenance unnerved her. "Another reason, on the long list of reasons, why that bastard needs to die." A violent sneeze shook Alastair, and his hand fisted.

Winnie's eyes flew wide, and she laughed incredulously. "You have the same affliction as Summer and Holly!" she crowed. "What is your—"

"Drop it, Winter."

She didn't dare defy his furious command, and yet... "I won't tell anyone. Just a hint."

He opened his mouth, and she expected him to blast her with his anger. She wasn't prepared for his honesty.

"Locusts."

Her hand flew to her mouth to hold back her giggles.

A wry smile graced his lips. "Go ahead and laugh, but if you tell the others, I'll find some dire punishment for you."

"This stays between us, Uncle. Pinky promise."

She held out the pinky of her right hand. For a moment, he stared at her in bemusement before he grinned and hooked his pinky with hers.

He finished off his drink and placed the crystal glass on the table. "Don't be too hard on your young man, dear girl. A love as deep and true as the one you both share can make a man crazy in the best of circumstances. Jealousy and insecurity, two of the things that Zane is experiencing, are added to the mix."

"He questioned if our love was worth it."

"And you haven't? Isn't that what you are doing right now with your two bottles of wine?"

"Maybe."

Alastair rose but not before he conjured a jar of elixir. "GiGi's hangover remedy. Chances are, you are going to need that tomorrow. There's a double batch. I believe the Carlyle boy is going to need something to take the edge off the headache he'll have tomorrow, too."

"He's getting drunk?" she demanded.

Alastair laughed. "Aren't you?"

"Yes, but I'm home! I'm not in some bar where some skank might prey—"

He held up a hand for silence. "You might want to check the front porch. He never went home."

Her anger dissipated. "Zane's getting drunk on our front porch?"

"Go easy on him, child. The Carlyle men are a thick-headed lot." He came around the table and kissed her forehead. "Good night, dear girl. I thank the Goddess that Zane got to you in time."

"Thank you, Uncle Alastair," she managed past the emotion clogging her throat. "I love you."

Alastair's irises morphed into a brighter blue as he stared down at her. "I love you, too. But don't tell anyone I said so. They'll think I'm getting soft."

"Mum's the word."

His chuckle could be heard even after he teleported.

Winnie topped off her glass and meandered to the front window. Sure enough, Zane sat on the steps, a bottle of hard liquor in hand.

As Winnie watched, Zane sipped from the glass container. Seemed he had settled in and had no intention of leaving.

"You should talk to him," Spring said from behind her.

"I probably should."

"But you won't?"

"How would it look if I gave in, sister?"

Spring joined her at the window to peer out. "Like maybe you love him and care about his well-being."

Winnie gave Spring a rundown of what was said earlier.

"How can I trust that he loves me?" she asked.

"You didn't see him when you were taken by Lin, Winnie. He went out of his mind and started yelling at Dad and Uncle Alastair. Who does that if they aren't in love? It's a recipe for disaster." Spring hugged her and kissed her cheek. "Anyone can have misgivings. You, yourself, had some. Give him a chance. He's already proved it in everything he's done. What more do you want from him?"

"I don't know. I guess I'm scared," she confessed.

"Go to him, sister. Ease his mind."

Winnie's eyes drifted to the lone figure on the steps. "It's all too intense, Spring."

"Think how he feels. You've known you've loved him for years and years. He was hit over the head with it when your spell was broken."

"How is it we never noticed you were the grown-up one of the family?" Winnie asked dryly.

"I keep a low profile."

Winnie sighed and took a sip of wine. "Fine. I'll talk to him."

ZANE HAD TAKEN ANOTHER LONG CHUG FROM HIS WHISKY BOTTLE, just as the massive mahogany door swung open. He glanced up, not expecting to see Winnie standing there.

Politeness and ingrained manners said he should rise to greet her, but instead, he twisted to rest his back against the railing and gestured with the bottle to the open space across from him.

Wordlessly, she mirrored his pose.

They sat in silence for a short while, each sipping their drinks, staring across the expanse of the steps at one another.

"Why are you still here, Zane?" Winnie finally asked.

"Where else was I supposed to go?"

"Home?"

He grimaced and took another pull of his drink. "I have no home without you, Win."

She closed her eyes, and a single tear escaped down her cheek. "Oh, Zane. You make this impossible."

"This, as in us, or this, as in rejecting me?"

"Us." Winnie focused on him. "I want you to *know* we're worth it. Not wonder."

"You've never had doubts, Win?" He pinned her with a stare. "Not once?"

"Of course I did. I wondered if you were in any way the man I thought you were. My misgivings were whether we would work as a couple, and it was only *after* you kissed another woman."

"How many times can I apologize for that?"

"I'm not asking you to," she stressed. "I'm only saying that's when I had my doubts."

"If you're doubt free now, then why insist on this separation?"

"Because I'm not doubt free. Yes, I love you, but I need more time to decide if this constant push and pull is what I want. I'm tired of being at odds with you, Zane."

"You want to know the funny part? I thought we were finally in-sync with our feelings. I thought the confrontation with Lin put everything in perspective. I guess I was wrong."

"Then why hide in the bathroom and ask if it's all worth it?" she stood as she shouted.

He gained his feet and lurched forward to tangle his hands in her thick, dark mane. "Because it killed me to see you that way!" he shouted in return. "Don't you get it, Win? I'm fucking crazy about you! Crazy being the key word. I'm not that guy." He forcefully calmed himself and rested his forehead against hers. "I don't yell. I don't go off half-cocked to murder people. I'm actually fairly mellow."

She giggled and triggered Zane's laughter.

"I *am*," he insisted.

"I've yet to see it, Counselor. As of right now, it's all hearsay."

He snorted and rubbed his nose gently against hers. "As of right now, the evidence is stacked against me to be sure. But I promise to prove my case, Your Honor."

"Well, you aren't going to solve anything shouting at each other out here on the porch." They both started at the sound of Autumn's voice.

"That's your cue to take her to bed," Keaton said over his wife's shoulder. "Bedding your woman solves everything." He grunted when Autumn's elbow found his ribs.

"Hush, you tool. I'm trying to help them."

"So was I," Keaton defended as he rubbed his abused middle.

"Ignore him," Autumn told them. "What I was about to say, before I was so rudely interrupted, was that only time and considera-tion for one another is going to solve your insecurities." She smiled when Keaton's arms drew her back against his chest. "No one had a bumpier road than us. I have faith that the Goddess put you together for a reason."

Zane met Winnie's thoughtful gaze. "Okay."

"Okay?" Winnie asked.

"Okay. I'll give you the time you need."

He could swear she looked disappointed at his announcement.

"Does this means you aren't bedding your woman?" she asked in a hushed voice.

Zane leaned close to whisper, "I *so* want to bed my woman. But I also want to give her what she truly needs. When you're ready, babe, I'm going to rock your world and not let you come up for air for days."

Winnie gripped his biceps and whimpered.

Unable to resist, he closed his mouth over hers and poured all he wanted to say into a single kiss. Her arms curled around his neck, and her fingers dug into his scalp. Her soft moan almost changed his mind about leaving.

As he pulled back, he noticed they were once again alone. "I love you, Winter Rose Thorne. There won't be a day that goes by that I won't think it, say it, or feel it down to my very soul." He dropped a light kiss on her lips. "May I call you tomorrow?"

Winnie nodded, wide-eyed with her fingertips caressing her mouth.

"Go up to bed, babe. I won't leave until you are safe inside."

She stopped when she got to the door. "Zane?"

"Yeah?"

"I love you, too."

"I'm glad, Win. It'll make my courtship of you that much easier."

"Courtship?"

"I figure it's time I did it up right."

The wide, happy smile that blossomed on her face went a long way in healing Zane's bruised ego.

"Hey?" he called.

"Yeah?"

"How's Rafe?"

"Better. Flirting with Aunt GiGi and Spring."

"And you?"

"No, he knows where my true heart lies."

"Good, maybe I won't have to hurt him when he recovers."

Winnie laughed and opened the door. "Oh, I almost forgot! Alastair left some of Aunt GiGi's elixir."

He frowned his confusion.

With a nod toward the whisky bottle on the step, she said, "It's a hangover remedy."

"Ah, yes. I've heard about that from Keaton. The one that tastes like dirt?"

"That's the one. Should I get it for you?"

"Nah. I can't seem to get drunk. Something happened to my metabolism when I got my powers." He shrugged.

"Not even a buzz?"

"Nope. Believe me, I've tried tonight."

"That's truly sad," she smiled.

"You ain't lyin', babe." Zane blew her a kiss. "Good night, my love."

"Good night."

After she'd gone inside, Zane dumped his whisky out on the ground and picked up her wine glass to set both items on a nearby table. With one last, long look up at her bedroom window, he teleported to the clearing.

He conjured a flashlight and a pocket knife then found the oak with his and Winnie's initials. Underneath his initial carving, he etched out the word *forever*.

"I was going to do the same thing."

Zane turned to find Winnie with a flashlight in one hand and a pocketknife in the other.

"Great minds," he stated. "I thought you were supposed to stay within the safety of Thorne Manor so I wouldn't worry about you."

"I can't stay caged up forever, Zane. Besides..." She lifted her hands and twirled in a circle. "This is sacred land. I'm as safe here as I am at home."

"What am I going to do about you, Win?" He approached her and tugged at the first button of her shirt. When it unfastened, he moved to the second.

"What do you want to do?" she asked huskily.

"I was going to give you the time you wanted. But then you come out here in those short daisy dukes and this low-cut top. What's a man supposed to do?"

"Hopefully, take advantage of the situation."

"Well, if that's what you're hoping for, who am I to disappoint?"

28

*W*innie drank in Zane's roguish grin. Two seconds after she'd closed the dark mahogany door of Thorne Manor, she knew she'd made a mistake in sending him away. All she wanted was to be in his arms, and it seemed he wanted the same.

As he unbuttoned the third fastening of her shirt, she smiled.

"I need you to listen up to what I have to say." When she had his full attention, she said, "It doesn't happen often, but when I'm wrong, I can admit it."

One of his dark blond brows shot up. "Oh?"

"Yes. I was wrong to say we need time apart."

Zane pursed his lips and nodded thoughtfully. "I see."

Another button parted from its matching buttonhole.

"Do you?" she asked, worried she'd prodded the sleeping tiger inside him again. Worried she'd appear like a crazy person with the push and pull of her emotions.

"Mmhmm. If I understand you correctly, and I'm hoping I do, you really came out here so I'd follow up on that offer to rock your world. That about right?" His lips trailed along her throat.

"Yep! That's got it."

One of his long, lean fingers hooked the edge of her top and drew it down her shoulder, exposing her collarbone. He nuzzled the hollow he exposed. When his teeth nipped her skin, she let out a soft yelp.

"Good. Do you want to conjure us a mattress or shall I?"

"A mattress?"

"I feel like sleeping out under the stars tonight, Win. Care to join me?"

"It's forty degrees!" she protested.

"And yet here you are, flaunting your perfect ass in those short shorts." He pulled back to gaze down at the rosy nipple he'd laid bare. "Hmm, maybe you are cold."

"Nope. Not at all." And she wasn't. Between her witchy ability to heat up her cells and the loving Zane was providing, she was toasty as could be.

Zane dipped his head to capture her nipple in his mouth. He suckled as he massaged the fullness of her breast. As he pulled back, he grazed the tip with his teeth. "Conjure the bed, Win," he growled.

A snap of her fingers provided a soft mattress perfectly suited to their needs.

He guided her backwards until they tumbled onto the bed.

Winnie laughed as she clung to him. "So much finesse!"

"Shut it and get naked."

"Like this?" With a simple snap of her fingers, her clothes were no more.

"That works," he murmured approvingly. He paused and raked her body with his hot gaze. "I was such an idiot to think—"

Winnie placed two fingers over his mouth to cut off his self-recriminations. "The past is no more, Zane. We are moving forward. We'll both try to be better people."

"You make me better, Win."

"Stop spoiling the moment with sentiment and do me," she ordered and offered up a wicked grin.

"Your sexual wishes are my command."

Zane trailed his fingertips across the curved plane of her midriff. Her muscles tightened and danced in reaction. His lips followed the path of his fingers, and the sensitive skin along her abdomen quivered in response.

As his tongue teased and swirled across her opening, she gasped her delight. And when he joined his body with hers, she cried out his name. Instead of the wild, fast-paced sex Winnie had been expecting, Zane took his time. Each stroke slow and steady, each caress worshiping her. Every kiss tender and packed full of promise. In return, she poured her feelings into every touch of his skin. When their eyes met, he could be in no doubt of her love.

When she climaxed, he refused to let her look away, insisting on seeing into her soul. And when he came, she saw his heart reflected in his warm, chocolaty eyes.

In that moment, she was truly loved and surrendered her soul to him in return.

As they cuddled under the open sky of the clearing, Zane sighed his contentment.

"What was that for?" Winnie asked as she twisted to see his expression.

He met her inquiring eyes and spoke his truth, "I don't know if I've ever been happier than in this moment."

Her eyes glowed with her emotion. "Me either."

Zane tightened his arms around her. "I don't want to spend another day apart, Win. Move in with me."

"I have a better idea," she said. "Move in with me."

"Won't it be crowded?"

"No more than your home." She shifted and rested her head in her elbow to look down at him. "Summer lives in North Carolina now. Autumn is living with Keaton and Chloe at Carlyle House. Dad is gone most days. That leaves only Spring and me. With my workshop on the Thorne estate, it makes it easier all around."

"Is this what you truly want? I'm not rushing you? It's okay to tell me if I am."

Her beatific smile filled the cracked holes in his heart that he hadn't been aware existed.

"I'm sure, Zane."

"I know we've had our ups and downs, Win. But I'm never happier than when I'm with you. I need you to know that."

"I feel the exact same way about you. Please tell me we are past the anger and jealousy, and any stupid games of revenge. I couldn't take it if tomorrow you walk away and it's all been another way to get even for what I did."

"We are well past it all. I can't say I won't get jealous when men try to capture your attention in the future—I'm human—but I promise to try to curtail any pettiness or anger on my part."

"There will never be any reason for jealousy on your part. I promise not to kiss any more men while we're together."

Zane went still. "Kiss any more men *while we're together?* Who did you kiss since we've been dating?"

She sat up and grimaced at her slip. Apprehension was written all over Winnie's face. "I…"

He jackknifed into a sitting position and faced her. With one fingertip, he tilted her head up. "Tell me, Win. Who did you kiss?"

"Technically, you and I weren't together," she hedged.

"Rafe," Zane stated flatly. "Just as I was starting to like the guy. Now I have to kill him."

"Zane! It's not like that. It was the morning after you kissed that chick in the bar. I was hurt and angry. He kissed me, and I let him. It meant nothing."

He let the silence drag out as he turned over the fairness of his anger. Her breathing kicked up with her nervousness. If he were to be honest with himself, he had no right to be upset, and yet, the territorial side he'd never been aware of before becoming lovers with Winnie kicked in with a vengeance.

"Come here," he ordered.

As she shifted toward him, he dragged her the rest of the way to straddle his lap. "You get this one pass because I was stupid. But if you ever kiss another man for the rest of your life, I'll rip his tongue from his head. Are we clear?"

"Is this like a wedding ceremony where I repeat the vow?" she teased.

"That works for me." He smoothed back the long hair from her face with the backs of his fingers and draped it behind her shoulder. "I, Zane Carlyle, take thee, Winter Thorne, to be my forever love. I promise to annihilate any man who touches you and rip out the tongue of any man looking to get overly familiar with your tonsils."

She laughed and kissed him. "I, Winter Thorne, take thee, Zane Carlyle, to be my forever love. I promise to rip out the hair of any woman who touches you and turn any female looking to get overly familiar with *any* part of your anatomy into a wart on a donkey's behind."

Zane grinned and kissed her in return. "I think this is the perfect commitment ceremony, don't you?"

"I do."

He snorted at her play on words. "Now tell me how sucky Rafe kisses, and we can get back to our lovely evening together."

Winnie's giggle cheered him.

"He had sweaty palms, didn't he? And he slobbered?"

"I swear, he doesn't kiss half as good as you," she said as she drew an X over her heart.

"I'll have to settle for that, I suppose. I can afford to feel magnanimous toward the poor guy. He lost."

"More importantly, you and I won."

With a slow, tender kiss, Zane confirmed her words. "We did indeed. I love you, Win. More than words can say."

"I love you, too." She buried her face against his throat and placed a light kiss on the skin there. After a wide yawn, she said, "Can we take a nap before we make love again? It's been a long day."

"Sleep, babe."

Within minutes, she gave over to the dream state that beckoned to her.

Zane held her to his chest and eased back into a supine position, careful not to jostle her. Soon enough, his eyes drifted shut and he joined Winnie in slumber.

our mornings later, Zane jogged downstairs to find Winnie rolling out the dough for another batch of her incredible cinnamon rolls. "How come you don't conjure them?" he asked.

"I enjoy making them from scratch. It helps me center myself and make a mental schedule of all I need to accomplish for the day."

"Do you have extra I can bring to Penny? I don't think she eats enough."

Winnie frowned and glanced up. "Why do you say that?"

"Just a feeling. She's never said, but based on some digging I've done, I don't think she and her little brother have had a happy life so far."

"Oh, Zane. Yet, she's so bubbly all the time. How does she do it?"

"I don't know. But she's kept my office running during all this mess with searching for the amulet. I'm going to give her a raise and hire her on permanently."

"I think you should. How old is her brother?"

"Sixteen."

"I could hire him after school to help with deliveries if you think it might be something he wants to do."

Zane wondered at her purity of heart. Never had he met anyone as generous in spirit as Winnie. "That's an awesome idea, babe."

"Why don't you tell her today when you get to the office? Have her brother stop by later this afternoon or tomorrow if he's interested."

Zane wrapped his arms around her and nuzzled into her thick, upswept hair before he dropped a kiss on the nape of her neck.

"I saw Rafe was up and around last night. How's the healing process coming along?"

"I checked on him this morning. His color is back to normal. Another day or two, and he should be good as new. He seems to have hit it off with Aunt GiGi."

"Think your uncle will be upset?"

"Uncle Ryker?" At his nod, she continued. "I don't know. They've been separated a long time."

"But as a Thorne, doesn't your aunt fall under the family legend of only one soulmate?"

"Yeah. I don't know that she'd get over her love for Uncle Ryker, but I think she's lonely. She should be able to find comfort if she can."

A knock on the front door startled them both. Zane glanced at his watch. "Who the hell is here at seven-thirty a.m.?"

Winnie rinsed her hands and followed Zane to the foyer, where he opened the door. On the other side, stood a petite blonde woman with a manila envelope in hand.

"Hi. I'm Liz. I'm looking for Rafe Xuereb. I was told by the Council he might be here."

Zane stood back and allowed her entry. He noticed her gaze flew immediately to Winnie to sum her up before she studied her surroundings.

"You seem familiar," Winnie said. "Have we met?"

"Once. When we were kids."

"I'm sorry, but you have me at a loss. I can't seem to remember."

Liz gave Winnie a half-smile. "I'm not surprised. You were about five or so at the time. I should clarify, my name is Elizabeth Thorne."

Winnie's jaw dropped. "Thorne?"

"We're second cousins. My grandfather was your grandfather's brother."

"Well, come in! Let me get you a cup of coffee, or do you prefer tea?"

"You don't have to go to any trouble. I'm only here to deliver this for Nash."

"Wait! You work for Nash at Thorne Industries?"

"Yes."

"I've left him messages, but he hasn't returned my calls." Zane voiced his surprise.

Winnie smiled sheepishly. "I wanted to invite him for Thanksgiving. He's Summer's brother. He should be around family for the holiday."

Liz's countenance visibly softened. "I agree. I'll do what I can to get him here."

When Winnie turned her beaming smile on Liz, Zane grinned. She'd made another conquest. He didn't know a single soul who didn't love his beautiful woman.

"Won't you join us too?" Winnie clasped one of Liz's hands in hers. "We'll have more than enough."

"I usually spend it with my parents and brothers," Liz demurred.

"They're more than welcome too," Winnie insisted. "I think it's past time we got to know your side of the family. I know my sisters would love to meet you and your brothers. Say you'll at least think about it."

"I'll at least think about—" Liz's promise was halted in her throat as her eyes were drawn to the man descending the stairs. Her amber eyes bulged, and a strangled cry escaped her. "You!"

Rafe's physical reaction was similar to Liz's. He'd stopped mid-descent and stared as if he'd seen a ghost.

Zane cozied up to Winnie. "Think there's a story there?"

"You know it. I'm a little hurt that Rafe kept it from me. I suspect Aunt GiGi is about to be kicked to the curb."

"How are you here?" Rafe's normally deep voice was hoarse as he continued to stare at Liz.

She had the presence of mind to lift the folder in her hand. "I was looking for Rafe Xuereb. The Council…"

"I'm he."

Liz shook her head in wonder. "I had no idea you were one and the same Rafe."

Rafe's dark gaze consumed Liz as it swept her petite frame from head to toe. "I work for the WC. It's why I had to leave that morning. I had no idea…" He trailed off and cast a side glance toward where Zane stood with his arms around Winnie and his chin resting on her head.

"Don't mind us," Zane laughed. "This is fascinating."

A dark flush stained Rafe's neck and moved to his cheeks. "Do you mind giving us some privacy, please."

Zane laughed again as Winnie shoved him toward the kitchen. "Oh, to be a fly on the wall," he murmured in her ear.

"I know! Did you see their faces? I'm guessing one-night stand, but he took off without an explanation."

Zane peeked around the door frame to see Rafe approach Liz, and Liz back up. "I think you could be correct."

"Hold on."

Winnie locked hands with Zane and voiced a quick spell. When warmth fully surrounded him, he raised a brow in question.

"Cloaking spell. Now we can spy on them."

"Why, Winter Thorne! You are one sneaky little minx."

She grinned, and Zane was helpless not to kiss her.

"This was how I spied on you in the shower during high school."

"Ah, so this was how it was done. Clever."

"Shhh, let's go, or we'll miss the best part."

"Wait! When you spied on me in the locker room, did you spy on the other guys too?"

She waved a hand in dismissal. "I didn't even look at the others. I was too busy watching you."

Somewhat mollified, he allowed her to drag him back into the foyer. He nearly snorted when she placed a finger to her lips to signal silence.

"I had no idea how to find you again," Rafe was saying. "*Qalbi*, I had no intention of hurting you."

Winnie gasped. "*Qalbi?* That's his nickname for me! That player!"

"Shhh. And he better cool it with the nicknames for you. Only I can use them from here on out."

Liz cast a sharp glance in their direction.

"Do you think she heard us?" Zane murmured in her ear.

"I'm not entirely certain. The cloak is supposed to come with soundproofing."

"Your indignant response to his pet name might have stretched the limitations of the cloaking spell."

"Shut it."

"Really, if you're attached to the endearment, babe, I can try to put it into play during our conversations," he continued to tease.

"Will you be quiet? I'm missing their conversation."

Zane's hand crept under Winnie's shirt and cupped her breast. "But I can think of a much better way for us to spend our time."

Winnie leaned back into him and ran her hand down the front of his slacks, pausing to rub his arousal. "What about work?"

"Screw work," he growled and teleported them to their bedroom.

WINNIE CAME DOWNSTAIRS FORTY MINUTES LATER TO FIND RAFE sipping coffee in the kitchen.

He smirked when he saw her and jutted his chin toward the fresh-baked cinnamon rolls on the stove. "I finished them for you."

A blush heated her face. "Uh, yeah, thanks. I got distracted."

Rafe chuckled and went back to reading the papers in his hand.

"Rafe?"

"Mmm?"

"You and Liz? What's going on there?"

He cast her a sharp glance. "Are you jealous, Winter?"

She shrugged as she plated up a roll for each of them. "No. I'm happy. I just felt I was missing something. Like you and my cousin had a deeper connection going on."

"Cousin? Liz is a Thorne?"

Surprised, she paused in eating. "You didn't know?"

"She took off before we could talk." His mouth twisted in disgust. "Do you know how I can find her?"

"Why would you want to?" she asked.

His dark, intense gaze burned into her.

"Ah. Okay. She works with my cousin, Nash, at Thorne Industries in North Carolina," Winnie offered up.

The wide smile he graced her with had Winnie sucking in her breath. The man was gorgeous, no doubt.

"I have a gift for you." Rafe laid an object on the flat wood surface and shoved it in her direction.

Her eyes widened as she locked onto the necklace. "The Uterine amulet! I thought Lin had it."

"Zane didn't tell you? I conjured a replica and switched them."

"Rafe!" Overcome, tears burned her eyes, and she had a hard time focusing through the blurry curtain. "You don't know what this means to me."

"I think I do. Just as you know finding Liz means something to me."

"What about the Council? You could lose your job."

He held up his papers. "It appears I already have." He gave an uncaring shrug. "That's what happens when the WC doesn't approve your decision to do the right thing."

"Oh, Rafe. I'm sorry."

"Don't be. I'd rather your mother be returned to you. Thank you for saving my life, Winter Thorne."

She smiled and reached across the table to grasp his hand. "It was entirely my pleasure."

"Why can't you keep your hands off my woman?" Zane complained as he entered the kitchen and poured a cup of coffee. "Every time I turn around, there you two are, flirting. It's giving me a serious complex."

Winnie and Rafe laughed at his teasing.

"On that note, I must bid you both goodbye. I'm heading home today," Rafe informed them as he rose and dumped the remains of his mug into the sink. "I owe you both a debt of gratitude. If you ever need me, I'll be there."

The two men shook hands.

Zane shook his head. "No, you don't owe us anything. It was a team effort to survive Lin. Don't forget to leave your number with Winnie. But no sexting."

Rafe conjured a piece of paper with his number and handed it to Winnie. After dropping a kiss on her cheek, he teleported away.

"I'm going to miss him," Winnie said. A great sadness gripped her. Rafe had become an important part of their lives in the last weeks.

Zane pulled her up from her seat and hugged her close. "Oddly enough, me, too. But you have his number, and I'm sure we'll see him again. I know he's not American, but that's no reason not to invite him for Thanksgiving."

"I love you. Thanks for understanding."

He reached past her to pinch off a piece of cinnamon roll and pop it into his mouth. "Damn! You did a great job on this batch, babe."

"Rafe made those. I was upstairs with you, remember?" she said dryly.

"Get him back here! We need him to cook for us!"

Zane laughed when Winnie swatted his chest.

"Get going to work. I need to call Alastair and let him know I have the amulet," she said.

After Zane left, she picked up the amulet and headed to her

room. Once there, she wrapped her hand around the tanzanite pendant her uncle had given her.

"I have a present for you, uncle dear."

"I'll be there this afternoon. Can you gather your sisters?"

"Consider it done."

"Thank you, child. I'll see you at three."

y three o'clock, the living room of Thorne Manor was packed with Thornes and Carlyles alike. Alastair stood off to one side in deep conversation with Winnie's uncle Ryker and her father. What the three men discussed in their low, hushed tones was anyone's guess.

GiGi served coffee and cookies while studiously avoiding looking in their direction. Winnie's heart ached for her. Her aunt obviously still bore an intense affection for Ryker, who paid her little heed.

Winnie's eyes met the tortured gaze of her aunt. "I'm sorry," she whispered. "I didn't know he'd be here when I messaged you earlier."

With a pat to Winnie's hand, GiGi conveyed her forgiveness and understanding.

Alastair called the meeting to order when Holly arrived followed closely by a scowling Quentin.

Zane lifted Winnie to sit, then pulled her back down onto his lap. The move caused Alastair to smile.

"It's time to discuss the next mission."

Everyone groaned.

"Sorry, kids, but we are on a tight schedule if we want to save Aurora."

"I suppose that means the next object on your list is for me to find," Spring said as she picked through the cookies on the tray.

Knox swiped a cookie she was reaching for. "*Us,* unless I miss my guess," he corrected. As soon as he took a bite, he spit the cookie into a napkin and glared at Spring.

Her wicked grin left little doubt that she'd turned the cookie to dirt. "I'm fine on my own."

"But as smart as you like to *think* you are, you missed the most important factor. A couple has to retrieve the object."

"A couple in *love* most likely. That leaves us out altogether, doesn't it?" Spring faced Alastair. "So, do Holly and Quentin go on the next mission?"

Holly sputtered her denial which the entire room ignored with a collective eye roll. Alastair held up a hand to cut her off.

"Relax, child. You're not going."

Winnie noticed her sister's relief and Quentin's amusement. Secretly, she was rooting for Quentin. The poor man was crazy for Holly, and Holly was the only one who refused to see it.

"To get back to your earlier statement, Spring, I will require you and Knox to retrieve Thor's Hammer." He passed out what information he had on the item. "There is very little to go on with this particular artifact. Here is a rough sketch drawn by Summer's ape."

"Morty?" Summer questioned as she took a second look at the paper in front of her.

"Yes. And based on his landscape paintings, all of which you've seen, I'm going to say the location is somewhere in the jungles of South America."

"That doesn't sound safe," Winnie protested.

"I intend to oversee this particular retrieval from the beginning. Lin won't get the upper hand again."

"I have contacts at the Council," Knox told him. "I can see what I can find out."

"Try not to alert them of our interest. I suspect there is a spy in their midst. How else does Lin continue to get the drop on us?" Preston said.

Winnie was surprised to hear her father mention anything remotely negative about the Witches' Council. Until recently, he'd been an advocate of the WC. Why that had changed was anyone's guess.

"We think he somehow placed a tracking spell on me in Malta," Winnie said with a gesture to include Zane. "Based on something he said, I believe you're right. But you should all know, he's connected. He's also the descendent of Serqet. It gives him the added edge for his mindless pursuit in destroying our family."

"Who is Serqet?" Coop asked.

"She was Isis's sister," Spring volunteered. "She sinned against mankind and her punishment was great. Ra stripped her powers. It's a painful process from what I've read in the older passages of our grimoire."

Autumn rounded on her. "Wait, you can read the older stuff? Is that a recent development?"

"Yes. Actually, Rafe helped me. He'd caught a glimpse of a similar writing in the antechamber of Isis's temple. The symbols matched the Uterine amulet. I was able to decipher some of the runes."

Zane leaned in to whisper, "Your younger sister is like Rain Man smart, isn't she?"

"Mmhmm. She also has a gift for languages," Winnie replied, careful to keep her voice low. Raising her voice for the others, she said, "Lin had a set of bracelets created that allows him to harness the wearer's abilities for himself. I think we need a few engineers on the team to figure out how to counter that little weapon."

Preston moved forward and placed a hand on Winnie's shoulder, squeezing lightly. "Ryker and I are working on that. He was able to steal some information from Lin's camp when he was disguised as Jolly."

"I'm still not happy with you for letting them throw me in that damned dungeon," Autumn told Ryker. She shuddered. "Those skeletons still give me nightmares."

Their uncle uncrossed his arms and shoved off the wall to join the discussion. "I didn't have a choice, Autumn. If I intervened other than to provide Alastair with the key, I would've been found out. As it is, my cover was blown helping everyone escape with Winnie."

GiGi finally looked in Ryker's direction. "Is that where you've been all this time?"

Their eyes met, and everyone in the room felt the ripple of energy indicating their hurt and anger with one another.

"Mostly," Ryker said in a non-committal way. His eyes lingered on GiGi for another breath before he purposefully looked away, his face a mask of indifference.

Winnie's heart broke for them. She couldn't imagine being separated from Zane after sharing such a legendary love as GiGi and Ryker had been reported to have.

"You could apologize to her," GiGi snapped. Her anger created another ripple in the room.

Without answering or acknowledging his wife in any way other than move to where Autumn stood, Ryker took Autumn's hand in his and pulled her into his embrace. "I'm sorry for what you went through, Tums. If I could take away the horrible memories, I would."

"Thank you, Uncle Ryker." Autumn returned his hug. "I appreciate the sentiment. But let's get back to the matter at hand. I want to know how we kill Lin."

To anyone on the outside, Autumn seemed a bit bloodthirsty, but she'd said what everyone in the room was thinking. Lin was responsible for their mother's and Autumn's stasis; he nearly killed two young children—one of which was Autumn's stepdaughter; and lastly, he'd strangled Winnie and left her for dead.

Winnie's gaze connected with Autumn's across the room. Both sisters had a score to settle with that bastard. Winnie nodded her understanding. From here on, the two of them would work day and night to come up with a solution to take him out.

Winnie shifted her attention to Alastair, who had been silently studying her.

"Are you okay, child?"

"Perfectly fine, uncle. Just picturing the Karma bus driving over Lin's body—multiple times."

Delighted laughter poured out of him, and the entire room went silent to witness this rare phenomenon. When he sobered, a small smile playing about his mouth was the only tell-tale sign he'd been amused at all.

"I'll do more research this week. Maybe I'll be able to find the last known location of Thor's Hammer." Spring brought the conversation back to the beginning topic. "If it really is in South America, that works for me because I have a replanting project scheduled for the middle of next week."

"If Coop and Keaton can manage the horses, I can be ready to leave then, too," Knox added.

"I haven't agreed to let you accompany me," she replied.

"You don't have a choice."

Spring rounded on him. "I most certainly do, and I don't want you to go."

"Stop being a stubborn idiot and—Gah!" Knox spit out the dirt she'd magically stuffed into his mouth. "You do that one more time, and I'm turning you over my knee like the spoiled brat you are."

"Try it, and you'll be buried six feet under," she snarled. "Trust me, I have the power to do it."

As the two of them faced off, Autumn conjured popcorn and sat back to enjoy the show. Summer bit her lip to keep her laughter at bay, and Winnie placed a hand over her mouth to hold back her giggles. Holly didn't bother to stem her amusement. All the men sat stupefied by the shrew who had possessed Spring.

"I've never heard her raise her voice before today," Zane said in awe.

"That's what makes this so hilarious," Winnie laughed.

Knox rose to his feet and glared down at Spring from his imposing height. "You say you're not a kid anymore, but you only ever act like a child. Maybe if you behaved like an adult, people would treat you like one."

Spring's expressive green eyes lost their light and turned to a mossy shade. Winnie imagined she saw the sheen of tears, but as quickly as they appeared, they were gone.

Spring glanced around the room at all the watchful expressions. When she faced Knox, her chin rose a good two inches and a polite smile graced her heartbreakingly beautiful face. "You're right. I apologize." She turned to Alastair. "If you'll excuse me, Uncle, I'll start that research so we can get a jump on the location."

Winnie hadn't been aware of squeezing Zane's hand until he surreptitiously loosened her fingers. She sent him a silent apology for cutting off his circulation. "I'll go see what I can do to help Spring look."

As she jogged up the stairs to the attic, Winnie wracked her brain, trying to find the words to soothe her sister's hurt and embarrassment. She came up with nothing. Spring had been Knox's shadow in their younger years. The two had been as thick as thieves until Spring developed into the bombshell she currently was. It seemed once Knox had realized her sister wasn't a child anymore, his friendly attitude toward Spring had dried up.

Winnie found Spring staring out the large bay window.

"Sister," she called softly.

"I'm okay, Winnie. I'm used to his contempt." Spring rested her forehead against the cool pane of glass and closed her eyes. "I don't understand why Alastair is forcing him on me when anyone with two eyes can see he hates me."

"He doesn't hate you, Spring."

"Oh, he absolutely does. Do you remember this summer when Autumn and I went to retrieve Eddie?" At Winnie's nod, she continued. "After Autumn left to meet you and Summer downtown, Knox caught me by the pool." Spring swallowed hard, and Winnie had the urge to offer comfort. Her sister charged on with her story. "I practically threw myself at him. I flaunted my body in my tiny bathing suit and flirted for all I was worth."

"What happened?"

"He shoved me in the water next to Eddie and asked me if I had any pride. He told me that one day, if I kept acting like a slut, some guy was going to take me up on my offer. That the man would take what he wanted and leave me cold." Spring knuckled the moisture from her eyes. "I thought I loved him, but in that moment, I hated him."

"Oh, Spring," Winnie cried softly, hurting for her baby sister.

"But he wasn't wrong, sister. When I got home, I took a good long look at myself. I didn't like what I saw. I was needy and trying to cling to someone who didn't give two shits about who I am as a person."

"I'm sure that's not true!" How could Spring believe she wasn't lovable? It defied imagination. Spring was as lovely on the inside as she was on the outside.

"It is. Six years, Winnie. Six years I tried to get him to see me as a woman and not a little girl." Her tears flowed faster, and she viciously swiped them away. "And there I was today, acting like the child he accused me of being. I don't know what it is about him that brings out the worst side of me."

"Do you still love him?"

Spring shook her head, but whether it was in denial or confusion, it was hard to say.

"I don't know what love is," Spring said and collapsed on the edge of a nearby chair. "I truly don't. I thought perhaps I did. I was attracted to his handsomeness. His kindness to a lonely kid. But I've started dating other men. I figure I'll learn a little more about myself in the process. What I want or don't want in a guy. Maybe I'll even fall in love with one." She rose and toyed with the edge of the family grimoire. "It might be nice to date an average guy and not one so beautiful it hurts to look at him."

Winnie didn't have the heart to point out that everything Spring was saying convinced her that her sister was indeed in love with Knox. Instead she asked, "How are you going to be able to work with him to find the artifact for Uncle Alastair?"

"An herbal form of Xanax?"

"Marijuana?"

Spring snorted her laughter. "I was going for valerian root, but I like the way you think."

"Do you want me and Zane to go after Thor's Hammer? He'll do it if I ask him."

"Oh, Winnie." Spring rushed across the space and hugged her tight. "Thank you for your offer, but I can't ask that of you. So far we've been successful because Uncle Alastair has picked the perfect pair to retrieve what he needs. I'm sure he has a reason for what he does."

"Matchmaking?" Autumn said from behind Winnie.

Spring paled. "Goddess, I hope not."

Almost certain her older sister was right but loathe to say it, Winnie hugged Spring a second time. "You're the smartest of us, sister. I'm sure you're going to teleport in and out in a matter of minutes to retrieve Uncle Alastair's item."

Summer and Holly joined their group, laptops at the ready.

"Where do we start?" Holly asked.

As her sisters grouped around the center table, Winnie unconsciously wrapped her hand around the tanzanite stone at the base of her throat. A sense of well-being struck. They were all strong women in their own right. Intelligent, driven, and innately kind. She had no doubt that this group of women, along with their male counterparts, would be able to accomplish any task Alastair could think up.

"That's what I believe as well, child."

"I'll pass this necklace to Spring, shall I?"

His soft chuckle sounded in her mind. *"Yes. Do that, I have the feeling I'll find her thought process fascinating."*

"I love you, Uncle Alastair."

"I love you, too, Winter."

When she felt their connection ebb, she called out to him one last time. *"Uncle?"*

"Yes?"

"Do you think maybe, when you've finished matchmaking with

my sisters, you could do something to help Aunt GiGi and Uncle Ryker?"

A long silence greeted her question, and Winnie assumed he'd already disconnected their link.

His voice came as she was about to release the stone. *"I'll see what I can do."*

EPILOGUE

*W*innie hummed a tune as she hand-whipped her latest batch of arthritis relief cream. She measured out the peppermint in a miserly fashion and capped the bottle.

"Miss Win?"

She glanced over her shoulder and smiled at the teenage boy. "Hey, Justin. You can stack those boxes in the van. Come back when you're done with that. We'll raid the kitchen."

His elated grin warmed Winnie's heart to see. Five months ago, when he'd shown up to work, there was little resemblance to his bubbly sister, Penny. Justin had been sullen and sarcastic at every turn. But each day he had mellowed a little bit more until the boy was almost as happy-go-lucky as Penny.

Just then, Spring walked by on her way to her gardens and waved, gracing Justin with a soft smile.

And three, two, one…

Justin fumbled the boxes in his arms with a strangled cry— almost a daily occurrence. With a flick of her wrist, Winnie saved her products from an undignified end and Justin from a face plant into to dirt.

Embarrassment colored his cheeks as he straightened, boxes secure in his arms once more. "Sorry, Win."

"She's gorgeous. I'd be surprised if you didn't trip over yourself when you saw her," Winnie laughed as she joined him by the van.

Justin stroked the jagged scar on the side of his face. "Is that a glam thing? Like does she make herself that beautiful on purpose?"

"No. She's naturally that beautiful."

Winnie watched as her sister strolled the Thorne gardens in the distance, stroking a plant here or there to restore its vitality. A sense of sadness pervaded Winnie's heart. If only Spring's mind could be restored as easily.

Spring hadn't been the same since she returned from her journey to South America, and Winnie missed her younger sister desperately. If she could turn back time, Winnie would've taken Spring's place in searching for Thor's Hammer—if only to save her from the horrible tortures she'd endured.

Winnie sighed and lifted the top box from Justin's stack. If she dwelled on what had happened to Spring, she'd wallow in guilt and pain. Spring needed to heal from her ordeal in her own time.

With a side glance in Justin's direction, Winnie said, "I didn't realize your scar still bothered you."

"If I could get rid of it, I would. No one wants to look like a freak," he mumbled the last as he shoved the boxes into the cargo part of the vehicle.

"Come with me," she ordered.

When they were back in her shop, Winnie gathered ingredients together. "I'm short an herb. Can you run and ask Spring for broadleaf plantain? Tell her it's for an ointment I'm making. She'll give you the proper amount."

His hand flew to his cheek again.

"She doesn't see your scars, Justin. She has too many of her own that she's dealing with."

"She doesn't have any scars," he argued.

"None visible anymore, but she has plenty inside. Go. Get the herb and hurry back. You need to make those deliveries before three."

As he jogged across the courtyard toward the garden, Winnie turned back to her worktable.

"You're good with the boy."

She nearly fumbled the aloe plant in her hand. "When are you going to stop scaring me and start giving me warning when you're coming over, Uncle Alastair?"

"And ruin my only form of entertainment?" he teased and dropped a kiss on her cheek. He walked to the front window and stared across the way. "How is your sister?"

"The same."

"Does the family blame me?" he asked. Only because she'd been listening closely, did she hear the uncertainty in his voice.

"No, uncle. No one blames you. She chose to go and find Thor's Hammer for our mother's recovery." Winnie walked up and placed a hand on his back. While he stiffened, he didn't pull away. "Truthfully, I don't think you could've stopped her from going."

"Thank you, child." Alastair turned from the window and perched on the sill with his long legs crossed at the ankles in front of him. "Have you and Zane set a date?"

Winnie glanced down at the engagement ring on her finger. A wide grin took over her entire face. "Not yet."

"Why the delay? You're sure of your feelings, correct?"

She met his inquiring gaze and nodded. "Absolutely sure. And of his. But I thought it might be nice to wait for Mama to wake, you know, so she could be there, too." Her voice cracked as it always did when she thought of her mother in stasis.

"I think that's a fine plan."

Justin came running back in and skidded to a halt when he saw Alastair. "Uh, I've got the plant, Miss Win."

Alastair's dark blond brows shot up when he saw what Justin held. "Broadleaf plantain? Who needs to be healed?"

"I was going to make a salve for Justin's scars," Winnie told him.

Alastair's quiet, contemplative stare unnerved Justin to the point of stammering. "You d-don't have t-to, Miss Win." He ducked his head and scuffed the toe of one of his Chuck Taylors across the wood floor.

"Do you not want it gone, Justin?" she asked gently, thinking perhaps she'd confused his desire to be rid of the scar.

He blushed and nodded.

"Come here, boy," Alastair ordered.

Justin did as he was commanded and scooted closer.

"Am I to understand that you want this removed?" Alastair gestured to the teen's cheek.

Again, Justin's color heightened and he nodded.

"I can't hear you, son."

"Y-yes, sir."

To Winnie, Alastair said, "Winter, make your salve for the boy." He returned his attention to Justin. "What's your name, son?"

"Justin."

"You know what I am and what I can do?"

"Y-yes, sir."

"Then with your permission, I'd like to heal your face."

Justin's head came up. "You can do that?" A bubble of excitement coated his words.

"I can. But there's a catch."

"I'll do whatever you say, sir," Justin promised.

"I'll heal your scars. In the immediate, the tightness of the skin will disappear as well as any discomfort that you currently have. However, the visual appearance will still take weeks to change."

Disappointment clouded Justin's gray eyes.

"But not when *you* look in the mirror."

"I don't understand, sir."

Alastair shot a glance in Winnie's direction. She understood his silent request that she explain. "Justin, what Alastair means is that he will heal your scar completely. But to the outside world, it needs to look like it's gradually disappearing, or it will seem odd. I don't mind if you tell people the salve is responsible. It would've worked that way had you used it. But you must know, we have to keep secret what we can do for the safety of our family."

"I haven't told anyone since I found out, Miss Win," he said with endearing earnestness. "I swear I haven't."

Winnie hugged him to her, and he didn't struggle in her embrace, though she sensed he wanted to. She loved that the teen was learning to trust.

"I know you haven't. Now, let's get started."

Alastair approached Justin and gripped his chin to turn the teen's face this way and that. When Alastair was satisfied by his examination, he said, "This might burn slightly, son. It's okay to cry out if you need to. No one will think less of you." So saying, he went to work healing Justin's disfigured face.

Other than an occasional hiss of pain, Justin bore the discomfort of the intense magical healing, never once flinching when the red arc of light crackled between them and touched on his skin. When Alastair was done, all that remained of the jagged keloid was a bright pink outline where the scar had been.

"Have a look," Alastair encouraged.

Justin ran to the bathroom and cried out his joy. When he returned, he held out a hand to Alastair, his eyes bright with unshed tears. "Thank you, sir. I can never repay you."

Alastair cleared his throat and took the proffered hand. "You're most welcome, son."

"Now go make those deliveries." Winnie rumpled Justin's strawberry-blond hair. "After you're done, you can stop and show Penny if you want." She scribbled a spell on a piece of paper and handed Justin a charm. "Use this for those you want to show, but only Penny and Derek, do you understand? No one else. The spell only lasts a few minutes."

"I can show Derek, too?" he asked in excitement.

"Derek, too."

Winnie had been happy when the two teens hit it off. And although Justin was a few years older than Derek, they both had discovered common ground over their deadbeat, abusive fathers.

"Cool. Thanks, Miss Win. Sir." With a nod in Alastair's direction, Justin was off and running again.

"Does he know what he is?" Alastair asked as he watched the van pull away.

"No. Neither does Penny from what I can gather. But they both learned what we are. Zane swore them to secrecy, and so far, they've kept a lid on it."

"Another set of parents believing binding their children was for the best," Alastair said in disgust. "It causes nothing but problems when they grow up."

"Do you think I should tell him?"

"That is strictly up to you, child."

"Actually, I'll leave it up to Zane. As someone who had his powers bound, he might have insight."

"Fair enough. I must be going."

"Uncle Alastair? Why did you stop by today?"

His eyes sought out Spring in the garden. "Guilt."

"You couldn't have known."

"No, but I had no right putting her in harm's way for my own selfish needs."

"Maybe, but like I said earlier, she would've gone anyway even if you were never involved. She wanted to save our mother just as much as the rest of us."

Alastair grimaced and changed the subject. "Have you heard from the Maltese roué?"

"Rafe? Yes, he went to work for Nash." Winnie cocked her head. "But I suspect you already knew that. Like Aunt GiGi, you know everything."

"I know enough, but not all. I'm too busy to keep tabs on him. I have enough to do in keeping tabs on you kids."

"We aren't kids, Uncle."

"You will always be kids to me, child."

Winnie's hand went to her lower abdomen. "You'll have another one to keep tabs on soon."

His dark sapphire irises brightened. "I look forward to it." He leaned in close. "But you should make plans for more than one."

Shock slackened her features. "Two? Twins?"

"Triplets."

"Ohdeargod." Winnie's knees gave out, but Alastair was quick to conjure a chair. Her butt came down hard on the cushioned seat. "How am I going to care for triplets?"

"With patience and love, child. You don't need more than that."

"I have to tell Zane we're having triplets," she babbled.

A hard thud sounded behind her. When she turned, Zane was sitting in the center of the floor with his head between his legs.

"I believe you already did," Alastair chuckled. He strode to where Zane sat and squatted on his haunches. "Careful what you wish for, son."

"I'm never going to tease about baby making again," Zane croaked.

"That would be wise. Isis is always listening."

LOVE WHAT YOU'VE READ? TURN THE PAGE FOR AN EXCERPT FROM SPRING MAGIC.

SPRING MAGIC EXCERPT

a banging on the door disturbed Knox Carlyle in the middle of his scrying. He shoved aside the small kernel of irritation. "One second!"

He closed his eyes, inhaled to the count of four, and released. Privacy at the Carlyle estate was a joke. He really should consider moving into his own place—*soon.*

Again, the banging started, more urgent this time.

Knox cast one last long glance at the woman reflected back at him then swiped a hand over the mirror. All was well for the moment. He could relax his guard.

"Knox? What gives, man? Open the damned door."

As he swung open the door, his cousin was poised with his fist in the air, ready to pound on the wood again. Impatience was alive and well in the Carlyle clan.

"Seriously, man? My 'one second' wasn't good enough?" Knox demanded.

Keaton's lips quirked in a sheepish grin. "Yeah, sorry. I need to know if you can watch Chloe. C.C. is in North Carolina, and Zane had an emergency pop up. Autumn and I had planned on a private dinner."

Keaton didn't need to stress how important his dinner with his new wife was to him. They'd only recently taken up where they left off years before due to a colossal misunderstanding. Finding their way back to one another had been a long, arduous journey.

"Sure. Go have fun. Chloe and I can either conjure something or grab a bite at Monica's." Knox referred to a local downtown diner that featured desserts to die for. His young cousin was always up for the triple chocolate layer cake.

"You're a lifesaver, man."

"I'm tallying up all the favors. One day I may need a kidney or something."

Keaton flashed an amused grin. "Thanks, Knox. Have I told you how much I like having you here?"

A snort escaped. "Because what's better than your own built-in babysitter?"

An outraged cry had both men ducking their heads into the hall.

Chloe's face screwed up in indignation. "I'm not a baby!"

Knox and Keaton shared a panicked look.

"I know you're not." Knox stepped up to the plate to soothe his eight-year-old cousin. "I didn't mean it that way, Chloe. It's a standard term for watching someone's kid." He scooped her up in his arms and blew a raspberry against her cheek. "Forgive me?"

She giggled and nodded as she wrapped her arms around his neck. He ignored the accidental pull of his hair.

"I forgive you, Knox."

"Good, because I have a special project I need your help with."

"You do?" Her honey-hued eyes flew wide.

"Indeed, I do, peanut." He tilted his head and made a face to indicate her dad. "But it has to wait until he's gone. This is Top Secret, I-could-tell-you-but-then-I'd-have-to-kill-you type stuff."

"Gotcha!"

"Now I want to stay and find out," Keaton complained.

"Nope. Only Chloe is allowed to know. I need her keen intellect and eye for detail," Knox swung her around for a piggyback ride. When the time came for Chloe's million questions—and it wouldn't be far off—Knox hoped like hell he could come up with something fun and creative to keep her occupied. Sometimes dealing with a highly intelligent kid was torturous.

"Fine. But don't think she won't spill her guts for a twenty and a bag of candy," Keaton informed him.

"I'm not a rat, Daddy!"

Autumn's arrival cut off the current line of discussion.

"There's my beautiful wife." Keaton's smile practically lit up the hallway. The man was head over heels.

"Well, don't keep her waiting. Chloe and I have things to do." After Keaton and Autumn kissed Chloe and left, Knox glanced over his shoulder at his young cousin. "Dinner at Monica's first?"

"Can I get a hot fudge sundae?"

"Is the sky blue?"

Chloe's scrawny arms tightened around his neck. "You're the best, Knox."

"I know. But for saying it, you get dessert first." He started humming the Mission Impossible theme as he crept down the halls of the sprawling two-story home. "Do we drive or teleport?"

Her excited squeak made him smile. Chloe was taking to magic like a duck to water, but there were still things her father refused to allow her to do without adult supervision, and teleporting was one.

"Will Dad get mad?"

"Not at you, and that's all that matters," he assured her. "So we doing this?"

By "this" he meant teleporting to the alley behind the diner. Knox knew the alley was usually abandoned except for the occasional stray animal, but he sent out a magical feeler first to be sure they had the all clear. It wouldn't do for their abilities to come to light in Smalltown, USA.

"Yeah!"

"Hang on tight, kid."

They arrived in the blink of an eye—much to Chloe's delight.

Hand-in-hand, they crept around the corner of the building and made a run for the front door of Monica's Diner, laughing the entire way.

The sight that greeted him stopped Knox short.

Spring Thorne.

She leaned her elbows back against the long counter, which had the effect of pushing out her perfect, pert breasts, as she flirted with Tommy Tomlinson.

But looks could be deceiving. They certainly were on the part of Spring. One had only to look at her to see a sultry siren with tawny hair and dancing jade-green eyes. But Knox knew she was far from the sexy goddess she appeared. Spring's bright-white aura was untouched, a clear indication of her virgin status.

Yet, based on the invitation in her eyes, she was clearly trying to rectify that little problem with Tommy.

Fury unlike any he'd ever known swamped him. It also confused him. He didn't want the complication that came with a relationship, and he absolutely didn't want the complication of Spring's innocence to contend with. But the sight of her making the moves on Tommy woke the beast in Knox.

When she threw back her head and laughed, her long, lean throat was exposed. That creamy expanse of skin was temptation itself. It begged a man to taste the silky sweetness there, to suck on her throat and to mark her as taken as a warning to all other men.

"Knox?" Chloe's uncertain voice penetrated the angry haze clouding his brain.

With great difficulty, he tore his gaze from Spring's beautiful body and glanced down. "Table, booth, or bar?" he asked.

"Booth in the back. Can we ask Miss Spring to have dinner with us?"

He suppressed a grimace. Chloe was a fan of all things Spring related: the flower shop, the Thorne gardens, the infuriating woman herself.

"It looks like she's busy."

"No, she's coming this way."

Knox's head whipped up. Sure enough, Spring sashayed in their direction with a wide, welcoming smile directed toward his little cousin. *Was it possible to be jealous of a kid?*

"Chloe!" she cried as if the sight of the child was the most delightful thing she'd ever experienced. And that was the crux of Knox's obsession with her. If she found the simple everyday that joy-filled, what would the serious aspects of life draw from her? He could only imagine what her enjoyment of sex would bring.

Chloe released his hand to run forward for a warm hug. "Did you already eat, Miss Spring? Do you want to join us?"

Wary eyes rose to connect with his gaze across the short distance. "I don't want to interrupt your dinner," she said in her soft, hesitant voice.

Knox should've demurred and told her that she wasn't interrupting, but he couldn't bring himself to offer up the social niceties.

"Knox doesn't mind. Do you, Knox?" Chloe turned wide, pleading eyes on him.

He forced a smile. "Of course not."

Spring squatted and, with the tip of her finger, tapped Chloe's nose. "Then I'll gladly accept."

As she rose, Tommy stepped forward and rested a hand on her waist. "I'll see you tomorrow?"

"Yes. I'll be there," Spring agreed.

Tommy's hand lingered as he tried to delay his departure.

The desire to sever that hand from Tommy's body just about caused Knox's head to explode. "Come on, Chloe. Let's leave these two alone for a minute."

"We'll be back there, Miss Spring," Chloe called over her shoulder as Knox practically shoved her toward the back booth.

With any luck, Spring would change her mind and head off with Tommy. While the image of the two of them together tore at his sanity, Knox silently hoped Spring would find another man to attach herself to. For the last six years, she'd taken every opportunity to throw herself at Knox. Each and every time, his answer was the same, "Not going to happen." She was like a pit bull with a bone and refused to accept no.

Remembering the sight of her on his doorstep in her tiny emerald bikini caused his saliva glands to dry up and his brain to malfunction. The gentle slope of her breast had scarcely been covered by the triangular scrap of material, and his hands had itched with the need to touch. The open longing in her bright green gaze had nearly been his downfall.

But he'd stuck to his guns. When she stalked away, he caved to his inner male-chauvinist pig and watched her ass twitch its angry rhythm until she was out of sight. He might have a strict policy of not getting romantically involved, but he wasn't dead. Any man with a pulse wouldn't have been able to tear his gaze from those firm ass cheeks.

He swallowed hard at the memory and pretended interest in the menu before him.

"I guess Miss Spring doesn't want to date you anymore, Knox," Chloe said as she openly watched her idol from across the room.

He stared in open-mouthed wonder at Chloe. *The kid was right!* Spring hadn't given him the time of day since the incident in her driveway about three months ago when he'd dumped a vase of water over her head. Maybe even before that, if he cared to examine the timeline.

Knox whipped his head around to where Spring stood with her hand over Tommy's heart. *Sonofabitch! She'd moved on!*

FROM THE AUTHOR...

Thank you for taking the time to read *WINTER MAGIC*. If you love what you've read, please leave a brief review. To find out about what's happening next in the world of The Thorne Witches, be sure to subscribe my newsletter.

www.tmcromer.com/newsletter

Books in The Thorne Witches Series:

SUMMER MAGIC
AUTUMN MAGIC
WINTER MAGIC
SPRING MAGIC
REKINDLED MAGIC
LONG LOST MAGIC
FOREVER MAGIC
ESSENTIAL MAGIC

You can find my online media sites here:

Website: www.tmcromer.com
Facebook: www.facebook.com/tmcromer
TM Cromer's Reader Group: www.facebook.com/groups/tmcromer-
fanpage
Twitter: www.twitter.com/tmcromer
Instagram: www.instagram.com/tmcromer

How to stay up-to-date on releases, news and other events…

✓ *Join my mailing list. My newsletter is filled with news on current releases, potential sales, new-to-you author introductions, and contests each month. But if it gets to be too much, you can unsubscribe at any time. Your information will always be kept private. No spam here!*
www. tmcromer.com/newsletter

✓ *Sign up for text alerts. This is a great way to get a quick, no-nonsense message for when my books are released or go on sale. These texts are no more frequently than every few months. Text TMCBOOKS to 24587.*

✓ *Follow me on BookBub. If you are into the quick notification method, this one is perfect. They notify you when a new book is released. No long email to read, just a simple "Hey, T.M.'s book is out today!" www.bookbub.com/authors/t-m-cromer*

✓ *Follow me on retailer sites. If you buy most of your books in digital format, this is a perfect way to stay current on my new releases. Again, like BookBub, it is a simple release-day notification.*

✓ *Join my Facebook Reader Group. While the standard pages and profiles on Facebook are not always the most reliable, I have created a group for fans who like to interact. This group entitles readers to*

"reader group only" contests, as well as an exclusive first look at covers, excerpts and more. The Reader Group is the most fun way to follow yet! I hope to see you there!
www.facebook.com/groups/tmcromerfanpage

Lightning Source UK Ltd.
Milton Keynes UK
UKHW021815061019

351114UK00017B/485/P